FRIDAYS

by

MARY   BAKER

A CIP catalogue record of this book can be obtained from the British Library

Published in Great Britain by
Cam Publications

Cover design by Felicity Jane Laws

For
Paul

Also by Mary Baker

According to Noreen Kemp, the world was yet again on the brink of nuclear war, as so often in the 1960s, even though Australia's sun continued to shine, making the air smell of road tar and turning green paddocks to yellow as spring approached summer. Mankind was about to be annihilated, but Noreen's eleven-year-old daughter Hester faced an infinitely worse prospect than imminent death. Her mother, on a self-appointed mission to save humanity, was going to make a speech at a school: the very school that Hester herself attended.

"You can't!" she wailed.

"Why not?" asked Noreen, puzzled by Hester's shocked reaction to the news. "Everyone's got to know how to survive radioactive fallout. It's really important. I said that to your headmistress, and she agreed."

"You don't understand," cried Hester.

Noreen had never understood school life. As a child in England during the Second World War, she had, like so many other London children, been sent out of the city in 1939 and entrusted to the care of strangers, only to return home a few months later because nothing much appeared to be happening. Then the blitz started, and Noreen was again dispatched to the countryside until things quietened down, but once more fled London as doodlebugs began to fall from the sky: the flying bombs that killed her parents and abruptly ended childhood. Those nomadic early years meant that Noreen's patchy education had taken place in many different schools where she was the permanent new girl, always an outsider, always without allies, continually teased and taunted, her accent mocked, her lack of local knowledge ridiculed. The result was that, when war ended and Noreen went back to London to live with her grandmother, a fourteen-year-old girl gladly abandoned education in favour of a shop job. By sixteen, the thin and mousy child had been transformed into a plump and pretty brunette who married before her eighteenth birthday, had a baby at twenty-one and settled into a rut of routine, her life on a collision course with the mundane reality of housework in a damp and dark Shepherd's Bush terrace, an area noticeable for its dearth of both shepherds and bushes.

Then a leaflet came clattering through the letterbox to change Noreen Kemp's destiny forever.

She had known about the atom bomb, everyone did, but it took that leaflet to make Noreen understand for the first time mankind's probable fate. "We'll die when they drop an atom bomb on us," she gasped. "We'll all die."

"We'd die whatever sort of bomb dropped on our heads." Colin Kemp was a factory engineer, a man who recalled his time in the RAF at the end of the Second World War with increasing nostalgia the older he grew, and Noreen's dramatics amused Colin in those days, but in those days she still praised him, marvelling at his tall handsomeness, and lamenting that their daughter had failed to inherit Colin's blondly Nordic appearance, taking instead Noreen's brown hair along with her plumpness, the worst choice any girl could make in Noreen's opinion. Not that Hester was conscious of having made a choice, but it still felt like her fault that she had not managed to glean more valued aspects of the family heritage available.

Drawing a homework picture of country cottages that the seven-year-old Hester had only ever seen in fairy-tale illustrations, she tried not to hear her parents talk of bombs and death, but it was too cold for a retreat upstairs because only the front-room fire was ever lit, its heat often overpowering while the rest of the narrow house filled with icy blasts that forced their way through draughty window frames. Hester tried to hum a song she had learnt in school that day about banishing dull care, but still the voices persisted.

"It isn't just a matter of dying because you're near the explosion," continued Noreen, overwhelmed by the leaflet's doomsday scenario. "There's radioactive fallout too, and no one can go outside the house for years, not even to get a doctor. And a doctor wouldn't be able to cure you of radiation sickness anyway."

"Then let's hope that your bomb does descend on our heads after all," remarked Colin. "Instant annihilation would save such a lot of hassle."

"You never take anything seriously," said Noreen, trying and failing to laugh. "This is terrible: the end of the world."

"And that's why nobody will ever start a nuclear war. They'd die as well."

"Hitler would have blown Europe to bits in 1945 if he'd had an atom bomb. It'll only take a single crazed dictator to obliterate the entire planet. It says so on this leaflet."

"If a madman's intent on destroying the earth, then he probably will and there's nothing we can do to stop him."

Colin turned a page of the book he was reading and went back to someone else's world, but Noreen found herself unable to cope with the helplessness of waiting for death without the chance to live a reasonable lifetime. She, who had never bothered voting in any election, began to listen to the political news on radio bulletins as well as gathering information about anti-radiation measures.

"We've got to dig a shelter in the basement," Noreen concluded after much investigation, triumphant to discover that she need not be a passive victim of fate like her parents but a potential survivor. "I know exactly what we want: a bunker at least twenty feet underground with walls and ceiling of reinforced concrete, the whole thing lined with lead."

"Is that all?" enquired Colin, entertained by the diligence of Noreen's research. "Silly question, of course. There has to be an underground bathroom, lead-lined as well. Why not a library too? And a ballroom."

Noreen frowned at the levity, although she would have felt even more anxious had Colin taken her fears seriously. "A water supply's

7

our main problem. I can stock up on tinned food, but tap water's going to be contaminated so I'll have to buy lots of containers and fill them with drinking water beforehand."

"Why bother? Those atom bombs will probably start exploding long before you've dug your way down twenty feet. Accept it; we're doomed."

"We might be able to survive inside the house by living on the stairs, if we keep all the doors shut, as long as there isn't too much radiation around," conceded Noreen, but it was a paltry consolation prize.

"I'm not going to live on a stair," said Colin.

"Then we've got to build our own shelter," declared Noreen.

Hester put fingers in ears as she attempted to learn a list of spellings for the next day's test, but still the parental conversation managed to seep through, making her heart thud with apprehension. Life was already blighted by having been lumbered with an old-fashioned name inherited from a grandmother, and Hester's days were complicated enough with school intrigues. An exploding atom bomb would be the absolute final straw.

"What's the point of a lead-lined cellar if we have to stay in it for the rest of our lives?" asked Colin. "We couldn't possibly store enough food or water anyway. Doesn't radiation hang around for centuries?"

"Yes," admitted Noreen, "but the wind can blow it somewhere else."

"How would we know that the wind had obligingly done its job, if we were twenty feet below ground and everyone else dead?"

"The people who'd built shelters like ours would still be alive," Noreen pointed out. "And scientists will be monitoring radiation levels."

"How?"

"I don't know; they just will, according to that leaflet. And men are going to come around to tell us when it's safe to be outside again."

"What men?"

"Air-raid wardens, I suppose, like in the war."

"But how would they find us, if we're entombed?"

"We'd have registered our shelter somewhere."

"Let's hope the register hasn't melted, along with everything else," said Colin.

"London might not get a direct hit," argued Noreen. "It depends how far off the explosion is, and the wind direction."

"If the USA nukes Russia, the Russians will launch their retaliation before an American bomb's anywhere near Soviet airspace, and London's right in the middle between Moscow and Washington whichever way the wind blows."

Colin was talking sense, and Noreen knew it, but admitting defeat and accepting premature death as inevitable was simply too terrifying to contemplate. "If the wind's from the north or south that day, we could be all right, but we've got to do something now. It's too late to dig a shelter after the bombs are in the air. We'll only have five minutes at most to get to safety."

"Then I'd better start training to run a four-minute mile in case I'm at work when your bombs begin exploding."

"We'll have to move," decided Noreen. "Yes, we've got to move house. We must always be close enough to our shelter to get back there within a minute: two minutes at the most."

"For the rest of our lives?" Colin laughed at the idea of such self-imposed limitations, although he realized that Noreen no longer thought in terms of decades. For her, the danger was immediate, and required the survival mentality that she had known during childhood: a strategy of getting through each air raid with the future looking after itself. "I sleep badly enough as it is," Colin reminded his wife. "You're not going to offload the end of the world onto me, or I'll stop sleeping altogether."

"I'll make a list," said Noreen, to gain some control over the horrors she pictured: horrors waiting to pounce ever since a bomb, that could have dropped from the sky anywhere in south-east England, had chosen to kill her parents. She picked up the pencil that Hester had been using for her arithmetic homework, and Noreen started to write.

Move house. Dig shelter. Buy tinned food. Get water barrel. Noreen's list was scribbled on the back of a brown envelope and pinned to the kitchen door, turning survival into a recipe.

****

Kilburn was a name that worried Noreen as it sounded horribly like an omen of nuclear destruction, but Colin's job was in Kilburn, and so Kilburn would have to be the next Kemp address. Colin put on a show of protest about moving there, but any change in the monotony of his routine was welcome, and the century-old terrace house, new to them, pleased him. He no longer had to hang around at bus stops on wet days or trudge home after hours of persuading outdated print machines to continue working, and Colin relished his extra spare time.

The move meant changes for Hester as well, particularly the disruptiveness of having to attend a different school, and she regretted the lost freedom of the lengthier journey that had once separated her two lives. Now she only had to walk a few steps to the corner of a road to find herself abruptly in front of the new school's dirty yellow brick, but Noreen was happier and ready to tackle the next item on her list: digging their very own nuclear bunker.

"I asked at the Council Offices, and a man there told me that we've got to get planning permission before we can even begin to dig our shelter," Noreen told Colin, neglecting to mention the clerk's undisguised amusement while he listened to her request for information.

"It'd cost a lot," warned Colin, certain that expense would end the scheme and restore Noreen to her senses.

"Being alive is more important than money. Anyway, I can economize."

"You already do."

"Then I'll economize even more. We'll just have to make a few sacrifices, that's all."

However, the family standard of living remained unthreatened. Apparently it was downright illegal to survive nuclear devastation without planning permission, and that permission was refused.

"This is stupid!" protested Noreen. "They can't refuse."

"They can and have, but a Council's got to consider things like underground pipes and house foundations," said Colin, glad that Noreen was so easily thwarted, and thankful that a raid on his bank account had been foiled. "Nobody's going to risk an entire terrace of houses collapsing in a heap of rubble and dust. That's why they make us apply for planning permission in the first place."

"Yet those planners gave themselves permission to build nuclear shelters under every single Town Hall in the country. I've read about it in the newspapers. Those hypocrites have made sure that they survive, but won't give the rest of us a chance."

"If I had to spend years underground in the company of Councillors and Aldermen, I wouldn't want to go on living," declared Colin. "Their fate will be worse than ours. So, that's that. No anti-nuke bunker for us."

"Let's dig one anyway" said Noreen, determined not to be cheated out of a future by selfish bureaucracy. "There's no need to tell anybody what we're doing. It's our business how we survive, not the Council's, when they won't lift a finger to help anyone except each other."

"Nobody can disguise building work; it's impossible. The neighbours would hear the noise, and word soon gets about. The Council would be down on us like a ton of bricks. Although that might be a bonus: save on the cost of actually having to buy bricks."

The whole world now seemed to be part of the conspiracy to frustrate Noreen's survival plan, and she glared at Colin who shrugged and then tried to make amends. "We could get hold of some cheap lead, and line the house with it. Would that suit you? Lead's always being nicked from church roofs, and thieves presumably steal it to sell."

Noreen dithered for a moment before shaking her head. She came from a superstitious background that her parents had imagined was a religious one, and God's wrath had to be averted as much as any atom bomb. "Church lead would bring us bad luck. We'll have to pay the proper price, and buy a little at a time. I just hope we can get enough lead together before the bombs start exploding. We need to line the walls, doors and roof with it, and seal the floors as well as cover all the windows."

"I'm not living in a house with no windows," Colin decreed. "I refuse to cower in stygian darkness, and I don't care how many of your atom bombs score a direct hit on my head."

"We can leave covering the windows until last," pleaded Noreen. "Or perhaps get lead shutters made."

Colin sighed, wearying of an emergency that, in his opinion, existed only in Noreen's fanciful mind. He had been called up for wartime military service in 1944, joined the RAF, faced the possibility of his death and survived, which had left him with a sense of immortality that no amount of doomsday talk could shake. It seemed plain to Colin that Noreen was panicking over nothing, but to humour his wife was an easier option than a confrontation about her delusions, and Colin had got into the habit of dealing with Noreen's nuclear histrionics by trying to turn the lethal-fallout obsession into jokes that rarely amused her. However the price of lead meant that World War Three would have to be considerate enough to wait for at least a century before commencing its activities, and by then radiation would no longer be a pressing problem for the Kemp family, but Noreen was unable to sit back and simply hope for the best.

"An atom bomb could explode at any time, and now there are hydrogen bombs too," she wailed, subconscious adamant that the abrupt end of her parents' lives might be a genetic trait. "We could be obliterated any day: any day at all."

"Not any day," said Colin. "Friday."

"Friday? Why Friday?"

"It's obvious. If we're destined to be fried to a crisp, we'll be fried on a fry day."

"That isn't funny," snapped Noreen.

"I'm not trying to be funny. I'm merely stating a fact. How else did the day get its name?"

Colin made his pronouncement on Wednesday evening, and a whole day of lessons, lunch, more lessons and then homework separated nine-year-old Hester from death. There such an immense amount of time stretching out between her and Friday that she felt reassured to have so many hours left to live. Noreen's insistence that atom bombs could start dropping at any instant had made the earth a permanently hazardous place, but Colin's scenario meant that should Hester survive a Friday, she had another week of life, and a week took forever to get through. Each Saturday morning became a reprieve, a second chance, and although Noreen claimed they were on borrowed time, time was one thing that could never be given back. Each extra week was a gift, not a loan.

As the grasping purveyors of lead and the narrow-minded local Council were determined that the Kemp family should die, Noreen searched frantically for an alternative strategy, and Hester provided it on a late-February afternoon by coming home from school with a postcard of eucalyptus trees that contained some scornful-looking koala bears. "It's from Rita Hooper. She sent me this picture all the way from Australia."

13

Hester had once sat at the same desk as Rita, who was under instructions to look after the new girl, but Hooper family members were no more to be seen in Kilburn, having departed for the Antipodes at the end of the previous summer, and Australia was so far away from London that Rita seemed to have disappeared from life itself, yet Hester held postcard proof that Rita could still communicate from the other world with those left behind. One bulky envelope postmarked two months earlier had been sent by ship to Rita's old school, its contents to be distributed among her former best friends, and ex-fifth-best-friend Hester Kemp had benefited.

'Dad says we got two summers in one year,' Rita had printed in wobbly letters, perhaps having run out of news by the time she reached postcard number five, but the magic of a message from another country, practically another universe, awed Hester.

"Miss Creel said that the postcards had travelled twelve thousand miles on a boat, right from the opposite side of the world, and it's true. She showed us where Australia is on the big globe in the classroom."

"The Hoopers are so lucky," commented Noreen, still brooding on Council obtuseness and the extortionate price of lead. "I heard somewhere that Victoria in Australia will be the very last place on earth affected by radiation after the nuclear war."

Noreen paused, wide-eyed and open-mouthed, astonished to have found a startlingly simple solution that would stymie the death sentence passed with such callousness on the Kemp family by the machinations of both a self-serving Council and those avaricious vendors of lead.

"No," said Colin.

"No what?" Noreen asked, although she already knew the answer to her question.

"No, I won't move house again, and definitely not to a house twelve thousand miles away."

14

"Lots of people emigrate to Australia."

"Yes, but presumably because they want to go there. I don't."

"Why not?"

"It isn't our home."

"It would be if we lived there," argued Noreen. "And think of the opportunities."

"What opportunities?"

"Well, we wouldn't have to worry about nuclear war."

"I don't worry about it now," Colin pointed out.

"Australia's the golden land of opportunity," declared Noreen, swiftly changing tack. "Australia's the future. It says so in all the newspapers."

"Only because the Australian Government pays them to say it. That's not news, just adverts."

Advertisements that had failed to entice Noreen until that moment. She grew up expecting nothing from life beyond what she already had, and hoping for yet more would have been described as 'getting fancy ideas' by her grandmother. Noreen had become a housewife in a backstreet London terrace because that was her destiny, a fate as inevitable as World War Three itself, but suddenly Noreen realized she might have a way of gaining power over the future. There was hope, glimmering far away on the horizon, but still hope despite the distance, and she had to beat a path towards it as nothing would ever come voluntarily to her.

"There are lots of job vacancies in Australia, I've heard, well-paid jobs: no unemployment at all. We've got too many people in England, but they need workers in Australia, and we wouldn't even have to pay the boat fare because the Australian Government does that for you. And it's like summer there the whole year round."

Noreen's campaign began with half-remembered stories of a magical land: legends picked up in shop queues and at the launderette. Everybody in London seemed to have a sister or cousin who had emigrated to Australia, and tales circulated about swimming-pools in back gardens and cars parked in garages by the side of detached bungalows, tales repeated by Noreen as soon as Colin walked into the house each day after work.

"London's our home," said Colin. "We're English."

"So are Australians," claimed Noreen. "They all emigrated there."

"Apart from the ones who got transported as cut-throats and thieves."

"That lot are dead, and have been for centuries." Noreen found she had an answer to each objection Colin made, and she was encouraged by such unexpected debating skills after years of failing to persuade him to take the nuclear-war threat seriously. The thought of moving so far away frightened her, but death would be a move that took Noreen even further from everything familiar, and she wanted to avoid that departure for as long as humanly possible.

Because the idea of emigrating was linked to Noreen's doomsday insanity, Colin automatically opposed her at first, immune to the lure of a sunlit land and Christmas Day on the beach, but there was a weak point in his armour. He had worked at the same printer's factory since being demobbed from the RAF, and spent dull days repairing faulty machines and filling out order forms, but it was a secure job and Colin told himself that he should be grateful when so many ex-servicemen were rootless and unemployed on their return to civilian life. He had rushed into marriage to start living after the missed freedom of his youth, only to realize that those war years in uniform were actually the time when he had felt most intensely alive, and now he appeared to be sleepwalking through the rest of his life. Had Colin been appreciated at work, he might have ignored any nostalgia, but promotion and pay rises twice passed him by: rejections that humiliated Colin. He always did his best, yet his best was apparently not considered good enough, even though neither of the promoted men had been as painstaking as he was, but both were younger than Colin: a sign of additional snubs ahead.

England had more workers than jobs for them: in fact, so many possible workers that employers knew nobody was irreplaceable and therefore they need never prize an individual. But Australia wanted workers, Australia was desperate for workers, and the country might offer Colin a second chance to live instead of wasting further time with a company that failed to recognize the value of effort and experience. In Australia, Colin could be a success, get as much promotion as he chose to accept, and earn better wages. There was also the enticement of travel. Colin had seen something of the world during his RAF days, and he would be able to see even more on the month-long voyage to a new life. For once, Noreen's atom-bomb hysterics had produced a result that might actually be worth following up.

"Odd if I do find myself going to live in Australia one day," remarked Colin. "It must be my fate. I was nearly sent out there at the advanced age of twelve."

"Why?" asked Noreen. "Did someone think you had relatives in Australia?"

"No. Orphans were shipped off to the dear old Colonies in those days. Perhaps it still happens. Australia wanted us and England certainly didn't, but I got measles and missed the boat. I was ill for ages afterwards, and Australia had no intention of being lumbered with a weakling. When I finally de-measled, I was old enough to leave the Home and got dispatched to a London factory rather than a sheep station in the outback."

"It's a sign that we're meant to emigrate," Noreen decided.

"Or a warning that it'll all go wrong," suggested Colin, to retain the right to say 'I told you so' should Noreen's plan turn into a disaster.

Colin always prepared an escape route for himself from blame, a strategy dating back to childhood. His parents had died young, like Noreen's, but unlike Noreen, there was no other relative to take over.

The Children's Home had been well-run, enlightened for its day, but still an orphanage, and Colin later returned to his early days in so many bad dreams that developing insomnia came as something of a relief to him. For his generation, nightmares would usually place them straight back in the Second World War, but RAF comradeship and purposefulness had appealed to Colin, adding to the glamorization of his war, and making him yearn for more adventures.

And Colin's next adventure arranged itself with ease.

The Australian migration process smiled on the Kemps who were in admirably good health, had the essential white skin stipulated by Canberra, and who slotted neatly into the age requirements for future citizens of the land brimming over with opportunity: glorious opportunities according to the glossy booklets that they were given to read and the Technicolor films shown to potential migrants in London's Australia House. The Kemp family would be following in the footsteps of those gold-diggers who had abandoned Britain a century earlier, but finding good fortune in the modern El Dorado was a lot less dicey than it once had been, and almost every penny of the fare for the ocean voyage would be paid by the Australian Government, so eager was the country for Colin Kemp's ability. He and Noreen only had to shell out ten pounds apiece, while Hester travelled entirely free, courtesy of Canberra, so for just twenty pounds sterling the whole family could cross the world to begin their new life: a new life with completely different prospects and expectations.

Like the Hooper family, the Kemps were to have two summers in one year. For Colin, emigration was a chance to recapture those lost hopes of 1945; for Noreen, it meant a possibility of surviving the 1960s. Nobody asked Hester for her opinion.

2

Bethanyville: so far south of Melbourne that a railway track was the area's main connection with the city. Bethanyville: a collection of small shops, a biscuit factory, a school, a migrant hostel and a hillside of square one-storey houses in square neat gardens lining the slope up to grandeur at the top, where a leftover colonial building with columned portico stood flamboyantly behind a stone-flagged courtyard that contained the unexpected sight of twin cannons facing each other, apparently prepared for their own personal war.

Rosebery Avenue, Bethanyville, Victoria. It sounded so like an address in a village back home that Noreen Kemp approved of the house even before she saw it, despite having found the English countryside bleak, muddy and lonely as a wartime evacuee. However, the years separating her from the 1940s meant that memories had been overtaken by Hollywood films, portraying a quaint England of picturesque cottages with a profusion of roses and berries around latticed windows.

The reality of Rosebery Avenue was a suburban street, but a street beyond anything that the Kemp family could have expected to inhabit during their London days. The new house was a detached bungalow surrounded by garden on three sides with a driveway that led to a garage on the fourth, mightily impressing the Kemps who had never aspired to owning a car. The word *home* still evoked a backstreet terrace with front doors opening directly onto pavement in a road without greenery, and where sunlight only managed to find a path between high walls at midday, but in Rosebery Avenue all seemed sunshine and space. Bethanyville's State School was a brief walk up the hill, and there were jobs for both Colin and Noreen a few minutes away in the opposite direction down by the railway station, where shops had started to gather around Barton's biscuit factory as more and more identical bungalows appeared in the area. Mordialloc beach was a mere twenty-minute ride on a bus, Melbourne half an hour by train, and because Noreen had begun to relax a little about radiation now that they were so far from the perilous Northern Hemisphere, there was the possibility of family outings. The Kemps could start to put down roots in a new country.

Rosebery Avenue was incredible luxury after their first Australian dwelling: two rooms inside a six-room Nissen hut on Bethanyville Migrant Hostel. During the war, Noreen had occasionally encountered European refugee children in the villages that were her temporary home, and now she was the stranger in a strange land: a stranger living in a Nissen hut that became an oven whenever the sun was shining, which meant every day because the sun shone gloriously from morning until night, and shone with a heat that wilted newcomers. Yet their time on the Hostel turned out to be the happiest that the Kemps would know as a family. Hester was comforted by the way that hostel children closed ranks to become staunch allies at school, a novelty for an only child; a canteen freed Noreen from the boredom of preparing meals, and Colin enjoyed the thought of so many choices still ahead. It seemed that anything could be achieved in a country where a few years work would give migrants a standard of living unattainable in Britain after a lifetime, but Technicolor Australia offered a future as radiant as its sun.

"It's warmer here at the end of winter than during summer back home," said Noreen, thoroughly approving of a land that gave her the first peace of mind she had known for years. "It isn't a winter at all: not what we call winter anyway. And they say that you soon get used to the really hot weather."

Nobody said it on Bethanyville Hostel, but still there was a sense of being on holiday, despite work and school. The Nissen huts were just one of life's transitory phases, because migrants had new lives stretching before them with golden prospects, and so an ex-army camp of shower blocks, toilet blocks, laundry block, a steamy canteen and little privacy could be tolerated when the future promised so much. On his second morning in Bethanyville, Colin had a job in Barton's biscuit factory, the following day Noreen started work in the local newsagent's, and Hester was dispatched to school, walking up a hill called Rosebery Avenue in the midst of a herd of hostel children, a school within a school. Noreen had gained confidence by challenging destiny and taking control of her own life, but Hester found so many changes more troubling than exhilarating at first, conscious of being an outsider who had no idea of the rules, whether on the Hostel or in school. Then even newer migrant families arrived, and Hester was an old hand, rushing around with cronies and sharing jokes.

"Barton's will give me a pay rise if I promise to stay at the factory for a year," reported Colin, proud to be so valued after the experience of working in overpopulated England where anybody could be replaced and keeping a job meant kow-towing to bosses even when they were wrong. To see an employer approach him and then offer inducements, in the hope that Colin Kemp would be persuaded to stay, was a pleasing novelty and one that made Colin feel important. Back home, he had been an anonymous worker; in Australia, the boss knew his name, and such recognition was as gratifying as it was surprising. Colin felt appreciated, and it began to change the way he thought about himself.

That year on the Hostel felt like living in a part of England, with British accents all around, and the identical migrant experience of travelling from a country still called home to a distant land led to instant friendships, which meant that Noreen was glad to be moving only a short distance away because the sheer size of Australia daunted her. The continent was too big and too empty for a Londoner used to noise and people, and the prospect of being able to revisit the Hostel was a comfort, even though she knew that the friends there would soon be scattered across Victoria as far as the New South Wales border, but those hostel Nissen huts were the last link with England,

and Noreen was reluctant to stray too far after so many drastic changes in her life.

The evening before a Kemp exodus from Bethanyville Hostel, friends dropped by the hut to say farewell, as if the family were about to leave for the moon instead of a house ten minutes away, and one of those friends unfortunately left a newspaper behind on the sofa that doubled as a bed.

"There's been a murder in Rosebery Avenue!" gasped Noreen, panicking at the thought of moving to so wild and lawless a street the very next day. "Some poor girl was murdered in Rosebery Avenue last night!"

"We're from London," Colin pointed out. "People get killed all the time back home. The book I'm reading is about those Jack the Ripper murders in Whitechapel."

"But we didn't live in Whitechapel. And a poor teenager's been murdered in what will be our street tomorrow morning," wailed Noreen. "This is awful. Do you think it's as sign?"

"A sign of what?"

"That we're making a terrible mistake, moving to Rosebery Avenue."

"The murdered teenager probably made all the mistakes that Rosebery Avenue needs to fill any quota, so don't blame the street. Most likely a boyfriend got dumped in favour of another heartthrob, and Mr Jealousy won't spend any of his time hanging around Rosebery Avenue just waiting for the police to arrest him; you can be quite sure of that. There's nothing for us to worry about, nothing at all, and the poor girl's problems are over."

"It looks such a nice road too, so calm and peaceful," lamented Noreen. "That's the worst of being in a strange country; you don't know which areas to avoid. Is it too late to cancel the house?"

"Much too late, and I don't particularly want to stay in a Nissen hut that'll become an oven in a month or so, when there's a bungalow we can move into tomorrow morning."

"I wish we'd chosen a house somewhere else, anywhere else." Noreen glanced at the newspaper again, and added, "She was so very pretty. Awful to think the poor girl had no idea when this photo was taken that it'd be printed in a newspaper along with a report of her murder."

"Much worse if she had known." Colin put down his book, lifted the newspaper out of Noreen's hand, and began to read aloud. "Blonde, twenty-five year old divorcée —"

"Twenty-five?" queried Noreen, distracted by trivia. "She looks a lot younger than twenty-five in the picture, more like seventeen. But even if she was in her mid-twenties, it must be a lot quicker and easier to get a divorce in Australia than England."

"So you'd advise me to watch my step." Colin glanced up, smiling at Noreen over the top of the newspaper.

"It's horrible to make jokes when some poor girl's just been killed."

"Some poor blonde divorcée's just been killed," amended Colin, returning to the newspaper article. Then he sat bolt upright. "My God! Sandra Stoddard! No, it can't be Sandra."

"The typist at the factory? Are you sure?"

"It can't be her. No, not Sandra." Colin stared at the paper, apparently convinced that the words must change if he waited long enough. "No, it couldn't be Sandra; it can't be."

"This is dreadful!" Noreen gasped again at the thought of a connection, no matter how slight, to a murder victim. An anonymous body in Rosebery Avenue would have been bad enough, but someone they had actually known was nightmarish. "I'd no idea that Sandra lived there. Did you?"

Colin shrugged absently, frowning as he continued to stare at the newspaper. "It can't be Sandra; it can't be. The picture's of a kid."

Noreen sighed in sympathy, but she was thinking less of Sandra than herself and the next day's move. Sandra Stoddard had been someone who occasionally came into the shop where Noreen worked, just another customer, although Sandra's voluptuous appearance had ensured that she would never be unnoticed, and Noreen shook her head in wonder at the randomness of fate, despite having once known a whole family of neighbours who had been killed during the Second World War alongside her parents. "If we'd moved into the house only a week or two ago, we could have met Sandra properly: been friends with her."

Colin was silent, distressed by the wide-eyed and confident smile on display in the newspaper picture. When seventeen years old, Sandra Stoddard had been at the very peak of prettiness, her attractive looks shining through the then-fashionable heavy make-up, mascara-black eyelashes and rigid curls. It had clearly not been a casual snapshot, but a professional photograph requiring careful preparation, and Noreen sighed again.

However, Sandra Stoddard might have found her only comfort in the charm of that newspaper picture as she had devoted much of her time to appearance, and the photograph belonged to pre-marriage pre-divorce days: Sandra at seventeen, hopes high of becoming a fashion model. Her abrupt death was a sad waste of a life that had been thoroughly enjoyed, despite the inevitable snags that mar the happiest of existences. Self-assured, energetically extrovert, valuing pleasure far above discretion and prudence, Sandra had breezed through her days, leaving behind gossip of wild parties and reckless affairs that seemed very out-of-place in so tidily respectable a street as Rosebery Avenue.

****

"Sandra Stoddard had one man after another, and acted like she was still a teenager. She got rid of her husband, and didn't have any children. In fact, she had no responsibilities at all," said Opal Teal, the new next-door neighbour, turning information into a complaint. "That Stoddard woman thought she could do whatever she wanted and get away with anything. But she was wrong, and finally had to pay the price."

It sounded severe retribution for a young woman who had simply chosen fun rather than convention, but Noreen was unwilling to argue the point over a wattle hedge with a newly-met neighbour on the first day of acquaintanceship especially as Opal and her family were English, which felt almost like discovering long-lost relatives, and long-lost relatives who had had an identical experience of Australian life. The Teal family, Opal, husband Derek and daughter Charmian had also left Tilbury for the month-long sea voyage and stayed on a migrant hostel before moving to Rosebery Avenue. To complete the match, Charmian and Hester were more or less the same age, although Opal was nearly five years younger than Noreen.

"I was just a child myself when I had Charmian," explained Opal, and a childlike air still lingered about her. She was small and fair, with a pink-and-white complexion carefully guarded from sunshine, and a delicate figure that made her look too fragile to be the mother of sturdy Charmian, who was already several inches taller than Opal. Charmian took after dark-haired and well-built Derek who towered over his wife and laughed at the contrast between them, but Opal rarely found the world an amusing place. She seemed overwhelmed by the complexity of a life that Noreen regarded as easy because the Teals had speedily acquired a washing-machine, refrigerator, hoover, television, radiogram and car, even though Opal had never gone out to work and Derek was a factory hand who would be earning far less money than Colin.

"I wish I was capable like you and had a job, but I think that a child needs a mother at home," claimed Opal, making Noreen feel guilty despite guessing that the words were empty. Opal Teal had no desire whatsoever to change herself, although she made the wistful tone sound genuine. Sandra Stoddard had been criticized for living a shallow existence, but Opal's own life was merely one of accumulating more and more possessions, and anything considered in the slightest way tarnished or shabby was immediately replaced.

Noreen's outlook had been formed by a family struggling through the Depression of the 1930s, wartime rationing in the 1940s, and then 1950s austerity, which meant that nothing was ever replaced until it had fallen apart, and Opal's acquisitions represented the sort of luxury Noreen only saw in Hollywood films, but she dared to hope for a house that might one day be equally full of labour-saving novelties in spite of Colin's disheartening tendency to remark "Something else to go wrong," whenever his wife admired a new gadget.

"My parents were furious that I married beneath me, as they called it, but I was a mere child and wouldn't listen," sighed Opal, proud to be the one-time heroine of so romantic a tale. However, the romance of Derek Teal had quickly worn off when Opal realized that her husband would be unable to provide the lifestyle she had unthinkingly anticipated, and Opal now regarded herself as having somehow been cheated out of fundamental rights.

"My parents died during the war, but my grandmother hated Colin at first sight. She claimed that he had shifty eyes and couldn't be trusted," said Noreen, smiling at the memory of a much-loved domestic dictator who had expected her only surviving granddaughter to shun the devious conman for no better reason than his eyes were pale blue.

"Yet Colin's an engineer." Opal looked impressed, but she was not thinking of achievement. "He must make good money."

"He certainly does in Australia."

"Derek's never had any ambition. He didn't even bother to learn a trade."

"Nor did Colin, until he got interested in machines and engines when he was in the RAF."

"Derek did his National Service in the Army," said Opal, the fact apparently explaining all in her mind. Derek Teal had only one ambition: to drift through life with a minimum of work, and such easy-going indolence would probably not have troubled Opal but for the low wages accompanying Derek's refusal to do overtime. He earned enough money for their daily needs, and saw no reason to acquire anything more, while Opal measured herself against other people by the number of possessions she could amass.

When she met Derek Teal, Opal Grainger had been going through a rebellious phase, bored with school and even more bored by the dreary choice between an office job or continuing her education. An early marriage was the only way to avoid both lacklustre prospects, and sporting an engagement ring at school offered a status that Opal prized more than passing any exam. Derek was twenty, with his National Service just completed, and he already had a job as a factory hand, which meant that Opal could abandon school for a whirlwind romance as she hustled the obliging fiancé towards their wedding. Her parents expected a daughter's future to be marriage and, although Derek was not the son-in-law of their former hopes, nobody suggested that Opal might be too young to set her life in stone, and she thought no further than a dress, veil and bouquet with the bride as star, the centre of attention, the envy of those still trapped by lessons and homework. Opal would have her own happy-ever-after ending exactly like a Hollywood film, and life would be a permanent summer holiday. The End, with cascading strings and oboe flourish.

Unfortunately, marriage meant that meals had to be prepared as well as laundry done, and the final disillusionment was Charmian's determination to be born despite Opal's own determination not to get pregnant and risk her figure. Money could have bought freedom with cleaners and a nanny but Derek's wages, riches beyond rubies to a schoolgirl, were too paltry to fund an escape route for a housewife. Opal was trapped, and resented every second she spent in her failed fairy-tale.

Opal Teal imagined that she had sunk to the lowest level of humiliation, but worse was to follow. The girls left at school desks, and once so envious of the lucky Opal, were beginning to acquire their own husbands, husbands with career prospects, and former dullards unable to parade a boyfriend at Opal's wedding now lived in expensive areas where she could only be a visitor. It was obvious that these ex-friends must scorn her, rejoicing in Opal Teal's downfall as they laughed behind her back, because that was what she would have done if the situations were reversed, and fleeing such an intolerable state of affairs became Opal's obsession. Australia was so far away that nobody could check whether or not details in letters sent back home were accurate, and according to migration advertisements, even idle Derek could earn good money in Australia. No advert sullied itself with a description of migrant-hostel huts, but after that blip, Opal's antipodean scheme began to work out, and she could mail fantasies about their fabulously-successful new life in their fabulously-expensive new house. Then the Kemp family arrived to live next door.

It seemed particularly unfair that Noreen's husband should be a well-paid engineer while Opal, who was much better-looking than Noreen, had been lumbered with Derek, a man lacking ambition to be anything more than he already was. Derek had let Opal down in so many ways that she despised him, but very little could be said openly because her life had to appear perfect so that people would envy and admire the gorgeous Opal Teal. It was part of the act.

Noreen had no need to pretend. Fate, usually unkind, seemed to be mocking Noreen Kemp. She had a detached house with a garden in a country that never experienced the bitter chill of an English winter, and Noreen also had more money than she would once have believed possible; in fact, Noreen was being given everything she could ever want, while knowing it was worthless because of that split atom: a threat rarely far from her mind. Other people were able to get along by ignoring the danger, by ignoring death itself, but Noreen was unable to push the knowledge away, and wondered how she could ever have been feckless enough to bring a child into a world with no future. That was the real guilt, not leaving a young daughter to fend for herself during school holidays, but having condemned Hester to a slow death from the radiation poisoning that would inexorably make its way to Australia. The Kemp family had had a temporary stay of execution, but future destruction was inevitable.

****

The first visitor to the Kemp's Rosebery Avenue home was a policeman, but Constable Albert Fulton was so relaxed and smiling that it appeared to be a social call, despite an initial question about the unfortunate Sandra Stoddard. Fair-haired and tall, handsome Albie had worked in his job for less than a year, but could have posed for a reassuring advertisement on behalf of Victoria's police to offset the record number of civilians shot by the force, and Noreen found herself smiling back at him, even though he was making enquiries about a murder. "We only moved into the house this morning, so none of us were here when poor Sandra died."

"You're from England," declared Albie, leaning against the doorframe and ready for a pleasant chat. "I recognized your accent straight off. My parents came from England as well: London."

"We're from London too," said Noreen, feeling welcomed to the road by such a coincidence. "It's a small world. Well, not really when it took us four weeks to get to Australia, but you know what I mean. Which part of London did your parents come from?"

"Rotherhithe, and they were lucky to leave because the Germans blitzed the street a couple of years later."

"It must have been sad news for them." The August day was warm and bright, Australia's concept of winter, but Noreen felt suddenly chilled, fearing that an unexpected reminder of war's devastation from the first person to knock at their new front door might be an omen of impending disaster. "We lived in Shepherd's Bush and then Kilburn."

"Is that near Rotherhithe?"

"Not particularly near, although not too far away if you go by tube train."

Albie nodded, but had no idea of comparative distances in London and he reverted to business. "So you didn't know Sandra Stoddard."

"Actually, I did. We were living on Bethanyville Hostel until this morning, and I work in the newsagent's by Barton's factory. At least, when I say that I knew Sandra, it was just the occasional hello each time she came into the shop. We never had a real chat, and I only found out what happened to her from a paper last night because we arranged the move with our days off-work. I couldn't believe it; I just couldn't believe it. She was such a nice person." However, Noreen was well aware that nice people came off worse when they encountered someone decidedly not nice, and Sandra had been no exception. A friendly woman, open-handed and cheerful, Sandra Stoddard had laughed at life, and life rewarded her with a brutal and untimely departure.

"You didn't know her friends? Any of the men she went around with?" The words sounded like questions, but Albie had already closed his notebook.

"We don't know anything much about Sandra. My husband's an engineer at Barton's, and I suppose she could have typed up some orders or reports for him, but he hardly knew her, although Colin's as

30

shocked about poor Sandra's death as I am. He thinks that a jealous boyfriend probably killed her, and I imagine Colin's right, isn't he?"

"We're still gathering evidence," replied Albie. "I reckon you'll know my Aunt Brenda. She and her husband Lenny own a shop: the one that sells lollies and ice-cream on the other side of the station."

"The Deans? Yes, I know them," said Noreen, feeling less of an outsider in Rosebery Avenue, merely because the first Kemp visitor had a connection to the life she was already starting to make for herself in Bethanyville. "You'll be Ginevra's cousin then. She's in the same grade at school as my daughter. In fact, Hester went to Ginevra's birthday party last month."

"Yes, I'm Gin's cousin all right," agreed Albie, his face so rueful that Noreen laughed. "Well, I reckon I'd best get a move on, or my Sergeant will be on the warpath."

"I do hope you catch the murderer soon: very soon. It feels so horrible knowing what happened to poor Sandra, and that she was killed only a little further up the street from here. It's awful."

"Don't worry. Whichever one of her men it was, he won't be planning to make any return visits: not with so many police officers in the area. He'll be at least a hundred miles away by now."

"That's what Colin says too." Noreen wanted to ask whether deaths like Sandra's were commonplace in Rosebery Avenue, but feared that the answer would give her worse insomnia than Colin's.

****

"What's this road like?" On a winter's day warm enough to pass as an English summer, Noreen was collecting letters from the Kemp's mailbox at their front gate when Derek Teal went by on his way home after a factory nightshift, and she finally dared to ask the question, knowing that he was unlikely to revel in exaggerating danger, and might actually be able to reassure her that she had not moved to the crime capital of Australia.

"The road? Oh, it's very smooth most of the time, but the tarmac melts in summer and sticks to your shoes," replied Derek, laughing. "The smell reminds me of having whooping cough when I was a kid. My mother took me to stand by a road that was being resurfaced because she claimed that breathing in tar fumes cured whooping cough. It doesn't."

"You know quite well what I meant," said Noreen, trying to smile. "Is there a lot of trouble in Rosebery Avenue? Have other people been murdered?"

Derek shook his head, abruptly and unwillingly sombre. "Nothing ever happens around here normally, and it shouldn't have happened to Sandra. She was a lovely girl."

"Yes, I know. Sandra often used to come into the shop where I work."

"You knew her?" Derek looked pleased, as if he had found a member of the same fan club and could share a fixation. "Sandra was nice, wasn't she? The nicest person I've ever known. Always pleasant and happy. I can't imagine anybody wanting to hurt her, not Sandra."

"Colin thinks that there must have been a jealous boyfriend. Perhaps Sandra tried to ditch a man who just wouldn't go away."

Derek shook his head again, Colin's theory emphatically rejected. "Everyone thought the world of Sandra. She was much too kind to upset anybody, and never left bad feeling behind her. Generous to a fault, that was Sandra."

She lived lightly and died darkly. Noreen could remember her grandmother quoting the words about a cousin who had been killed during the blitz. All thoughts and sympathy should be centred on Sandra Stoddard at so tragic a time, and Noreen felt ashamed to realize that she was still thinking of her own family's safety. "But nothing like this has ever happened in Rosebery Avenue before?"

"Not that I've heard of." However, Sandra's fate was at the forefront of Derek's mind, and he added, "She didn't go in for drama and pretence. Sandra just wanted to enjoy life without complications or entanglements. And why shouldn't she?"

Noreen's upbringing had taught her to regard marriage as the sole aim of female existence, and she was awed by the idea of Sandra's independence, although Noreen found herself compelled to offer an extenuating circumstance for such a drastic abandonment of the norm. "But Sandra had been married, hadn't she? It said divorcée in the newspaper."

"She told me that her first husband was also her last husband as she never made the same mistake twice." Derek smiled, the Sandra in his imagination alive and vital, free-thinking and free-spirited. "She stayed on good terms with her ex though, which must be some sort of record, but said that she'd served her time, and now she'd been released, she was never going to lock herself up in a prison again. Sandra ought to have had years and years more of freedom. I was so shocked to hear she was dead, I drove the car into our gate and knocked over the mailbox merely because the sun dazzled me a bit."

"Sounds like you knew her well," remarked Noreen.

"You only had to talk to Sandra for five minutes, and you knew her. She was the warmest and most straightforward person I've ever met." Derek sighed as he rejoined the present and recalled the reason why they were discussing Sandra Stoddard. "Life's very unfair; life's cruel."

"Yes, it is." Sandra might have been spared a lingering and painful death from radiation poisoning, but it seemed little recompense for someone who had filled every moment so vigorously, and Noreen was conscious of wasting far too much time worrying and working. She ought to enjoy herself more, make room for fun, and it was dreadful to suspect that perhaps she no longer knew how to have fun. The Kemp world was paying bills, sending a child to school, working for money that would finance another week of the same routine, and soon it would be too late for anybody to have fun. Sandra's outlook appeared sensible rather than frivolous, but Noreen failed to see how she could achieve a similar light-heartedness when her existence was one of responsibility in which recklessness played no part. The occasional day in Melbourne or an evening at the beach was as carefree as Noreen could get, and even then she fussed over details. A Sandra she would never be, and whatever lifespan was left to Noreen, it would be the poorer because of her timidity.

"There won't be another girl like Sandra Stoddard, not in a million years," said Derek. "There can't ever be another Sandra. She was a wonderful person: the best."

He seemed to have known Sandra very well indeed, thought Noreen with imagination supplying X-rated scenes that depicted the extent of Sandra and Derek's relationship.

****

Hester Kemp and Charmian Teal had been unenthusiastically acquainted for nearly a year, but they were now expected to become friends, expected to walk to school together, and expected to act almost like family simply because their parents had bought neighbouring houses. Even in Grade 6 they were supposed to be allies, despite a Rosebery Avenue address being one of the few things they had in common, but neither questioned the general assumption.

Charmian was belligerently competitive, determined to win at games and shine in school tests, despite very average abilities. She was unable to tolerate any rival who dared to approach what Charmian hoped would become her exalted status, and was annoyed by the apparent ease with which Hester managed to coast through lessons.

"People are saying that you cheat, just like Ginevra Dean," claimed Charmian.

"I don't cheat, so Ginevra probably doesn't either," said Hester.

"I didn't say that you cheated; it's what the others are saying. And Ginevra's a definite cheat. How else could she have come top in arithmetic last Friday? I'd tell Mrs Lang about her, but I'm no sneak."

"Ginevra could rob a bank, and you wouldn't sneak on her," laughed Hester. "She's Albie Fulton's cousin."

"I saw him first, so you'll have to find somebody else," decreed Charmian. Even if the chosen one remained unaware of his admirer, it was considered treachery in Bethanyville School for another girl to anguish over the same boy. The rules were very precise and inflexible on the point.

"I don't think I could ever have a crush on a policeman," remarked Hester.

"Why not?" Charmian demanded, sensing criticism of her choice.

"It must be such a horrible job, having to deal with murderers all the time. I'd be scared that he'd get killed."

"I'm not afraid because Albie's so clever, he can outsmart any criminal. Albie's the bravest man in the whole world. He keeps Australia safe for everybody else." Constable Albert Fulton was Charmian's hero, and she remained convinced that worshiping a man rather than a boy, even from afar, gave her lofty eminence in the school. Lesser girls could waste their time with adolescent nonentities, but Charmian Teal was experiencing adult passion. "Albie's going to solve Sandra Stoddard's murder all by himself, but that won't stop Ginevra being a cheat, and people think you're one as well."

Even after a year in Bethanyville, Hester was still regarded as something of an outsider in the midst of Australian children who had known each other since kindergarten, and attending her third school, she felt fated to repeat the Noreen pattern of rootlessness. It seemed unlikely that anyone would bother to gossip about so insignificant a member of Grade 6, but Hester was worried by the idea of being thought a cheat even if the insult existed only in Charmian Teal's slanderous imagination. "I'd sooner fail every single test every single Friday than cheat."

"You shouldn't get ten out of ten so often. It looks really suspicious," declared Charmian, eager to reduce competition at the top. "Everybody says that you can't possibly know a thing about Australia when you haven't been in the country five minutes. You're only eleven as well, and we're all twelve, yet you beat the rest of us in last week's history test."

"I just read that chapter about the First Fleet, like Mrs Lang told us to, and remembered what it said in the book; that's all."

"I believe you, but none of the others do." Charmian looked proud to be so trustingly charitable, and Hester resented the self-righteous superiority, but a quarrel with Charmian would make things too awkward when they were next-door neighbours, which meant that any hostility had to be hidden.

"I'll work even harder," vowed Hester. "I'll prove that I don't need to cheat."

"You'd just convince everybody that you must be cheating," said Charmian, alarmed at the prospect of her scheme backfiring and Hester Kemp waltzing off with an armful of end-of-year prizes in December. "Don't worry. I tell everyone that I don't think you're a cheat, even though they won't listen to me."

Charmian was probably lying, but she might not be. It was a horrible world, full of horrible people, and matters were about to get so much worse that Hester would soon begin to think mankind's approaching extinction might actually rank as good fortune.

Noreen had discovered a group of fellow radiation-obsessives, all determined to reduce Australia's population to their own state of quivering dread. *One in Five* served as both group aim and name, its zealots resolved to inform one in five people of the correct course of action to take when the air turned radioactive, and Noreen was more than ready to terrify others as she had been terrified, but all her horrors, all her nightmares, were nothing when compared with Hester's panic on hearing that Noreen's début speech was to be given at Bethanyville School.

"Mrs Hexham heard about *One in Five* and she asked for someone to speak to the older children at the beginning of December," said Noreen, surprised by Hester's agitated reaction to the news. "It's important that as many people as possible know what to do when radiation reaches Australia."

"But you've never made a speech before," cried Hester.

"I've got to start sometime. It's what *One in Five* is about; it's what the organization does. We tell people how to survive radioactive fallout." Noreen was free to scare people all she wanted; she could address the General Assembly of the United Nations on the subject of nuclear warfare if she chose, but a speech at Bethanyville State School was another matter entirely.

"Why does it have to be you?" wailed Hester.

"Because Friday's my afternoon off," replied Noreen, callously indifferent to the fact that her daughter's life would become a desolate wasteland, bleaker than a nuked desert, with utter humiliation threatening to devastate the rest of Hester's earthly existence.

It was all Mrs Hexham's fault. A woman bearing a strong resemblance to Queen Victoria in one of the old monarch's grumpier moods, Bethanyville School's dumpy and dictatorial Headteacher was apparently unaware of either radio or television, and seemed to believe that Bethanyville's youth had lives limited to school and homework. Mrs Hexham's belief came from her own isolation in the intellectual aridness of suburbia, where she attempted to enlighten the children of parents who cared more about money than poetry, and regarded school as a child-minding service that ended the instant a kid was old enough to go out to work.

A product of education that dated back to the 1920s, Mrs Hexham had yet to adapt herself to the 1960s, an era that brought politics along with the Vietnam War into most homes via radio or even television, and she persisted with a Friday afternoon tradition of guest speakers who would usher the world into an assembly hall: a tradition lingering from her own schooldays.

What One In Five People Ought To Know. Noreen's subject would go up on the notice-board outside Mrs Hexham's office, and there was likely to be idle speculation about the knowledge that one in five people ought to have, but as Friday afternoon talks were worthy rather than racy, none of the wilder suggestions would get more than a snigger. Hester could have given the speech herself from an exhaustive supply of data after years of indoctrination about radioactive fallout, and she suspected that the doom-laden scenario Noreen would relish presenting might turn her audience against the scaremonger's traumatized daughter or, even worse, reduce spirited Australian schoolchildren to helpless laughter while Noreen was in full-flow.

Always dark, its window shutters closed against sunlight that might otherwise dazzle anybody on the dais in front of captive listeners, the assembly hall would not be dark enough to hide the speaker from Hester's schoolmates. Noreen had never taken much interest in her daughter's education, and there might have been a chance that no one would realize the two Kemps were related, particularly as Noreen's accent was English and Hester had become an Australian chameleon imitating whoever spoke to her, but Charmian Teal would delight in exposing Noreen's identity. Indeed, Charmian Teal would rejoice in Hester Kemp's shame.

Uncertain and wary in a culture that was still alien, Hester had no idea how Bethanyville children would react to someone's mother striding onto the dais and describing a horror-film scenario, but Hester could easily imagine the taunts that any unfortunate child cursed with so visible a parent would have to face back home in England, where being inconspicuous was regarded as a virtue by both pupils and teachers. Australia might be a different country, but it seemed inevitable that the remainder of Hester Kemp's existence must be forever blighted by fallout more gruesome than the radioactivity that would be released by a simultaneous explosion of the world's entire atomic-bomb stash. Life, as Hester knew it, was about to end.

****

"I can't go to school that day," declared Hester. "I just can't. I won't."

"You've got to," decreed Colin. "Families always stick together, no matter what, and Mum's never made a speech before. You have to be in that hall to smile encouragingly at her, and clap like mad when she finishes. You've got to have a few questions ready as well, in case no one speaks when Mum asks if anybody wants to know more details."

"I couldn't stand up in front of everyone and ask a question," cried Hester, appalled at the mere thought of so public a demonstration of family solidarity. "They'll all know she's my mother."

"What's wrong with that? Are you saying none of the other kids would support their own mother?" Colin shook his head at such unspeakable treachery, and Hester felt worse. "We're not just here to fork out pocket money and birthday presents. Loyalty goes two ways, and this will be a time when you can do something for Mum."

As Colin's idea of family loyalty had come to him from books and films rather than experience, he could sound as stern as an outraged chapel elder on the subject of allegiance, turning into a stranger who laid down rules of behaviour that had never applied to him. Colin often used his forlorn time in a Children's Home as leverage to get Noreen and Hester to do what he wanted, and Colin expected them to live by higher standards than he would ever require of himself. Hester knew that there was no way out for her, when Dad had gone into lecture mode, but abandoning all hope was too defeated a move to contemplate.

"Mum won't be able to say a word," claimed Hester, in dire need of a respectable excuse to shun Noreen's launch as a public speaker. "I'll feel sick as anything for her. She'll be terrified."

"All the more reason for you to support her. You'll go to that talk, and afterwards you'll tell Mum what a brilliant speech she gave, and that you're proud of her. Do you understand?"

"Yes," mumbled Hester.

"Good. I don't want to hear any more of this nonsense."

Had Noreen put in an appearance at Barton's biscuit factory to address assembled workers on radiation-survival methods, Colin would undoubtedly have beaten an extremely hasty retreat, but Hester must not be a coward. Hester must do the right thing. The rules were different for her; Colin had his own set.

3

Instead of a front room and a back room as in their London home, the Kemps now enjoyed the prestige of a living-room and a dining-room, because both were in the front of the house and required separate names. The family had felt self-conscious at first, not to say pretentious, but the novelty soon wore off, and on the first of September, the Kemps were eating breakfast in their dining-room when Noreen glanced at the window to see a police car stop outside the Teal house.

There was very little traffic in Rosebery Avenue, everyday sounds often limited to cicadas and birdsong, making any sort of human activity unusual enough to notice: a very far cry from London. "It can't be anything urgent," Noreen decided. "The siren would have been switched on."

"The police only use a siren to warn cars to get out of the way," said Colin. "There aren't any other cars just now, and so no need for sirens to screech around Rosebery Avenue."

"It'll be to do with poor Sandra. More questions, I expect."

"Why? What would the Teals know about Sandra that the police don't?"

Mindful of Hester's presence in the room, Noreen shrugged, unwilling to share her guess about the exact nature of Derek's relationship with Sandra. "I was just thinking aloud. I haven't a clue why the police would call next door. Derek was on nightshift when Sandra died, and Opal told me that she watched television all evening before going to bed."

It chanced to be a Friday morning, and Hester felt shaky with panic because anything out of the ordinary on one of Colin's Fry Days alarmed her. However, the police were not there to warn the street about imminent radioactive annihilation; they were only interested in the Teal house. Two men got out of the car, consulted the number on the mailbox by the gate, and then began to walk up the driveway.

"Perhaps they've come to arrest and deport Charmian," said Colin. "It wouldn't surprise me in the least. I saw her tip the board over when she realized she was going to lose that game of Ludo, and Australians take fair play very seriously."

Hester laughed, and stood up to pack books into her schoolbag. The false alarm somehow guaranteed that particular Friday was not about to turn into The Fry Day after all, and she would be sitting the weekly tests as usual, Noreen could go to work, and Colin to bed after a nightshift among Barton's Biscuits.

"Don't wait for Charmian today," Noreen instructed Hester, while moving closer to the window and watching in fascination as the policemen approached the steps of the Teal verandah. "It'd look like we're nosey if you hang around the gate."

"And we're not a tiny bit nosey," added Colin, amused.

"Doesn't matter being nosey as long as you're not seen actually peering out of a window," said Noreen, smiling at the contradiction between her instructions and her actions. "Perhaps it's bad news from England. No, that'd come in a telegram and two policemen wouldn't deliver it."

"This will all fizzle out to nothing, the way things do," predicted Colin. "The police have probably mistaken the address. They'd closed the road when I left work, and someone said there'd been an accident, but that can't be anything to do with the Teals. It happened during the night, long before Derek would have left for the factory this morning."

Hester still believed that her father knew everything about the world and its workings, but he was wrong that day, very wrong. The policemen had found the right house and the right people.

****

Noreen's obsession with nuclear disaster had given Hester the idea that radiation was the main cause of death, and the absence of an atomic explosion equalled near-immortality for everyone on earth, but Derek Teal had been all too mortal, and something as old-fashioned and avoidable as walking in front of a car had ended his life without the least amount of radioactive involvement. "The wrong place at the wrong time," Colin said. "If Derek had stayed in England, he'd still be alive."

It was a reproach aimed at Noreen, even though the Kemp standard of living had improved beyond anything possible in London, where they would never have imagined themselves able to afford a detached bungalow surrounded by garden plus a garage waiting for the car that was another item on the list of possessions they expected to buy in a year or two. Britain would have meant a lifetime of damp houses in narrow backstreets that were darkened by centuries of soot, and Colin knew what he had left behind and what he could achieve with an Australian future, but still Colin teased Noreen by pretending to sigh nostalgically for the glow of shop windows seen through gloomy murk on December afternoons and he also claimed to miss the lingering twilight of English summers, despite having lambasted the British climate for as long as Hester could remember.

"The road was still closed when I went into the shop, and our customers were talking about a hit-and-run accident all morning, but no one knew that it was Derek," Noreen said at lunchtime, shocked by Colin's sensational news. "Where did it happen exactly?"

"Down by the Bush," replied Colin.

It sounded very rugged and Australian, but a patch of scrubland that stretched out at the foot of Rosebery Avenue in a tangle of gorse, broom and bramble was always called the Bush, despite shops and a railway station around the corner and another suburban street visible on the far side. What were once trackless plains now hosted a highway that eventually led to Melbourne, even though few cars were seen by day and fewer by night, which explained why the body of Derek Teal had lain undiscovered by the roadside for so many hours.

"He told Opal that he was doing a nightshift, although he actually had a few days off, but she didn't know it," reported Colin. "Opal's completely bewildered, and no wonder. When the police suggested a friend should be with her, she couldn't think of anyone but us, so I stayed next door most of the morning."

"Good," said Noreen. "Opal must be devastated. Was Derek seeing another woman?"

"It turns out gambling was his vice, rather than women. Opal told me that he'd often been fool enough to throw all his wages away on horse or dog races." Colin sounded self-righteous, equating lack of interest in betting with virtuous restraint. He could pride himself on being sensible with money and pose as a careful man with a careful mind, dragged halfway across the planet by a nagging and hysterical wife. In view of Derek's shortcomings, Colin chose to forget his own reasons for wanting change, especially as the Australian life now meant a routine similar to the English one, and he had difficulty resigning himself to factory work again after the excitement and luxury of a long sea voyage. Even the new house, a bungalow that would be the envy of those left behind in London, was losing its lustre. The Kemps had achieved the Australian dream, and Colin needed other worlds to conquer.

"Awful for the car driver," said Noreen.

"A whole lot worse for Derek."

"Yes, of course," Noreen agreed hastily. "It couldn't possibly be any worse. I suppose poor Derek was crossing the road just as a driver turned off the highway and there wasn't time to stop the car."

"Perhaps, but the driver didn't hang around to explain what happened." Colin shrugged at the cowardice of mankind, yet understanding why anyone confronted with the situation would panic, but he was still prepared to add instruction for his daughter's benefit.

"Derek shouldn't have crossed the road by the highway. Nobody should, and particularly when it's too dark for a driver to see clearly."

"Did Derek drink?" Noreen asked.

"Opal didn't mention it."

"If only he'd taken his own car instead of walking," lamented Noreen.

"Opal would have guessed that he wasn't going to the factory. The police had a look at Derek's car though."

"Why?" demanded Noreen. "Surely they can't think that Opal killed him?"

"Luckily she's never learned how to drive," said Colin, but he smiled at the idea of Opal, so fluffy and girlish, turning into a ruthless slayer of husbands. "I told the police that we saw car headlights whenever Derek drove in or out of the garage at night, and it's so quiet around here, a car engine always wakes me up, assuming I've managed to get to sleep in the first place."

"You can't say that a car *always* wakes you," objected Noreen. "There might be times when a car goes by and you don't hear it."

"That's what people call being pedantic. Anyway, an earthquake wouldn't disturb you once you're asleep, so you don't know what you're talking about. It's different with insomnia. If I'd been here, instead of on nightshift, I would have heard every single car that went by the house." Colin seemed to be boasting of a prowess worthy of celebration, and he was smiling proudly as he continued, "But the Teal car presumably stayed in its garage all night because there were no dents in the bodywork, or whatever the police thought they might see. Well, they asked about the dent in the bumper that Derek made when he drove into the mailbox, but I explained."

"It was his collision with the mailbox that made me ask if Derek drank," confessed Noreen. "He seemed the type somehow: loud and over-cheerful. But very nice," she added to avoid being suspected of criticizing the departed, although Noreen had liked outgoing and unpretentious Derek far more than his wife, put off by Opal's tendency to adopt a little-girl voice and her preoccupation with appearance. Noreen was too busy worrying about nuclear war on behalf of the human race to have time for lesser concerns, and Opal's perfect hair, expensive clothes and manicured fingernails were flummery in comparison with mankind's looming destruction.

"Well, it doesn't matter now whether Derek was a drunk or not," remarked Colin.

"I'm sure he wasn't," declared Noreen, aware of the traditional obligation to defend the dead. "Is Opal managing all right?"

"She's in shock. I don't think she'll be able to cope with any of it."

"No, probably not. Poor Opal. She must feel so alone. And Rosebery Avenue isn't having much luck either right now. First Sandra, and then Derek. I hope it doesn't mean there's another death coming, but everyone says that things happen in threes." Noreen shook her head at the harshness of fate, removing two people who had both delighted in being alive. The world was a poorer place without them, yet there was no choice but to go on. "At least Opal can count on us for support."

"That's what I told her," said Colin.

****

"The next time you see Charmian, don't mention her Dad," Noreen instructed Hester. "If she talks about him, just say how sorry you are. Charmian won't want to hear anything more because she'll be far too upset."

The prospect of dealing with a grief-stricken Charmian in floods of tears appalled Hester, and made her avoid going out into the garden in case Charmian should be on the other side of the wattle hedge. Hester also delayed her departure for school until the last possible moment each day, reconnoitring the road from a window to be certain that there was no sign of Charmian, before Hester felt able to dash past the Teal house in a pretence of being too late to walk.

However, Charmian reappeared at school one day, acting as though nothing had happened, and the other children took their cue from her. After all, parents were very much in the background when Grade 6 buzzed with gossip about who no longer spoke to a former best friend and which girl was in love with which boy: a petty world that absorbed everyone's attention and gave Charmian a holiday from the memories she would have to cope with at home.

"Opal might go back to England," suggested Noreen, after waiting days to hear of a level-headed response to Derek's death from Opal.

"No," said Colin. "Her mother's the only relative over there now, and she criticizes everything that Opal does. They haven't bothered with each other in years."

"Australia's a better place for Opal anyway. It'll be easier for her to find a job out here than back home, and she's probably getting short of money." Noreen frowned at the difficulty of picturing Opal Teal in employment, and then added, "I suppose she could work in a clothes shop."

"Opal couldn't work in a shop," scoffed Colin.

"Why not?"

"She isn't the type."

Colin's tone was so dismissive that Noreen laughed. "I've only ever worked in shops. What type am I?"

"The type who can add up money in her head and know the total's right," said Colin, realizing that he should move onto safer ground. "Opal isn't the practical or capable sort, and she's never had a job."

"It doesn't mean that she couldn't get one out here when there's such a shortage of workers." Noreen imagined Opal with her wide skirts and pencil-thin heels on a factory floor, and was positive that such an anomalous sight would never become reality, but Derek might have been well-insured, enabling Opal to carry on living the only life she knew. "Did she mention any life-insurance policies?"

"Yes, you're definitely the down-to-earth type," Colin declared, smiling. "I don't think Opal's got around to looking that far ahead. She's still too bewildered."

Perhaps all bewildered and recently bereaved widows concentrated on hair and make-up, rather than finances, because Opal's sleekly groomed appearance never altered. The Opal Teal form of stiff-upper-lip, Noreen concluded, wondering if Opal would react to the news of atomic warfare by checking her make-up, unable to tolerate the thought of being vaporized with smudged lipstick or shiny nose.

"Opal's so vulnerable," continued Colin. "She's got no idea how the world works or what she should do next."

"Opal will muddle through as long as she's got enough money," Noreen predicted. "Let's hope Derek didn't gamble it all away."

"That's a distinct possibility. I don't think he was very kind to her."

"Of course Derek would have been kind. Easy-going people always are. What makes you think that he wasn't?"

"Just the impression I got. I doubt he ever considered how Opal would manage if he died young."

"None of us do enough planning for death," Noreen declared, sent straight back into her nuclear fixation. "People pretend that nothing's ever going to change, but one day the worst will happen and we should all prepare for it."

"Too late to tell Derek," said Colin.

"Exactly! He probably assumed that he was immortal, the way most people do." Noreen sounded triumphant, even though she knew that Derek Teal had been trapped in the path of a moving car without an atom bomb having blasted him there. However, Noreen still regarded her point as definitively made.

Hester stood on the sidewalk by the crimson-painted mailbox that rose on its wooden pole high above pink flower heads at the front of the Teal garden. She was waiting for Charmian to emerge from the bungalow, jump from verandah steps to driveway and then run to join Hester. Together, they would hurry up the hill on weekday mornings, and it was a journey that passed too quickly because they usually met other girls headed in the same direction, and much had to be said before they reached the wire fence surrounding Bethanyville's State School, a red-brick one-storey building fringed by prefabricated huts added to cope with the influx of migrant children. Charmian was normally late, which often meant the hill had to be tackled at a canter, but that morning she appeared on the verandah seconds after Hester's arrival and stamped furiously towards her, anger increasing with each step.

"I'm never going to speak to you again, Hester Kemp, never, not as long as I live. You won't get another single word out of me ever."

"Why not?" asked Hester.

"You know! And I never want to see you again either. You're a liar."

Hester shook her head, conscience clear. "I haven't a clue what you're talking about. What am I supposed to have done?"

"You know!" Charmian could barely get the words out, each one muffled by the rigidity of rage. Whatever Hester's transgression, it was obviously a major one. "Mum told me that you know."

"Know what?"

"Stop pretending!"

"I'm not. What do I know?"

"About your horrible father." The words were spat rather than said, and Charmian began to charge up the hill. Hester dithered, and then ran after her before Charmian got an opportunity to broadcast the grievance around Bethanyville schoolyard and turn Hester Kemp into a pariah.

"What about my Dad?" she demanded, breathless after the rush to catch up with Charmian.

"Your father's a filthy old man, and I'm not staying with them. I'll go back home to my grandmother, and if she doesn't want me either, I'll run away with Albie." Charmian stood still, gasping with the effort to breathe in enough air to continue her rant as she glared at Hester. "I told Mum how much I hate you. Don't think that we'll be sisters."

"But we aren't sisters," Hester pointed out.

"And never will be!" retorted Charmian. "It doesn't matter what your horrible father thinks."

"Why would he think that we were sisters?" asked Hester, wondering if Charmian had decided to act out an elaborate joke, even though her ferocity seemed genuine.

"Stop lying! Stop pretending!"

"I'm not," maintained Hester. "I really don't know what you're on about."

"How can you not know that your father's moving in with us?" demanded Charmian.

"But we've got our own home. Why would we move in with you?"

"Not you, him! He's going to marry my Mum."

"No, he isn't," laughed Hester. "He can't. He's already married."

"Have you never heard of divorce? Stupid old man, thinking that he can just walk into the house and take my Dad's place."

Charmian suddenly fled up the road, and Hester let her go, instinct adamant that anyone so incensed was not going to listen to reason. Charmian had invented a dramatic scenario entirely without foundations, something that she was inclined to do, and even a glance between two schoolfriends had often been interpreted as a diabolical plot against her, leaving Charmian free to enjoy hatching a counterplot against the supposed conspirators. Hester had left Colin and Noreen placidly discussing a trip into Melbourne at the weekend to see *South Pacific*, and Charmian could spread whatever story she liked around the school, because no one was going to be intrigued by a fictitious love affair when the people involved were as ancient as parents. Hester had a temporary reprieve until the dreaded Friday when Noreen's speech was destined to make her daughter a universal laughing-stock, but there were whole weeks to get through first in which anything could happen to avert so atrocious a calamity, and with luck Colin's Fry Day might arrive before the Noreen catastrophe.

****

Opal had decided that Colin needed a push to force him to see sense and leave Noreen. Without that push, he might be content to dally next door for a few hours and then saunter home afterwards to his wife. Telling Charmian that Colin would soon be moving in with them ensured the information being passed on to Hester who should promptly go running to her mother with the tale, and the result would be a screaming row guaranteed to drive Colin straight into Opal's consoling arms. It was a perfect strategy, and the contrast between a gently passive Opal and the screeching harridan of a Noreen would make Colin's choice inevitable.

If she had ever heard herself described as selfish and scheming, Opal would have been astonished. She was delicate and sensitive, incapable of facing life's difficulties without the protection of a man, and even more afraid of being thought unable to attract one: an insult to her enticing figure and beautiful face. Colin would probably be quite willing to stay with Noreen while enjoying the perks of an affair with a younger and more alluring woman, but Opal believed in marriage, especially when it included financial security with a husband unlikely to be feckless enough to leave her penniless after his death. The fact that Colin was somebody else's husband she could overlook, because Noreen had plainly failed to satisfy him and everyone was entitled to happiness. It would be a rescue for both Colin and Noreen, freeing them from a lacklustre relationship, offering everybody the chance to make a new start, and Noreen was a capable woman who would almost certainly find an unattached man in a country where males outnumbered females by ten to one. There was going to be a Hollywood happy ending, and all Opal had to do was wait.

She understood Colin so little that Opal had no idea her plan was an unnecessary effort, and she could have relaxed while she waited.

****

"We can move to any town in Australia," Colin had said, a few months earlier. "Why hang around Bethanyville?"

"Because everybody knows that Victoria will be one of the safest places on earth after the nuclear war, and living south of Melbourne is even better," Noreen reminded Colin. "Besides, we've got good jobs here, and Hester won't have to change schools if we stay in this area. Yes, it's sensible to look for a house in Bethanyville."

Sensible, and boring.

Colin sailed from England to enjoy a new life, and four weeks at sea onboard the *Strathnaver*, a luxurious P&O liner, had no precedent in his experience. A couple of rooms inside a Nissen hut on Bethanyville Migrant Hostel came as a stark contrast, but there was the companionship of families also on the brink of new lives filled with new hopes in a country where migrants could work at well-paid jobs of their choosing while they saved for golden futures. It was one excitement and novelty after another until, suddenly, Colin reached full stop.

He had arrived at the end of his voyage of discovery, and found himself once again imprisoned by routine. Colin walked down Rosebery Avenue to do a job that had already become tedious, and walked up the same road to return to the house he had left only hours before. A pattern for the next forty, perhaps even fifty, years was being established, and Colin felt trapped after the exhilaration of total change. He missed the feeling that it was in his power to alter everything, to escape, to feel free, but now it seemed that all he had done was swap a cold climate for a hot one, and Colin began to yearn for upheaval, for anything that would turn his world upside down again. He even thought of going back to England, although the voyage home was the attraction, rather than reliving a former existence, but Colin tried to persuade himself that he was nostalgic for rain and mist, for cloud and fog, while all the time knowing that he simply craved another adventure.

Then a beautiful woman made it plain that she desired him, and she changed Colin's life forever. After her, he could no longer tolerate monotony, and Colin knew that he had to hunt and capture any chance of the next adventure, not drift towards old age, yearning aimlessly for what might never happen unless he refused to accept conformity as his lot.

Eye-catching Opal greeted Colin as a hero, never challenging or questioning what he said; attentive Opal concentrated on him and ignored radioactive warfare; seductive Opal was in need of comfort and very willing to be comforted. She quickly turned into one of the remedies that Colin had been searching for, and Opal's adoration flattered his ego, adding intrigue to revive a stale existence. Opal seemed too fragile to flirt, too guileless and trusting to be manipulative, but Opal was also alone in her house when Colin called, and so anything and everything was possible.

When not at work, Noreen spent much of her time rushing out to anti-war groups or attending lectures about radiation survival, and she entirely missed her own domestic fallout: not even suspicious when Colin reclaimed his days by going onto permanent nights at the factory. A nightshift brought in more money, he said, and still Noreen failed to spot the dayshift taking place next door. Her life was so busy that she never noticed how dully repetitive Colin's had become or that he was avoiding her, and the idea of him seeking an escape route also eluded Noreen, as did his Opal-facilitated getaway. The long-dreaded atom bomb could not have exploded with more force than the shock produced when Noreen came home from work one afternoon in mid-September and saw that all Colin's belongings were gone.

Hester waited until Noreen had worked out matters for herself, before reluctantly offering the explanation. "Dad said to tell you that he's gone to stay next door."

4

"Tell Mum that I'll be staying next door," Colin had instructed Hester, assuming that an eleven-year-old girl was too immature to understand the full implications of his message. "Opal can't cope on her own, and needs somebody with her."

"She isn't alone; she's got Charmian," Hester pointed out.

"Charmian!" repeated Colin, making a face and evidently expecting his daughter to laugh with him. "I don't think Charmian Teal's much help to anyone at the best of times."

Colin had left school aged fourteen, and drifted through factory jobs before his RAF service, which was followed almost immediately by marriage. He had waited years to stage an adolescent-type rebellion, and relished every moment. Colin had not originally planned to desert Noreen so speedily, but she was competent as well as a fighter, determined to survive anything life hurled at her, and Hester was a sensible girl whose father would only be next door. By the time he and Opal moved house, Hester would be used to the situation, and as girls married young in Australia, she might only be a few years away from taking flight herself. Everything would work out sooner or later, and but one snag existed: Charmian.

Charmian Teal was an unpleasant child, spoilt and prone to tantrums. Opal tried, but she was too gentle to restrain her strong-minded daughter, and Colin congratulated himself on Hester's superior upbringing that had resulted in a self-controlled girl who was inclined to keep quiet about her emotions: a most convenient secretiveness when a father had no intention of feeling guilty.

"You want me to be happy, don't you?" Colin stated rather than asked. They were walking in Melbourne's Botanical Gardens, a place that Hester would never revisit, their faces scorched by a north wind as blistering as air from an open furnace. "I know that you don't want me to go through life being unhappy."

"No," Hester replied automatically, unable to turn the question around and ask whether Colin cared about his daughter's happiness.

"When a marriage is over, it's dishonest to go on pretending. That'd be exactly the same thing as lying, and you know telling lies is wrong."

Everybody, from parents to teachers, condemned deceit and so Hester nodded, but it was just as wrong to despise your father for being a second-rate person, and Colin must have sensed her unspoken protest because he continued, "You're lucky, Hester, very lucky. You've got two parents: family. You're not stuck in an orphanage, no one caring if you live or die."

Colin's favourite and most effective weapon, the Children's Home, had been an inevitable addition to the lecture, his voice implying years of neglect and starvation in a Dickensian workhouse, and he never failed to make Hester miserable with guilt for not being perpetually thankful, but hostility refused to be dislodged so easily.

"None of this will make any difference to us. We'll see each other all the time," Colin claimed. "They have drive-in movies over here, just like in America, so you, me, Opal and Charmian can pile into the Teal car and go to see a film one weekend. That'll be fun, won't it?"

No, thought Hester.

****

Colin had never seemed the womanizing type and Noreen tried to blame Opal, but felt that any censure should probably be directed at herself. She had been too confident, too trusting, too convinced that marriage was for life, and so Colin could go into Opal's house or into any woman's house without consequences. Perhaps Opal had seductive wiles unknown to Noreen, but it was more likely that Colin had become bored with his wife. He might also tire of Opal in a few years, as he was clearly a fickle man, yet the thought failed to bring much consolation with it, especially as Noreen was well aware that hurt pride rather than a broken heart was the main reason for the pain she experienced, leaving her ashamed to be so petty. Had she ever really loved Colin? Noreen was a typical product of a generation who were expected to marry young, and it had been something of a competition among her friends to be the first one to get an engagement ring. Colin Kemp had a steady job, would be a good provider, and was so handsome that the teenage Noreen could show him off as a prize, but if he had switched his attention to another female in those days, she would simply have started the husband-hunt all over again without overwhelming trauma or shattered dreams. It was humiliating to realize how shallow she must be, but at least the insight might prevent her making the same mistake twice. Noreen knew that she would never again be able to trust a man or any vows he might make, but she had more pressing matters to occupy her than the loss of adolescent illusions.

Noreen had an initial panic about money and how she would manage alone financially, but a few sums reassured her, and Noreen was surprised to realize that she could cope, despite the expense of a dependent child. There might not be many luxuries or treats, but both Noreen and Hester would be fed, clothed and housed, even if Colin went back on yet another promise and failed to support his daughter. He might soon consider himself divorced from Hester as well as Noreen, but they would survive his desertion, whatever future choices Colin made.

Hester felt less optimistic, and longed for a quick way out of a horrible mess. If she and Noreen moved house, things might become endurable; if Colin left Rosebery Avenue along with Opal and Charmian, it would be a positive relief, but the stalemate of next-door houses was excruciating. Then Walt Disney provided a possible solution in *The Parent Trap*, a film that told the story of identical twins who successfully reunited estranged parents by overthrowing the devious other woman in pursuit of their father, and the Hayley Mills strategy was simple: arrange for a few animals and reptiles to rout Opal, surely an easy enough task given Australia's feisty wildlife, and remind Colin and Noreen of the time they met, the music they had heard, the dates that led to romance. The result would be a guaranteed happy ending.

"You met Dad at a party," Hester remarked casually that evening, as she turned the radio dial from station to station in an attempt to find one broadcasting music capable of lulling Noreen into suitably nostalgic mood. "That's what you said, wasn't it? A party?"

"I don't want to talk about him." Noreen greatly regretted having taken Hester to see the latest Hayley Mills film in Melbourne because *The Parent Trap* had reminded both mother and daughter of everything that Noreen had hoped to escape for a few hours, and she guessed the purpose behind Hester's query. "Dad's gone and that's that."

"But he might come back."

"I don't want him back."

Colin had abandoned his daughter, and Hester's wishes apparently meant nothing to her mother either: a double rejection that hurt and made Hester feel very alone. Once she had belonged to a family, once she had been part of a solid unit, but it turned out that Hester Kemp was no Hayley Mills loved by her parents. Hester Kemp was a nonentity. "Dad's bound to get cheesed off with Opal soon, she's such a phoney. He could turn up at the front door tomorrow morning, tonight even. He might come back home any time now."

"I wouldn't let him in," Noreen stated.

"But if Dad opened the front door, he —"

"He can't. I had the locks changed, remember, and he hasn't got a key."

But Hester had one, and she would open the door for her father if there seemed to be any chance at all of the old life resuming, although Colin was a lesser man than he had once been. However, surely even he must eventually see Opal as the outsider she was, and then Colin would want to come home again instead of living in somebody else's house. Anyone would hate to be a permanent guest, whatever the attractions of an Opal, and no matter how Hester tried, she was unable to understand Colin's decision. The thought of nuclear war had once kept Hester awake at night, but now it would be a holiday to face annihilation and forget everything else.

"Why did he do it?" demanded Hester, suddenly angry with Colin's stupidity. "Why did he go? Opal's horrible. Why can't he see that?"

"Because he doesn't want to," replied Noreen.

"Then he's a dim-wit."

"Not half as dim-witted as me," Noreen muttered.

****

It was not in a daughter's power to control parents, yet Hester felt nervous at the thought of going to school again. There might be other girls whose fathers had moved out, but those girls did not have Charmian Teal spreading lies about them or their defaulting Dads.

"Is it true that your father murdered Sandra Stoddard?" Ginevra Dean, wide-eyed and breathless, sounded more awed than shocked as she stood in Hester's way to prevent any escape. It was a magnificent piece of gossip and tiny thin-faced Ginevra, light-brown hair tied up in bunches, hopped from one foot to the other, unable to be still while awaiting such a crucial answer.

"My Dad's never killed anybody in his whole life, not one single time, not even in the RAF during the war." Hester tried to laugh but she was very aware of sounding awkwardly defensive, despite the accusation's absurdity. "We didn't really know Sandra, because we were still living on Bethanyville Hostel when she got killed."

"She worked in the same factory that your Dad does."

"So do hundreds of people."

"I know, but they didn't buy her spiders."

"Spiders?" queried Hester, taken aback.

"Yes, spiders. Your Dad bought Sandra lots of spiders in our shop. In fact, he bought her one after work on the very night that she was murdered. Mum said so, and she told my cousin Albie all about it. He's a policeman."

"Yes, I know he is. But why would my Dad buy anybody a spider?" Even after a year, Australian culture was often incomprehensible to Hester, but never more baffling than at that particular moment. "Why would anyone buy a spider?"

"Don't you like them?"

"No, I don't: not at all."

"Sandra did. Your Dad was always buying them for her."

Red-back spiders, funnel-web spiders, white-tailed spiders, trapdoor spiders, black widow spiders, wolf spiders; Australia's venomous list went on and on. The antipodean spider had little in common with innocuous English counterparts, but was instead a lethal executioner lurking in gleeful wait for its next victim, and Hester could only marvel at the extraordinary tastes of the late Sandra Stoddard.

"And your Dad visited her house at night," Ginevra continued. "He spent every night with her."

"No, he didn't."

"How would you know? You'd be asleep," Ginevra pointed` out, determined to cling to the intriguing scandal. "Charmian saw your Dad go into Sandra's house lots of times. And Charmian says that he's going to kill her mother next."

Good, thought Hester.

"And Charmian keeps a knife in her schoolbag now, in case your Dad tries to kill her as well."

The idea of both Opal and Charmian being summarily executed was an attractive scenario, and Hester felt that she could forgive Colin anything if only he would turn into the killer of Ginevra's imagination. The fantasy was so enticing that Hester sighed for the might-have-been, but unwillingly forced herself back to reality. "What a load of old rubbish! Charmian's having you on."

"She's got evidence," Ginevra said triumphantly.

"What evidence?" scoffed Hester.

"Charmian wouldn't say, but she's giving it to the police."

"If my Dad's planning to kill Charmian Teal, why hasn't she given her stupid evidence to the police already?"

"I don't know," admitted Ginevra, but she was not to be daunted by commonsense. "And Charmian says that your Dad drove into her father and killed him, as well as murdering Sandra."

"Dad doesn't have a car."

"Charmian saw him steal one."

"Charmian Teal's a liar."

"She said you'd say that."

"Because she knows that I know she's lying."

However, Hester could tell that Ginevra had not the slightest intention of being talked out of Charmian's story, and nor did anyone else in the school. To Hester's surprise, she found herself an instant celebrity who was accompanied by awed glances that led on to more popularity than Hester had ever known or would know again. The legend of the Kelly Gang lived on in Victoria, and children born there grew up automatically accepting murderers as heroes, which resulted in Hester's Dad acquiring the debonair status of a rebel who cheerfully scorned authority: an outcome that left Charmian furious, particularly because her own father was seen as a victim, and victims were weaklings who had failed to fight back and trounce their foes. Hester's Dad, in contrast, had glamour and was plainly a man freed from society's petty restrictions. In fact, Hester's mythical father was a truer Australian than many of the men reared in the country, and Colin's spirited reputation expanded as tales of his supposed exploits were embellished throughout Bethanyville State School.

"He bought Hester a ruby necklace and a sapphire ring after he robbed a bank in Melbourne. I asked her about it, but she wouldn't tell me a thing. I reckon Hester's been sworn to secrecy by her Dad, and she's too loyal to say a word. Even a detective inspector won't be able to get her to talk." Ginevra had a band of followers who chose to believe every syllable she uttered, and perhaps Ginevra was also a believer in the tales that she embroidered so lavishly while ignoring the material's flimsy origin.

The lack of rationality gave Hester a chance to bask in reflected glory without telling any actual lies out loud, and even though her conscience occasionally prickled, she was glad that Charmian's plot had turned itself upside-down so superbly. Australia was indeed a foreign country for both Hester and Charmian: a country in which strategies that might have worked in an English school were entirely routed by an alien ethos. Charmian had no idea why her enemy was now an acclaimed heroine, and the resentment festered.

****

Colin Kemp seemed to have died along with Sandra Stoddard and Derek Teal, the third death that Noreen had so dreaded. She was unable to recognize the man a teenager called Noreen Randal thought she had married, because that Colin Kemp was supposed to be considerate, somebody who put his family first, somebody who could be relied on. The stranger who had taken Colin's place was a liar and a coward without the guts to tell Noreen to her face that he was leaving, but even in the midst of shock and depression, one comfort remained. Noreen's grandmother would never be able to say that she had warned her granddaughter about the shifty-eyed Colin Kemp, and to find any consolation in the death of the greatly loved woman, who had tried to protect her, made Noreen miserable with remorse.

Nearly a decade had been wasted on fear, fear of nuclear war, of radiation, of suffering, of dying, but Colin had freed Noreen as life no longer seemed worth clinging to. His rejection left her feeling ugly and aimless: a woman with little to look forward to, a woman who might be trapped in isolation with empty years of loneliness to fill after Hester ventured out into the world. Losing that life would be no great trauma, and death unexpectedly began to appear in the guise of the release that Noreen had often heard it called: a release without the power to terrify. The idea brought freedom, almost as much freedom as Noreen had enjoyed in the days before a leaflet dropped through the letterbox of a dark and drab London house in Shepherd's Bush, because nuclear war and its aftermath would liberate her from both old age and humiliation, and humiliation was the hardest thing of all to bear. Colin had spurned his wife for someone who was nothing more than a face and figure, leaving Noreen bewildered that such a vapid female should have attracted Colin. To be replaced by so bogus a woman was the final blow, and Noreen felt too despondent and worthless to help anybody, therefore Australians would have to educate themselves about surviving radiation. She had returned to the mindset of her childhood, the mindset of the Second World War, when tomorrow had no existence and the thought of never feeling anything again was a consolation. What had once been Noreen's worst nightmare became her lifeline. She would still have tried to save herself, in the event of a nuclear attack, but failure might also feel like victory.

"Why does he like her?" asked Hester.

"She's good-looking," replied Noreen. Better looking than Noreen. Better figure than Noreen. Probably a better cook than Noreen, and presumably better in bed.

"There are lots of good-looking women. Why her?"

If Noreen had known the answer to that question, perhaps Colin would never have wandered off. "It just happens sometimes."

"But she's nobody special." Hester tried to find other words, but they refused to form themselves in her mind even though she knew that Opal was show without substance. Colin ought to have used his intelligence instead of seeing no further than the pretty colours of a shell, and Hester was disappointed in her father for having been so easily duped into throwing away his family. "Can we go back to England? I don't want to stay here any more."

"I can't take you out of the country unless your Dad agrees."

"He wouldn't mind. He doesn't care about me."

It was plainly true although Noreen tried to object, but Hester was beyond the age of believing in fairy-tales, knew that she had been left behind just as much as her mother, and saw no reason to pretend otherwise. Noreen wished that she could reassure Hester, but the girl was right when she said, "We're in the way now, and he'd be glad if we didn't live next door."

Noreen would be glad too, and the idea of returning home was attractive. Not to Kilburn or Shepherd's Bush, far too painful explaining to friends that Colin had flitted off to greener and younger pastures, but England was bigger than London and starting to acquire an allure that Noreen had never noticed when she lived there. She was beginning to forget the bleakness of cold winters, bad-tempered people, high unemployment and low expectation because England had become a country of magnificent Regency streets, ancient towns, manor houses, ruined castles, daisy-speckled meadows, pretty villages and cornfields with poppies: photographs in a calendar that was pinned to the kitchen wall. The upheaval of a month's sea voyage and then yet another new life might have the power to stop Noreen brooding on her rejection but, even as she imagined such a future, she knew that none of it was going to happen. Colin would refuse to allow Hester to leave Australia because he wanted to fool himself that he was a devoted father.

"We could still move even if we don't go home," said Noreen. "There are plenty of jobs in Australia, and we might be able to get a house nearer the sea. They say it's a bit cooler on the coast and I'd like that. What about Mordialloc or Mentone?"

"Anywhere," declared Hester: "anywhere but here."

****

Charmian Teal hated everyone, everyone in the world, even people she would never meet, but she particularly hated her mother, Colin Kemp and his daughter. The other girls at school were traitors who still spoke to Hester, despite Charmian's best efforts at slander, which meant that nobody was on her side, and the loneliness felt unbearable without any release in sight from her torment. Revenge would be Charmian's only comfort, but fate stubbornly refused to oblige by delivering wholesale annihilation of her enemies, all of whom prospered happily regardless of Charmian's anguish, and the entire situation was utterly, totally and absolutely unfair. Life had no business whatsoever to trundle along as normal when Charmian Teal's existence was dust and ashes, but the springtime sun shone with even greater warmth as October approached, people laughed while they began to make plans for the Christmas holidays, and no one noticed or cared how Charmian suffered. The human race deserved to be obliterated in all its callousness, but the earth persisted in turning as though nothing had gone wrong.

Opal claimed that things were different in Australia, but Charmian was humiliated to have a mother who lived with a man married to another woman, and the fact that he happened to be Hester Kemp's father made everything worse. Because Charmian relished spreading lurid gossip, she assumed that Hester must be repeating scandal about Opal's behaviour, and although living in sin might be an Australian norm, Charmian was still English with her full share of rigidly English narrow-mindedness, and that narrow-mindedness cringed at the idea of everybody knowing of Opal's disgrace. Hester could boast a virtuously wronged mother, but Charmian's was a Jezebel: a Jezebel who cared nothing for her daughter's shame.

It was even more unfair that a strange man should have taken up residence in Charmian's home, making her seem like an outsider. No, not *seem* like an outsider, she *was* an outsider. Opal thought only of Colin and Colin thought only of Opal, which left Charmian in the way and very aware that they preferred her absence to her presence because she no longer had a family; she was on her own. Charmian considered running away, but there was nowhere for her to run to, and so she would have to endure a prison sentence without a crime on her conscience, unless Colin could somehow be dislodged and defeated.

"The police are going to arrest him any minute now," Charmian remarked casually one evening, as the front door closed behind Colin on his way to a factory shift. "Everybody says that he killed Sandra."

"Don't be so stupid!" Opal had been relaxing in an armchair as she sipped a glass of lemonade, but suddenly she was bolt upright and blazingly angry. "Colin never even knew the woman. That Stoddard slut got killed by one of her boyfriends. She was nothing more than a tart. Everybody knows that, everybody."

"*He* was the boyfriend who killed Sandra," declared Charmian, jerking a thumb in the direction of the front door. She was a little taken aback by the fury of Opal's reaction, but quite prepared to stand her ground. "Everyone's saying that *he* killed Sandra."

"Rubbish!" snapped Opal. "The woman got what she deserved, fooling around with all those men. I told you, Colin didn't even know her."

"That's what you think. Hester Kemp says her mother was glad to see the back of him because he had girlfriend after girlfriend long before Sandra."

"Then Hester Kemp is a liar!" Opal's face was pink with rage, and lemonade spilled from her glass onto the floor. "You're a liar as well, to say things like that."

"I'm only telling you what everyone else knows. The police will probably arrest him tonight: tomorrow at the latest."

"Nobody's going to arrest Colin, nobody at all," cried Opal. "And just look what you've made me do. Get a cloth, quick, before this lemonade spoils the wood varnish."

Opal knelt down and scrubbed at the floor with a handkerchief that was too femininely small to be anything but decoration: a flimsy piece of lace already lemonade-sodden when Opal's tears abruptly started. "If you loved me the least little bit, you wouldn't try to ruin the only happiness I've known in decades."

Tears had always been an Opal speciality, turned on and off with such ease that there might have been a tap installed behind each eye, but Charmian had witnessed many similar displays of emotion and long since become immune to them. "You don't know a thing about him. He could have killed lots of people before Sandra. How do you know that he isn't one of those mass murderers?"

"Don't be silly. Colin wouldn't have been allowed to emigrate to Australia."

"That just proves the police didn't catch him, and it's probably why he killed poor Sandra. She knew too much about the murderer, and he silenced her."

"Why are you so cruel?" sobbed Opal. "Why am I cursed with a daughter who cares nothing for my feelings, my happiness?"

As Opal clearly cared nothing for Charmian's feelings or happiness, it was a question not deserving an answer. "Facts are facts, and they stay facts even when you don't like them."

Charmian decamped to her room, content to have had the last word, and pleased to give weeping Opal time to brood on what had been said. It was a comfort to know that someone else felt miserable, and although Opal's copious tears would speedily dry after Charmian closed her bedroom door, those few moments of revenge helped, and there was a chance that doubts might start to nag at the back of Opal's mind about Colin Kemp's past. He was a contemptible man, in Charmian's opinion, whether or not he had actually killed Sandra

Stoddard, because a trustworthy man would never abandon his wife and daughter, something Opal should have known, enabling her to see despicably deceitful Colin Kemp as the villain he really was. However, Charmian had overlooked the extent of Opal's willingness to sacrifice other people's lives for her own advantage.

The tears dried up even more quickly than Charmian imagined, and Opal was already checking her make-up to be certain that no urgent repairs were required after the rush of emotion. She had named her daughter Charmian, but the ungrateful girl seemed to react against anything to do with charm despite Opal's best efforts to instil the values of good grooming and deportment. Charmian was a disappointment on every level: not pretty, not slender, not elegant, not even graceful. In fact, Derek Teal's daughter was a blight on her mother's life, and a blight that Opal bitterly regretted having given birth to.

5

Detective Sergeant Earl Lanyon had very little faith in the reliability of gossip, but gossip shaped much of the information about Derek Teal and his background. It was a fact that Derek's widow was now living with Colin Kemp, and tales from Rosebery Avenue as well as the Barton biscuit makers linked Colin to Sandra Stoddard. The Rosebery Avenue rumours came later than the factory ones, but all sources apparently agreed that Colin had had an affair with Sandra, according to Constable Albert Fulton.

"It's what people are saying," reported Albie, whose input was actually based on what his Aunt Brenda said, but she had always been in the know about local scandals and therefore considered a reliable source by Albie. "It seems very convenient that Derek Teal should get killed right after Kemp starts an affair with Opal Teal."

"Convenient, but not necessarily suspicious." Yet Earl had no difficulty in adding details of his own to the story, despite preferring solid evidence to speculation. He was a tall man and had once been thin, but office work and a car were already contributing to what would soon become a weight problem unlikely to be reduced because of his fixed belief that a sedentary life indicated a successful life. Earl was forty-three, plain with a lined face and receding brown hair, but well able to imagine the power that a handsome man might exert over women. With Sandra gone, Colin would be ready for a new affair, and in all likelihood Opal Teal was vulnerably in need of consolation. A car accident and a panicking driver still seemed to be the most probable explanation of Derek Teal's death, but with Colin Kemp apparently connected to both Sandra and Opal, there were questions that needed answers.

"My aunt and uncle run a shop by Barton's factory, and they say that Colin Kemp bought Sandra Stoddard a spider in there on the night she died," continued Albie, a constable with ambitions higher than his lowly rank, eager to display deductive abilities. "Of course it might have been coincidence, but the next thing Sandra Stoddard's dead, then Derek Teal's killed, and Colin Kemp's moved in with the widow."

One spider in a shop was hardly proof of a passionate affair, but it did indicate a relationship outside the factory, and there might also be significance in the fact that Sandra had been murdered two days before the Kemp family arrived in Rosebery Avenue: their new home conveniently, or maybe inconveniently, near to the late Sandra and with the live Opal next door. Earl was officially investigating Derek's death, but a connection to Sandra's murder ought not to be dismissed. "Did you tell Detective Sergeant Grissom about the spider?"

"Yes, but he wouldn't listen to me," grumbled Albie, resentful at the memory of a snub after he had gone out of his way to be helpful.

"Your aunt and uncle are sure it was Colin Kemp with Sandra on the night she died?" asked Earl.

"That's what they told me," said Albie. "They remember it because of hearing about Sandra Stoddard's death the next day, and they knew her well."

"Did they talk to Sandra that night?"

"Yes, and it was definitely her. And definitely Colin Kemp." Albie realized that a further venture into hearsay would not impress Detective Sergeant Lanyon, but was unable to resist adding, "Everyone says that Kemp and Stoddard were having an affair. He's the type. And so was she. You should talk to my aunt."

"Perhaps," conceded Earl, unwilling to acknowledge that a mere constable could have made a sensible suggestion, but the information about Colin Kemp and the spider might be worth following simply to see where it led.

****

Sandra Stoddard's notorious spider, courtesy of Colin Kemp, had not faded from memory. The event was recalled in awesome detail by both Lenny and Brenda Dean, who ran the small shop, scene of the infamous assignation.

"It was the very night that Sandra got killed. We knew her well because she often came in here after work, and joked with everyone." Leonard Dean sighed at the picture in his head of Sandra so vividly alive, laughing as she walked into the shop with Colin, and there was genuine sadness in Lenny's round face as he rested his bulk against the counter. "I never thought for one moment that I wouldn't ever see her again."

"I was surprised that she was with Colin Kemp. Not that Sandra ever lacked men buzzing around her, but the married ones aren't usually prepared to be so — well, so visible. He only stayed a few minutes though, and then fled, probably because I recognized him." Brenda's tone was cynical, implying a worldly knowledge of married men's devious transgressions, and her thin face was resigned as she contemplated Colin's duplicity.

"You're certain it was Colin Kemp?" Earl queried.

"His wife works in the newsagent's, so we know the Kemp family. Their daughter goes to the same school as our Ginevra, and came to her birthday party. Yes, we know Colin Kemp all right. One girlfriend dead and, five minutes later, he's moved in with a woman whose husband isn't cold in his grave." Shoulders bowed, Brenda shook her head at the fickleness, but then added more tolerantly, "Of course, people react to death in all sorts of odd ways, and Colin Kemp won't be an exception, but it still seems cold-hearted when he was clearly fond of Sandra, and she had a horrible end: one she didn't deserve."

"Sandra was wearing a blue dress," said Lenny, gazing at an empty chair in front of the counter: a chair that would now be forever Sandra's to him. "Her necklace was blue as well."

"You can be sure that every word of Len's description is accurate," Brenda declared with a sudden smile, her wiry figure upright again. "If Sandra had ever once looked in his direction, he'd have been off like a racehorse."

"But she never did glance at me, and nor does any other woman," said Lenny, in rueful recognition of his size and sandy-haired plainness "I reckon you're stuck with me, Bren."

"I'll survive, which is more than poor Sandra did. What's happening around here? First Sandra, and then Derek Teal." Brenda looked at Earl for an explanation, but he merely shrugged.

"I wouldn't have to bother you with questions if I already had the answers. Did you know Derek Teal?"

"Yes, we knew him. His daughter goes to school with our Ginevra as well, and was at the birthday party. Derek thanked us the next time he came into the shop. He was a good bloke."

"A good bloke," echoed Lenny.

"What about his wife?" asked Earl.

"Never met her," replied Brenda. "She probably goes to that Chadstone place to shop because I'd know her if she came in here."

"Sad, her losing such a good bloke, even though she's been quick to find a replacement," commented Lenny.

"Perhaps it doesn't seem all that quick to her," Brenda suggested, trying to be charitable.

****

A good bloke. By all accounts, Derek Teal had been a good bloke, and it offended Earl Lanyon's sense of justice when the world lost pleasant people like Sandra and Derek while the evil that had killed them remained very much alive. The certainties of Earl's childhood Presbyterian beliefs were gone, but no remnants of religion had ever cramped Walter Grissom's style because he was in charge of his life, without any need of heavenly intervention to help him achieve ambitions. Large, fair-haired, handsome Detective Sergeant Grissom had supreme confidence in himself and his abilities, which meant that

Walt happily anticipated the glory of further and rapid promotion. He was inclined to mock Earl Lanyon's subdued caution, but could still recognize the value of painstaking work, even though Walt tended to avoid the monotony of interviewing people who had little information to offer, yet would insist on talking at tedious length about whatever crime was being investigated. However, underlings could be delegated to get rid of timewasters, and free Walt to concentrate on the more important aspects of an enquiry, such as the one into Sandra Stoddard's death.

"Yes, I'd picked up the connection between Sandra and Colin Kemp," claimed Walt, not to be outshone, and he leaned back in his chair, pleased that two cases were apparently going to be solved simultaneously through his own analytical skills. "Kemp had an affair with Sandra Stoddard, and the moment she was out of the way, he moved in with the widow of a man who was murdered like Sandra."

"Derek Teal's death could have been an accident," Earl pointed out. There was only one chair in Walt's office, and perhaps deliberately so. Forced to stand on the wrong side of a desk, Earl felt that he had regressed to his schooldays: doubtless a Walt strategy to enhance the Grissom sense of importance. "It's just conjecture that Kemp had an affair with Sandra. There's no solid evidence yet."

"Whether they had an affair or not, he bought her a spider after work, probably trying to ingratiate himself, but when he went around to Sandra's house that night, she rejected him and he killed her."

"Possibly." Earl would have preferred some proof, but Walt was known for his lucky guesses, and Earl's own suspicions had already singled out Kemp for extra scrutiny.

"What's the merry widow like?" asked Walt.

"Not grief-stricken, unless she recovered in record-breaking time." Delicate Opal was the sort of woman who would turn to the strongest character available for help, but the speed of her turning made Earl look for another reason. "I reckon the Teal marriage wasn't a happy one."

"What marriages are, after the novelty's worn off?" Walt liked to pose as a dashing roué, but his wife was the one who had an affair and left him, an insult that still rankled. "Kemp's got a few questions to answer about both deaths."

"He appears to have been more than an acquaintance to Sandra, but we might not link him to either death if he hadn't moved in with Opal so quickly," said Earl. "Would Kemp have done something as stupid as that after he'd killed Sandra or Derek?"

"People don't commit murders expecting to be caught, or they wouldn't do them. Kemp's overconfident. He's probably killed before and got away with it." It was a considerable leap from one spider and one widow to compulsive murderer, but Walt had always relished a dramatic scenario. "Makes you wonder what else is hidden in Kemp's past."

"He doesn't have a criminal record," Earl remarked.

"Which simply means the English police never caught up with him, and now he believes he can get away with anything. I reckon Colin Kemp will be the man we charge with both murders," Walt declared, proud to show off his celebrated instinct. "Kemp's the link between Sandra and Derek. All three lived in the same road and all three worked at Barton's."

"Almost everyone in the area works for Barton's. And Kemp was still living on Bethanyville Hostel when Sandra died."

"He knew her though. Perhaps she threatened to tell his wife about the affair."

"Would that have worried Kemp?" queried Earl. "He left his wife for Opal Teal only weeks later."

"Perhaps he started an affair with Opal months ago, Sandra found out, got jealous, and there was a showdown. Whatever the reason, Kemp had to get rid of Sandra Stoddard."

Earl raised his eyebrows at the supposed passion surging behind Rosebery Avenue's placid suburban façade, but even though Colin had abandoned his wife for the widow next door, Walt's theory still seemed a little too fanciful. "Do you really believe that Kemp is Bethanyville's Vlad the Impaler?"

"I'll believe it if Opal Teal's murdered tonight," laughed Walt, but he would just as readily concoct a scenario involving Lenny Dean or anyone who had known both victims. "Sandra's other boyfriends — well, the ones we've identified so far — all seem to have alibis, but we're still checking. She was very popular, and everybody appears to have liked her."

"Someone didn't," Earl commented.

****

As a migrant in a country new to him, Colin Kemp would expect to be unknown wherever he went, but might have overestimated the chances of remaining anonymous in a small community, and perhaps an insignificant detail was going to be his downfall. The thought pleased Earl who was fond of details, and a killer being caught because of a minor purchase in a shop seemed to indicate that the cosmos was working alongside Detective Sergeant Earl Lanyon despite his long-lost belief that right would always triumph in the end. He was still reacting against the rigid-mindedness of an inflexibly Presbyterian upbringing, and he now equated religion with hypocrisy, but it was as much a part of him as any physical feature, and Colin Kemp's punishment would warm a soul taught to be grim from childhood.

Marriage had once been presented to Earl as a duty, full of responsibilities that wisely restricted both human nature and freedom, but the choices Colin Kemp and Opal Teal had made went further than Earl could condone, despite liberation from the views of his parents, and he was annoyed to experience even the slightest disapproval. Earl was divorced himself, although no third party had been involved because Greta simply walked out, claiming that he made her miserable with his silent criticisms, yet Earl felt he ought to be a man of the world, able to sympathize with the carefree Colin, but that stubbornly Presbyterian conditioning refused to be routed at the sight of Rosebery Avenue's scarlet woman.

Opal's smile was tremulous, emphasizing her fragility, as she opened the front door and saw the maroon Warrant Card in Earl's hand. "Not more questions, I hope."

"A few." Detective Sergeant Lanyon was no Hollywood hunk, but Opal blossomed at the sight of a man, any man, even when the occasion could scarcely be called a social one.

"What do you want to know?" Opal had not asked Earl into the house, but he took an invitation for granted, walked past her to the living-room, and settled in a chair before producing a notebook and biro.

"About Sandra Stoddard —"

Opal sank into the chair opposite Earl and she sighed, leaning back as though exhaustion had abruptly overtaken her at the mere thought of Sandra Stoddard. "What's she got to do with me?"

"Did you ever talk to Sandra?" Earl tried to sound bland, but his voice instinctively softened at Opal's vulnerability.

"I never had a conversation with *her*: not once," declared Opal, apparently responding to an accusation of impropriety. "Why would I speak to the Stoddard woman? We never met."

"But you knew Sandra by sight?"

"Everyone in Rosebery Avenue knew her by sight, as well as the many boyfriends constantly in attendance," said Opal, with an example of the girlish giggle that now infuriated Noreen Kemp. "The rest of us are very dull in comparison, and she was rather conspicuous. And that Stoddard woman liked to be conspicuous."

"Do you know the names of her boyfriends?"

"No, but it would have been tricky to keep up-to-date with them. She was with a different man every time I saw her. I think that it's ten men to every one woman in Australia, isn't it? Well, Sandra Stoddard certainly had more than her quota."

"What about Colin Kemp?" asked Earl, glancing up from his notebook to watch Opal's reaction.

"Colin? He didn't know Sandra Stoddard or her boyfriends. He wasn't living in Rosebery Avenue then."

"No, but he works at Barton's, and so did Sandra."

"This is all too silly for words," protested Opal, smiling. "Colin had nothing whatsoever to do with Sandra Stoddard. He's an engineer and she was just a typist, so I don't suppose they even spoke to each other once. What are you going to say next? That Colin was one of her boyfriends?"

"I'm just trying to learn more about Sandra's background," said Earl, noting the jump that Opal's mind had made from the improbability of an engineer and a typist encountering each other at work, and the possibility of Colin having been Sandra's lover. "I've got to ask questions. It's my job."

"Haven't I suffered enough without you trying to destroy my world yet again?" Opal wilted, victim of cruel fate, before she added, "All those Stoddard boyfriends had cars. She wasn't interested in any man without a car, and Colin doesn't drive."

"You mean that he doesn't own a car."

"It comes to the same thing. That Stoddard woman wouldn't have looked at him." Opal frowned at the memory of Sandra, so young, so self-assured, so outgoing, and so determined to enjoy life to the full in the company of a succession of attentive men. Opal had married too early to appreciate the fun on offer to an attractive woman free of both parental supervision and entanglements: a missed opportunity that had made Sandra's uninhibited behaviour seem part of a conspiracy to scoff at those constrained by other people's rules, and Opal had never coped well with mockery.

"Your husband Derek worked in Barton's factory too," Earl pointed out. "Did he know Sandra?"

"Only by sight, like me." Opal attempted another regretful sigh, but realized that too much grief at a reminder of the lost Derek would hardly appear convincing when he had already been replaced, and she wisely stuck to the topic of Sandra. "There's meant to be safety in numbers, but I suppose it was inevitable that one of the Stoddard boyfriends would get violently jealous sooner or later and kill her."

"We're still building up a picture of what happened to Sandra."

"The police continue their enquiries. That's what the newspapers always say, but everyone in Rosebery Avenue has played detective and knows exactly what happened to her. And why it happened." Opal smiled again, while shaking her head at Sandra's folly. "The Stoddard woman simply took one chance too many, I imagine, and had to pay the price of thinking that she could do whatever she liked."

As Opal was living with a man who had been a stranger a few weeks previously, Earl hoped that she would listen to her own criticism of Sandra's rashness, but he was there to ask questions, not issue warnings even to a woman possibly in urgent need of protection from Bethanyville's very own murderer. "Has Colin Kemp ever spoken to you about Sandra?"

"Never," replied Opal, standing up as she heard the front door open. "This will be Colin now, so he can tell you himself that he didn't know the woman. Colin! We're in here, and I'm being cross-examined by a detective. Come and rescue me. It's all to do with that Sandra Stoddard, but you never even spoke to her once, did you?"

Colin walked into the room, apparently untroubled at the prospect of police questioning, but Opal had given him valuable seconds to prepare, and Earl was not surprised that Colin should seem relaxed as he said, "I talked to Sandra every so often when we were at work. She occasionally did some typing for me."

"I never knew that," said Opal, taken aback to learn of even a slight connection with the disreputable Sandra.

"I would have told you, if you'd asked me. But I don't think we've ever mentioned Sandra, have we?"

"No, of course we haven't. Why should we talk about her? She was nothing to either of us." Opal turned to Earl and Colin sat down, at home in a house that had so recently been another man's territory. "It's quite clear we can't help any police enquiry, no matter how many questions you ask us."

Despite his absolute rejection of childhood indoctrination, Earl would always have to fight a tendency to regard someone with easy-going morals as capable of any crime, and attempts to keep an open mind failed. Colin was already guilty of having blithely abandoned wife and child in order to trespass on a dead man's terrain: an action with lascivious origins that might predate Derek Teal's death. "What did you talk to Sandra about, Mr Kemp?"

"Things at work," said Colin, dismissing the information with a shrug to demonstrate how insignificant it was.

"What things exactly?"

The words sounded like sarcasm, and Colin looked puzzled at Earl's reaction. "I'd talk to Sandra about forms or reports: things that she'd be typing up for me."

"What else would they be talking about?" Opal demanded. "They hardly knew each other."

"Sandra and I were just employees in the same factory," agreed Colin.

"I've been told that Sandra was involved with a married man," said Earl, half-heartedly endeavouring to keep his voice free of the contempt that he was ashamed to feel. "Can you supply the married man's name?"

"I never talked to Sandra about anything like that," said Colin.

"Anything like what?" asked Earl.

"Boyfriends. Her personal life. Sandra was someone else who worked at Barton's, that's all."

"Yet you bought her a spider on the night she was killed," remarked Earl.

The statement, more an accusation, was so bizarre that Colin shook his head in bewilderment. "A spider? I've never bought anyone a spider. Are they kept as pets over here? I thought Australian spiders were all poisonous."

Earl sighed, impatient with a migrant's possibly feigned ignorance, and he made Colin feel very conscious of being an alien in an alien land. "I'm talking about a mix of ice-cream and lemonade. It's called a spider."

"Why?" asked Colin.

"How should I know?" retorted Earl. "But you bought one for Sandra the night she was killed. You were seen in a shop together: the shop next to Barton's factory."

"Sandra had stayed after work to finish typing a report for me, and so I offered to buy her an ice-cream as a thank-you," explained Colin, Sandra Stoddard very much alive in his mind as she laughed and chatted in the shop with Brenda Dean. Bright and beautiful Sandra, blue dress matching the colour of her eyes, fair curls tied back in a pony-tail; voluptuous and vivacious Sandra, unaware that she was rapidly approaching the end of a happy life that should have lasted years longer, decades longer. "Actually, I thought she asked for cider, and as the drink came in a metal beaker with a straw, I simply assumed that Sandra had changed her mind about wanting some ice-cream."

"But you admit to buying her presents?"

"It wasn't a present, merely a thank-you," protested Colin. "You might have said that the day was cool, but to me it felt warmer than an English summer often is, so I bought myself an ice-lolly or icy-pole or whatever it is you call them over here, and then I went back to the Hostel, leaving Sandra in the shop."

"Did you regularly stay behind at the factory with her after work?" enquired Earl.

"What exactly are you implying now?" demanded Opal. "Colin wouldn't have had anything to do with that woman."

"How do you know?" asked Earl.

"I just do!" Opal declared, with such childlike and round-eyed naïveté that Earl wished she could be right.

"I only worked late with Sandra that one time," said Colin. "We clock in and out at Barton's, so you can check the factory's record."

"We have, and Sandra stayed in the factory after work more than once."

"Not with me," maintained Colin. "Sandra worked days, but I do all sorts of shifts."

"So you knew her schedule," commented Earl.

"Of course I did. If Sandra wasn't there, any paperwork had to wait until the next day to get typed."

"You never told me that you knew the Stoddard woman well enough to buy her presents," said Opal, and Earl felt sorry to witness the start of disillusionment with a man who must have seemed the only support left for Opal to cling to.

"I didn't buy Sandra presents; it was one drink." Colin knew he sounded defensive, and also knew that Detective Sergeant Lanyon was watching him. "Sandra had done me a favour by staying to type up that report, and I was grateful. I'd arranged to have a couple of days off because we were moving into the new house, and I wanted my report on the manager's desk before I left work that afternoon. And so I offered to buy Sandra an ice-cream. It was just a way of thanking her."

"Anybody would be grateful," agreed Opal. "Like leaving a tip for the waitress in a restaurant."

But Sandra Stoddard had been no anonymous waitress. Colin Kemp had known Sandra well enough to buy her a spider on the night she died: a night only thirty or so hours before he moved to Rosebery Avenue. Mere facts, not enough to convict Colin of anything, but still facts, and Earl approved of facts. "Where were you on the night that Derek Teal died?"

Opal gasped at the bluntness of the question, but Colin remained unfazed. "I was doing a shift at Barton's. Check the factory record."

"I have," said Earl.

"Then why ask?" demanded Opal. "This is persecution."

"No, it's a police investigation," said Colin. "He has to ask unpleasant things."

"Well, now that he's got his answers, he can go," retorted Opal.

****

As a wronged and deserted wife, Noreen should have had Earl Lanyon's sympathy, but something about her reminded him of his Bible-quoting mother, and he had difficulty in not snarling the questions at her as he sat in the Kemp living-room.

"Did you know that your husband knew Sandra Stoddard?"

"Yes. I knew her as well," replied Noreen. "She often came into the newsagent's. That's where I work."

"Did Sandra talk to you about your husband?"

"She never mentioned Colin, but I don't suppose she realized that I was married to him. The shop's always busy when a factory shift ends, so I didn't ever really chat with her."

Earl's mother would not have chatted to anyone either, when duty dictated that she concentrate on a job, and he frowned at the thought. "But you knew who Sandra was."

"Everybody knew her."

Earl wondered at Noreen's matter-of-fact answers and the way that she could mention a flown husband without apparent rancour, although her wounds would still be raw. His mother never displayed feelings to a stranger, and the many pamphlets that littered the room also damned Noreen because Earl imagined they were something to do with religion. Had he known that most of the leaflets concerned radiation poisoning and that Noreen would soon throw them out, Earl's disapproval might have increased as even harsh facts were preferable to fiction. Opal's excesses of ornaments and frills had appealed more to Earl, simply because of their contrast to the stark plainness of his childhood home.

"When you lived in England —" Earl paused, but there was no tactful way of asking the question. "Did your husband have women friends in London?"

"No." The answer came automatically, but Noreen was aware that she could no longer be sure of what had once seemed obvious. Opal might not have been the first because Colin had often worked late, or claimed to be working late, and Noreen was uncertain whether the idea of multiple duplicity hurt more than the comfort of knowing that Opal was just another floozy of whom Colin would tire sooner or later. The many attractions of Sandra Stoddard could also have enticed him, and the questions about her indicated that Detective Sergeant Lanyon thought a relationship between Sandra and Colin had been a possibility. So did Noreen, given recent events in the life of the man she had married.

"Did your husband ever mention meeting Sandra after work?" asked Earl.

"No. Did he?"

Earl pretended not to have heard Noreen, and scribbled in his notebook to allow time for the notion of a Colin-Sandra affair to take hold in Noreen's mind, even though Earl suspected her of being able to hide all emotion, assuming that she felt anything deeply. "So, as far as you know, your husband only met Sandra in the factory."

"That's right." But what did Noreen really know of Colin? Perhaps people had been laughing and gossiping behind her back from the start. There were always pretty typists like Sandra, young typists, attractive girls everywhere, and Noreen marvelled at her former smug confidence that she was the only woman Colin would ever want. Perhaps her complacency had driven him away, and he might have welcomed Noreen's obsession with nuclear war because it meant that her attention never focused on his own obsessions. "Did Colin have an affair with Sandra?"

The words were easier to say than Noreen would once have thought possible, and even easier to believe now that Colin was next door with Opal Teal. He had become a stranger, and capable of any betrayal.

"I have to ask personal questions," said Earl, knowing that his words would sound empty to Noreen. "It's just routine, nothing more. For example, does your husband drive?"

"Colin learnt in the RAF, but we — he's never owned a car." What was in Lanyon's mind? That Colin had killed Sandra Stoddard and then Derek Teal? Colin might have become a mystery to Noreen, yet she was unable to picture him as ruthless assassin, but presumably the police did and suspected Colin of removing an out-of-favour Sandra after he began an affair with Opal that had led him to eliminate the inconvenient Derek. Colin might now be a stranger to Noreen, but still she shook her head. "If you think that he had anything to do with the deaths of either Derek or Sandra, you're wrong."

"I don't think," Earl claimed. "I just go around asking questions. It's routine, as I said. Your husband was off-work the day following Sandra's death."

"So was I. We timed the move to Rosebery Avenue with a couple of days off, but Colin was working a nightshift when Derek was killed. You can check Barton's record."

"I have."

"You don't really think Colin sneaked out of the factory, do you? How could he know Derek was going to walk down the road just then? And where would Colin get hold of a car?"

The points were good ones. However, Colin might have arranged to meet Derek, despite a rendezvous at such a time and such a place being somewhat unlikely, and the reason given to Derek for the supposed encounter stayed elusive. But there had never previously been a murder in Bethanyville, and two deaths so close together of people who lived in the same street and who worked at the same factory indicated a single killer. Colin Kemp was linked to both victims, and two killers with entirely separate motives carried coincidence to extremes in Earl's judgment.

"Did your husband seem worried when he came home from work on the morning that Derek Teal died?"

"No. Colin wasn't any different. He'd seen police cars in the road on his way back, and heard something about an accident, but he didn't know it was Derek who'd been killed." Yet Noreen found herself adding details that she knew existed only in her imagination. Had Colin been truly upset by the news? He normally shunned emotional scenes, yet that morning he had hurried to Opal's side, perhaps so they could get their stories straight for the police. What Englishman would willingly and unnecessarily race next door to involve himself in another family's tragedy? Certainly not the man Noreen had married. "Colin was shocked by Derek's death, and so was I."

"Had you ever heard the Teals arguing?"

"No." Between work and nuclear war, Noreen had rarely made time to notice other people's lives, yet even the first suggestions by Colin of an unhappy Teal marriage had come as no surprise, because her suspicion of Derek's possible affair with Sandra predated his death. Derek had appeared easy-going, but Opal would always be discontented with her lot, wanting more and more, convinced with the tenacity of a determined toddler that screamed demands were going to produce results, and that would alienate any husband. The Teals had been an ill-matched couple from the start: just like Noreen and Colin, it seemed.

Australia had once been the refuge, the only place in the world where Noreen could feel safe, yet her personal world had exploded with a force rivalling that of any atom bomb, and she was bewildered by the speed with which so much had been destroyed. The Colin she married no longer existed, but could the stranger inhabiting his body have murdered both Sandra Stoddard and Derek Teal? A few days earlier Noreen would have laughed at the idea, but laughter had entirely deserted her, along with Colin. Yet why would he kill the lovely and spirited Sandra? Had she tried to end their affair? Was Opal Teal a mere consolation prize before Colin moved on again? What did he find so special about Opal that she lived but Sandra had died?

"I don't know anything," said Noreen.

But there was one thing that Noreen would know. "On the night that Sandra Stoddard died, was your husband with you the whole time?"

"Yes," replied Noreen. "Yes, I think so."

"You only *think* so?" queried Earl.

"It gets sticky and stuffy inside those hostel Nissen huts during hot weather. Colin doesn't sleep well, and he'd sometimes go down to the toilet block and take a shower, or sit outside on the hut steps." Even as she spoke, Noreen was aware of how very stupid she had been. The explanations given by Colin whenever she had awoken on his return to bed now sounded as phoney as he was.

"It wasn't hot when Sandra died; it was August: winter. Did he leave the hut that night?"

"I'm not sure. I don't remember."

"So you can't confirm he was with you all that night?"

"I think he was." Less than half a mile away, Sandra Stoddard's life had ended, but Noreen slept through the night undisturbed. In the morning, she would have gone to the Hostel canteen for breakfast, presumably done some packing for the next day's move, and definitely invited friends to what would become a farewell party in the hut that evening. But had Colin been with her the whole of the previous night?

"I don't really remember the actual night that Sandra died," Noreen admitted. It seemed callous and self-centred, but it was unfortunately true. "I remember the next night though, when we read about her death in a newspaper. I couldn't believe something so awful had happened to someone so nice," Noreen added, to prove that she was more sensitive that she might appear.

"How did your husband react to the news about Sandra?" asked Earl.

Colin's reaction? Had it been genuine shock, or a performance staged for Noreen's edification? At the time she had had no suspicion that he was anything but distressed; however, in those days Noreen had also assumed that she knew her husband.

"Colin was shocked, terribly shocked," Noreen decided, "just like me."

But no matter how shocked Noreen was to hear of Sandra's death, it had been nothing to the shock she experienced when Colin abandoned his marriage. Noreen was trudging through gloomily bleak days while the rest of Australia danced in sunlight, and coping with each morning, afternoon and evening was such an effort that she had no time to spare for anything else. Fear of nuclear disaster had given Noreen furious energy to try and thwart the warmongers, but now she was trapped in a fog that surrounded her alone, a fog colder and more disheartening than any London peasouper, leaving Noreen uncertain which direction she should take or what she ought to do next.

****

"Everything's been fingerprinted," said Walt, looking as complacent as if the investigative abilities of Detective Sergeant Walter Grissom, rather than a postman, had delivered the new evidence.

An open paperback book had Colin Kemp's name scrawled on its title page, and the six photographs beside the book were of Sandra Stoddard, the woman who had had a model's figure and stance but too much character ever to be one of the bland zombies draped across cars or furniture in magazines. Unmistakeably Sandra Stoddard, even though her face was obliterated with black ink on all the pictures: pictures deliberately and literally defaced. An assortment of blue stars had been drawn at the top of each photo, decorated stars as flamboyant as Sandra's short life, the symbols perhaps serving as a code that only the intended recipient would know how to interpret. In spite of these messages or possibly because of them, somebody had exulted in Sandra's death, and the photographs appeared to be a gloating memento, a souvenir of hatred.

"Now, who posted these to me?" said Walt, laying out the pictures to form a row across his desk. "That's the interesting bit. Who went to the bother of sending the book and photos to me?"

"Noreen Kemp," Earl decided. "She's the religious-fanatic type. Bitter, though she hides it well."

"All ex-wives are bitter," declared Walt, laughing. "Mine would point the finger at me for any crime, and gleefully manufacture the necessary evidence." Walt was wrong. His ex-wife had no resentment against him whatsoever, having relegated her philandering husband to the past when she fluttered off with a car mechanic from Bendigo. Walt was the spouse left with the bitterness of having been spurned, but tried to pretend even to himself that he was now happily free to satisfy the desire felt by every woman who had the good fortune to encounter him: a playboy, rather than a reject.

Earl picked up the book, its cover showing the silhouette of a top-hatted frock-coated man lurking in shadows below a blood-red title: *The Whitechapel Murderer.* A torn piece of brown paper had been used as wrapping, the police station's address was handwritten in capitals, and a local postmark covered far too many stamps. The sender had not wanted to take the package into a post office.

"The book and pictures could have been sent by one of the usual timewasters," Earl suggested.

"If we're dealing with a timewaster, he had a ready supply of Sandra Stoddard photographs," said Walt. "Although she had a ready supply of boyfriends: not as many as gossip maintains, but still quite a few."

"One of them could be trying to frame Kemp," Earl pointed out. "It might be less a timewaster than the killer himself. He must have hated Sandra to destroy her face in the pictures."

With the presumed exception of her killer, no one else had apparently hated Sandra Stoddard, despite a little righteous criticism of her behaviour, and the death might turn out to be the result of a stranger's random act of madness, but one thing was plain: somebody hated Colin Kemp and wanted to cause trouble for him.

"Were there any useful fingerprints?" asked Earl. "Though I reckon whoever sent the book and pictures would have to be downright stupid not to wear gloves."

"Sandra Stoddard handled the photos at one time, but that's not surprising. There were a few unidentified prints as well, so I need to get Colin Kemp's. If Sandra gave him the pictures, their relationship went further than one spider."

"Would he keep the photographs if he'd killed her?" Earl knew that he was looking for commonsense in a man capable of murder, and the pictures might have represented trophies to Colin Kemp as he gloated over his power to end the life of a woman no longer in favour; however, it still appeared most unlikely that he would be careless enough to leave damning evidence behind him for a ditched wife to discover and take her revenge by alerting the police. "Colin Kemp doesn't strike me as a fool."

"All killers are fools," decreed Walt. "No amount of hatred or vengeance could be worth risking the death penalty."

"If Kemp murdered Sandra, he'll probably have lost control, and not thought of consequences," said Earl, picking up the paperback book again and studying the signature inside it. "Odd that Noreen Kemp should act anonymously. I'd have reckoned she was the type who'd consider it her duty to get Kemp arrested and charged. I'm surprised that she didn't deliver the photos in person."

"Looks like I'll have solved Derek Teal's death for you, when I arrest Colin Kemp for murdering Sandra Stoddard," remarked Walt.

6

Opal Teal was happy. She had a handsome man in love with her: a handsome man who earned good money. Opal would have been attracted to Colin Kemp whatever his income, but high wages were a definite bonus. Colin could afford to be generous even after paying for Hester, and the girl should be going out to work in a couple of years. Charmian would also be gone at that same happy time, freeing Opal to concentrate on her new and wonderful life. The wasted years with Derek could be forgotten because Opal planned to move to the most expensive part of Melbourne and have smart clothes and smart friends. Noreen was a hick, but Opal would be at home in the sophisticated atmosphere of Toorak with a wealthy man who adored her. It was the happy ending promised by a Hollywood film, and Opal could at last look forward with confidence.

****

Charmian saw Hester further down the road: a lucky Hester able to hurry home from school to a house that had no outsider in it, and where she could tell her mother that yet again Hester Kemp had the glory of being top in every single one of the Friday tests. Hester would then add that Charmian Teal had made a fool of herself in those very same tests, and it meant revenge was the only solace left to Charmian. Eager to make someone else as unhappy as she was, Charmian ran to catch up with Hester.

"Your ghastly father killed Sandra Stoddard, and the whole school knows it."

"Only because you're a liar." Hester had caught a glimpse of the enemy while turning to cross a road, and assumed that Charmian would ignore her, but the breathless accusation had probably been inevitable and Hester was glad of an opportunity to prove that Charmian's slanders meant nothing to her.

"Your filthy father tried to move in with Sandra because he hates you and your mother, but Sandra refused point blank and so he killed her. I've got proof."

"You can't prove something that never happened."

"He collected photos of Sandra, and scribbled across her face in every single one of them: scribbled with vicious hatred."

"Instead of using a biro?" retorted Hester, trying to laugh. "Anyway, how could you know that it was Sandra in the photos if there isn't a face?"

Charmian had no intention of being sidetracked by feeble attempts at either ridicule or logic, and she continued relentlessly. "Then your horrible father put the photos in one of my Dad's books, trying to make it look like he killed Sandra, but nobody was fooled, and so your rotten father killed him too."

"My Dad doesn't have a car," scoffed Hester. "How could he run anyone down?"

"He stole our car on purpose to kill my Dad and get him blamed for Sandra's death. I'm going to tell Albie Fulton that I saw your murdering father sneak into our garage and drive the car away."

"Without its keys? Or is Dad supposed to have stolen them as well?"

"He didn't switch the engine or lights on. He took the brake off and let the car go down the hill so that my Dad wouldn't see or hear anything behind him."

"That's just stupid!" It was automatic loyalty, the words said merely to contradict Charmian, but Hester found that she was already doubting Colin. She no longer knew the father who had deserted wife and daughter for a separate existence that shut both of them out, because if Colin could do that, then he might be capable of any atrocity. "How did he get the car back into your garage? Push it all the way up the hill by himself?"

"Spot on!" declared Charmian, ready to accept any explanation of a purportedly-stolen car's continued presence inside the Teal garage. "Your evil father's going to be hanged."

So much would be solved by Colin's removal from Rosebery Avenue that, for a split-second, the idea of his death actually came as a relief. Then, spurred on by guilt at having wished her father to dangle lifelessly at the end of a rope, Hester rushed to defend him. "If you think that he could hurt anybody, you don't know the first thing about my Dad."

"I know everything about him, and he deserves all he gets."

Hester felt that she would prefer to be as dead as both Sandra Stoddard and Derek Teal rather than let Charmian know that Colin's daughter had agreed with her, if only for an instant, and Hester tried to laugh again. "Actually, it was your father who had an affair with Sandra. Ask anybody in Rosebery Avenue. All the neighbours know, and they talk about it the whole time. That's why your mother was glad to be rid of him, and find herself a much better man."

"You're a liar, Hester Kemp, just like your father. I saw him drive our car out of the garage to murder my Dad."

"Then you're the liar!"

"No, I'm not, and I'm going to tell the police everything about your killer of a father."

"They'll laugh just as loud as me," predicted Hester.

"Not now they've got proof," retorted Charmian, hurrying away so that she could comfort herself with the satisfaction of having had the last word.

****

The photographs of Sandra had been tossed into the Teal's garbage bin, along with a book about Monty's Double that once belonged to Derek, but the malevolence behind the obliteration of Sandra's face could never have been his, and Charmian knew exactly who to blame. Colin Kemp had wrecked her whole world and he deserved to be punished. Justice demanded that Kemp suffer the way she was suffering, and it seemed further proof of his warped nature that he had brought a book about Jack the Ripper into the Teal house to mock Charmian. The police should be able to work matters out for themselves, although nothing appeared to have happened, but Charmian had a plan guaranteed to force them into action and, even better, give her a reason to accost Albie Fulton.

****

At the end of Rosebery Avenue, close to the scrubland where Derek had died, there was a starkly square block of flats, three storeys high, but seeming even larger in contrast to the squat houses that dotted the rest of the hillside. Constable Albert Fulton rented one of those flats, and Charmian had often loitered outside the building in an attempt to meet him by chance, but at last she had a watertight excuse to stop her idol and talk to him, and the Kemp takeover of Charmian's home was almost worthwhile when it offered her such a glorious opportunity to ambush Albie Fulton.

The afternoon sun dazzled Charmian's eyes, but not as much as Albie did when he got out of his car. The song of both birds and cicadas had been overpowered by engine noise, but now the whole of Bethanyville seemed to be holding its breath, as if waiting for Hollywood-music accompaniment as Albie walked towards her. He was just as alluring close up as from afar, and Charmian, wearing best dress with sparkling necklace and hair tortured into curls, hoped Albie would assume that she was sixteen at the very least. He looked so gorgeous in blue jeans and open-necked purple shirt that Charmian's nerve almost failed her, but it was a case of now or never.

"I know who killed Sandra Stoddard." Charmian spoke too quickly, the words almost gabbled, but Albie stopped walking and stared at her, his face blank with surprise. "I'm a witness, a vital witness."

Albie continued to stare, and Charmian noted that his eyes were blue as she had expected, a blue dark as night skies, and to gaze at such perfection silenced her until Albie eventually asked, "Witness? How do you mean, witness? You're a witness to what?"

"I saw him," said Charmian, encouraged by gaining Albie's full attention. "I saw him steal our car."

"What car? What are you talking about?"

"Oh, I forgot to say that he murdered my Dad as well as Sandra. You have to arrest him, Albie, before he kills me too. And my mother."

Albie frowned in bewilderment. "You saw Sandra Stoddard die? You can't have."

"What I witnessed was him stealing our car to murder my Dad, but he killed Sandra as well, and you've got to arrest him."

"Then you didn't see Sandra Stoddard die?" ventured Albie, as he attempted to make sense of Charmian's jumbled story.

"I didn't actually *witness* him murder Sandra," Charmian conceded, "but everyone in Bethanyville knows that he did it. You ask anybody at the school. And then he killed my Dad as well. Ran him down with our very own car."

"So you didn't see Sandra Stoddard die?"

"No, but I definitely witnessed him stealing our car." Charmian wished that she could sound as calmly adult as she had intended, but her words tripped over each other in their rush to be spoken. "I'm Charmian, Derek Teal's daughter, and Colin Kemp killed my Dad. You've got to arrest him."

"Colin Kemp?" Albie demanded. "You saw Colin Kemp kill your father?"

"No," admitted Charmian. "But I did see him go into our garage and steal the car."

"What's that got to do with Sandra Stoddard?"

"Everything. He killed her."

"What makes you so certain?" Albie queried, after a pause that allowed Charmian to regain some self-assurance.

"Because Colin Kemp's a murderer. That's why he stole our car and killed my Dad." It was as straightforward as arithmetic, and Charmian hoped that she had impressed Albie with such matter-of-fact logic. The details were absolutely clear in her mind, and Charmian could tell that Albie was interested in every word she said, not dismissing her as a silly child. Perhaps he would get promoted because of the crucial evidence provided by Charmian Teal and be forever grateful to her. Ginevra Dean had mentioned Cousin Albie's ambition to become a detective, and Charmian yearned to help him achieve his goal. "I'll cross my heart and swear on the Bible, if you like. I saw Kemp steal our car and drive away in it to kill my Dad."

"How come you haven't said anything before?" enquired Albie, as he evaluated Charmian's claim. "How come you waited until now before telling anyone about Colin Kemp?"

"Nobody asked me. But I'll talk to anyone you like, anyone at all."

Albie nodded, but he looked doubtfully at Charmian, and she hurried to reassure him.

"I'm frightened of Colin Kemp, but I'll do anything to stop him killing my mother."

"Is he violent?"

"Yes, of course," replied Charmian, surprised that so obvious a fact needed to be stated. "He's murdered two people already. That's why I'm frightened of him."

Albie thought for a moment, and then said, "We'd need more evidence before he could be arrested and charged. It'd make the case against Kemp much stronger if you'd ever seen him with Sandra Stoddard."

It was very plain what information Albie wanted Charmian to supply, and she obliged. "Colin Kemp used to visit Sandra long before he moved to Rosebery Avenue."

"You saw him go inside her house?"

"Loads of times." And Charmian was easily able to picture Colin walking up the path lined with rosebushes to Sandra's door. Perhaps he even had a key. Yes, he would produce the key from a pocket and then open the front door, exactly the way he did at Charmian's house. The scene was as vivid as watching a film, but could be no Hollywood illusion because it had happened. It must have happened. How else had Colin Kemp got inside Sandra Stoddard's house and murdered her? "I saw him go up to Sandra's place and open the front door with a key. Yes, I saw him go inside her house heaps of times."

Albie smiled and Charmian smiled back, thrilled to have pleased him.

****

"Why hasn't she told anyone before now?" asked Earl.

"She's frightened of Colin Kemp." Inside a police station but wearing casual clothes, Albie could imagine the future Detective Inspector Albert Fulton and the meteoric rise that swept him to greatness. Even as a Constable, he revealed the initiative separating him from the mediocre because, instead of wasting time on routine and written reports, he had rushed vital information to one of the men able to act immediately on it, but the future Detective Inspector Albert Fulton was to be no sour-faced Earl Lanyon, sitting behind a desk and frowning at nothing. The future Detective Inspector Albert Fulton would already have left the building on his way to arrest Colin Kemp. "The kid couldn't talk to anyone while Kemp was around, and her mother's a fool about the man."

"You shouldn't have interviewed a kid on her own."

"I didn't interview her," protested Albie, taken aback to find himself rebuked rather than congratulated. "She just ran up to me and blurted the whole thing out. Kemp's at work, so I sent the kid home and said to stay there because someone would be around to see her before Kemp left Barton's.'"

If things seemed too good to be true, they usually were too good to be true, in Earl's experience. The sudden emergence of a witness who had seen Colin Kemp use his own key to go into Sandra Stoddard's house would be a giant step forward in Walt Grissom's investigation, but when that witness had also seen Colin Kemp steal a car on the night of Derek Teal's death, a night Kemp supposedly spent inside a factory, it was definitely too much good luck. Miracles happened, but not to Earl Lanyon, and they never would because he had no belief in them.

"Her story adds up," said Albie, impatient with Earl's cautiousness. "The kid was very sure of what she told me."

However, Earl knew that a child's testimony in the formality of a courtroom was unlikely to be delivered with confidence, even if the plethora of Colin Kemp sightings were genuine. The police would need a lot more evidence than Charmian's word before an arrest could be made. "There's no proof that the girl saw what she claims to have seen."

"Why would the kid make it up?" asked Albie, but the answer was all too obvious even to him. Charmian resented Colin Kemp's occupation of her home, and was plotting his removal. "Surely she wouldn't risk trouble with the police by weaving a web of lies."

As adults often had a tendency to weave more than one web of lies while talking to a policeman, it seemed doubtful that the next generation would have higher standards, but a statement from Charmian, whether true or false, could be useful for putting pressure on Colin Kemp, and Earl stood up.

"I'm not on duty right now, but I'll go with you, if you like," offered Albie. "The kid might talk more freely with me there."

Earl would prefer Charmian simply to stick to the facts, if there were any, rather than babble as profusely as a creek in full flow, and he shook his head.

"I think she trusts me," Albie argued, unwilling to relinquish his star witness to another handler. "After all, the kid chose to talk to me."

However, Earl wanted to see Charmian Teal's reaction to a stranger, and if the story changed to suit her audience. Spinning a tale to a gullibly young Constable could have encouraged Charmian to add details to impress him, assuming that there was any truth behind her claims, but questions from a sceptical older man of higher rank might intimidate Charmian out of any attempt to embellish either her facts or her fantasy.

"I'll deal with it," said Earl, ignoring Albie's offended glare.

****

"Oh, no, not again. Not another cross-examination by a policeman." Opal sighed with mock weariness at the sight of Earl, and then added a giggle to assure him that she was still ready to appreciate male company. "You'll have to put up with me on my own. Colin's at work."

Opal made it sound like an opportunity: a playful flirt who imagined that she was in control of any situation involving a man, and Earl could understand how easily she had been appropriated by Colin Kemp.

"I'm here to talk to your daughter." Earl hoped that the kid's yarn would at least alert Opal to the fact that she knew very little of Colin Kemp, even if Charmian had invented whatever she was going to say, but Earl suspected that Opal would cling to her new love, refusing to believe anything bad about him, no matter how much evidence against Colin later emerged.

"Charmian?" Opal was round-eyed with surprise to discover that a man's attention was diverted from her, especially when it had been transferred to an ungainly schoolgirl. "Why do you want to talk to Charmian?"

"Do you know Constable Albert Fulton?"

"I've never heard of him. What's he got to do with Charmian?" Opal smiled at the idea of a connection between her daughter and a policeman; then amusement abruptly changed to exasperation. "Has the silly girl been telling more of her lies about Colin? You can't credit a word she utters."

"I still want to talk to her." Earl made an attempt to keep his tone neutral, but he was already inclined to agree with Opal that listening to anything Charmian had to say would be a waste of time.

"If you must talk to her, then I suppose you must," said Opal, making no effort to hide the annoyance she felt. "But Charmian's a liar, and has been her whole life. That's all there is to it. She's totally self-centred; cares nothing at all for my happiness. You'd think that a daughter would have more compassion, but not Charmian; oh, no, not Charmian Teal."

Even if the girl had told the truth about Colin Kemp to Albert Fulton, her mother would reject the allegations, and Earl again felt sorry for Opal. She was the type of woman always targeted by conmen, and no amount of harsh experience was likely to make her less naïve. "Is Charmian here?" asked Earl before Opal's grievances could be elaborated.

"Of course she's here; she's always here. Charmian doesn't seem to have any friends at all, and that's understandable." Appalled at the extent of her daughter's meddling, Opal led the way into the living-room. "I hope you're not going to charge the stupid girl with wasting police time, but it'd serve her right if you did. Charmian! Come here! Come here at once."

Opal's command was delivered in a voice so weak that anybody more than a few feet away could hardly be expected to hear it, but Charmian must have been listening attentively from behind her bedroom door because she immediately appeared.

Earl had imagined he would see a junior version of Opal, but Charmian looked determined and capable, and also decidedly petulant. She had thought that Albie would be there to support and encourage her when she spoke to a detective, and the disappointment was acute.

"What lies have you been spreading about poor Colin?" asked Opal, wilting into a chair. "You're in real trouble now that the police have heard the terrible things you've been saying."

"It's the truth," Charmian informed Earl, turning her back on Opal. "I told Albie nothing but the truth."

"Albie?" Earl was usually uncomfortable when he had to question a kid, but Charmian was no frightened or vulnerable youngster, and Earl wondered how the gentle Opal managed to cope daily with so truculent a daughter. "Do you know Constable Fulton, Charmian?"

"Whether she knows this Albie or not, she told him a pack of lies," declared Opal. "Why are you so cruel, Charmian? Why are you trying to wreck my happiness?"

"You called Constable Fulton by his first name," Earl continued quickly, hoping to avert an emotional scene as Opal sounded close to tears. "Do you know him well, Charmian?"

"Yes. Albie's a friend of mine. Sort of."

"How much of a friend?"

"I know Albie's cousin Ginevra Dean, but she's a lot younger than me." Charmian straightened her back in an effort to look taller. No Detective Sergeant was going to refer to Charmian Teal as a child when Albie Fulton was around, if she could prevent it.

"Don't listen to a thing Charmian says," urged Opal. "She lies all the time."

"No, I don't. You're the liar. I saw Colin Kemp break into our garage and steal the car on the night he murdered Dad, and I saw him go into Sandra's house loads of times," Charmian maintained, obstinately determined not to let Albie down.

"Colin never stole anything in his life. He's the most honest man I've ever known," protested Opal. "And he barely recognized the Stoddard woman by sight."

"How would you know?" retorted Charmian. "He's a liar like you. I saw him with Sandra, and I saw him steal our car."

"The car's never been stolen, not once," scoffed Opal.

"He put it back in the garage after he'd killed Dad." Charmian pressed her lips together in defiance, not prepared to retreat an inch, and Earl was glad that his marriage had been childfree.

"How come none of the neighbours heard a car leave your garage or saw any headlights?" asked Earl, before recalling that Colin Kemp was the insomniac neighbour who claimed he always knew when the Teal car left its garage at night, and Colin Kemp had purportedly been at work among Barton's Biscuits when Derek died, according to factory records.

"That murderer was so sneaky, he didn't switch the engine or headlights on. He coasted along the path to our gate and then down the hill," said Charmian.

"How is Colin supposed to have returned the car?" enquired Opal, laughing derisively. "Did he coast uphill?"

"No, of course not." Charmian had given the matter extensive thought to make sure that there would be enough irrefutable evidence against Colin Kemp to guarantee his arrest, and she had worked out what was hopefully a more plausible theory than Hester's facetious idea. "He stole the car keys so that, after he'd murdered Dad, he could drive right to the very top of Rosebery Avenue, then coast down and turn into our driveway to get the car back inside the garage without anyone knowing it had gone."

"What an imagination you've got, Charmian." Opal forced another laugh, and glanced at Earl, obviously expecting him to share the ludicrous joke. "I hate to say it of my own daughter, but the girl must be mad."

"Charmian, why didn't you tell anyone about this before?" asked Earl.

"I did, but *she* wouldn't listen." Charmian glared at Opal, and complained, "She just won't believe that he's a murderer, so I told Albie instead. And Albie believes me."

"Then he's a fool," Opal looked distressed, and turned again to Earl for support. "I don't know why Charmian's such a liar, and she doesn't even invent credible stories. She can't possibly see the garage from her bedroom. It's on the other side of the house."

"I wasn't in my room; I was in the kitchen," said Charmian. "I woke up when the front door slammed, and went to get a drink of water."

"To see if there was any ice-cream in the fridge," amended Opal. "Charmian never stops eating. She won't have a shape soon; she'll just be a huge blob. Anyway, the wretched liar couldn't see anything outside with the kitchen light on. And the curtains would be drawn."

"I didn't put the light on," snarled Charmian. "I opened the curtains instead, and saw that murderer Kemp go into our garage. Then the car came out."

"How come you didn't wake your Mum and tell her that the car was being stolen?" asked Earl.

"Exactly!" Opal declared in triumph.

"Because I thought it was Dad." Charmian frowned, angry at having to admit that there might be any doubt of the figure's identity.

"So you can't be certain that you saw Colin Kemp," Earl pointed out. "Is the garage locked at night?"

"Yes," said Opal. "Well, usually. Sometimes. Please don't scold me. I know I'm being careless, but it's such a nuisance locking and unlocking the garage. I don't drive, but I keep the hoover there, so I'm in and out all the time. But no one went inside the garage that night. She'll be saying next that Colin murdered Sandra Stoddard."

"He did," snapped Charmian. "He had a key to her house. I saw him open the front door and go inside."

"You saw Colin Kemp go into Sandra's house?" enquired Earl, bored with Charmian's creativity, and wondering why he had listened to a constable. "When did you see this happen?"

"Millions of times," stated Charmian, and then, all at once, her surly face was alive with sudden inspiration. "I found a key, and it isn't ours. I bet it's the one he used to get into Sandra's house."

"And what did you do with this key?" asked Earl, resignedly preparing himself to hear yet another of Charmian Teal's convoluted stories.

"Nothing, nothing at all. The key's in my room this very second. I'll go and get it." Charmian rushed out, as though she could provide proof positive of Colin Kemp's infamy, and Opal shrugged helplessly.

"Charmian hates Colin, and doesn't care in the least about my happiness. Is it even possible to make a car go without its engine switched on? I never learnt to drive, so haven't a clue about cars. Will Charmian get into trouble because of the rigmarole she's spinning?"

"I have to investigate everything anyone tells me," explained Earl. "But don't worry. Charmian's just a kid, and getting Constable Fulton's attention might be behind all of this."

"The celebrated Albie? More problems." Opal made a rueful face and shook her head despondently. "I'm rapidly reaching my wit's end because of that girl. I simply don't know what to do with Charmian these days. I suppose she'll grow up eventually, and I really can't wait for that glorious moment to arrive."

"Here it is." Charmian hurried back into the room, a key held aloft like a prize that she then awarded to Earl. "I forgot to tell Albie I found it. On the kitchen floor. Last week. Yes, I found it on the kitchen floor last Friday."

"More likely she found it in the street, if you ask me," commented Opal.

"No, it was on the kitchen floor right after *he* went out to work," Charmian maintained, smugly aware of having produced a trump card. "That key will open Sandra's front door; you'll see."

"No, you'll see what a liar Charmian is," predicted Opal.

****

The grass in Sandra Stoddard's garden was withering to brown after weeks of neglect in relentless sunshine, and the rosebushes that lined her driveway were starting to drop shrivelled yellow buds onto parched earth: a red clay now too arid even to support weeds. Earl was conscious of a neighbour watching him from behind a window as he climbed the verandah steps to the front door, and equally conscious that he was being manipulated by a kid who hated everyone around her with the possible exception of Constable Albert Fulton. Earl put Charmian's key into the lock, expecting it to stick, but the key slotted in smoothly, and Sandra Stoddard's front door opened.

7

"Back again?" There was no need for Opal to make her words sound like a question, because merely opening a door had revealed Earl Lanyon on the verandah. "I hope you're going to tell Charmian off for inventing such dreadful lies."

"No, I'm here to ask her again where she found that key."

"Why? What's so important about finding a key? She'll only tell you another pack of lies, and I can't do anything with her. I don't know why Charmian turned out the way she is. I did my best. I couldn't have done more. Please don't blame me."

Opal leaned against the doorframe as though the weight of worry had become too much to bear, and tears filled her eyes. Earl felt sorry for Opal, but he never coped well with female distress. His wife had once told Earl that he could take woodenness to championship level, and Opal's sensibility repelled him.

"I want to see the kitchen," said Earl, walking past Opal into the house.

"The kitchen? Why? Surely you're not going to pay any attention to Charmian's rubbish about someone stealing a car that's never gone missing."

The kitchen door was open, and even from the hallway Earl could see that there was a clear view of the garage and driveway from the window above the sink. Sandra Stoddard's key had opened more than just a door, and Earl tried to picture a scenario based on the assumption that there might actually be some truth behind Charmian's unlikely claims. "She said the front door slammed and woke her up."

"Charmian says a lot of things that are all lies," declared Opal, tears stopping abruptly as she hurried after Earl.

"What time did your husband leave the house?"

"I don't know. I was asleep, and he wouldn't have slammed a door anyway. He always sneaked out, hoping I wouldn't know he'd left.

It wasn't an easy marriage, but I prefer to keep quiet about my suffering." Opal struggled to continue speaking, but her voice faltered before she managed to regain control and force a brave smile. "Derek was a gambler. That's why it's so wonderful to have found a dependable man at last."

Dependable was a word unlikely to be used by either Colin Kemp's wife or daughter when describing him, but Opal lived in a childish world centred on herself, and plainly believed what she wanted to believe. The many lies Charmian told were an inheritance, thought Earl; then he remembered that the girl had given him a key to Sandra's front door, and also became aware that Charmian was standing in the hall, glaring at Opal.

"You're the liar. Dad wasn't a gambler, never ever."

"She doesn't know of the anguish I went through. I regarded it as my duty to keep the worst from her." Opal's tone was resignedly self-sacrificing, and infuriated Charmian.

"She didn't go through anything. She just demanded more and more money."

"I protected her from the true situation," sighed Opal.

"There was no situation. She whined on and on at Dad because she wanted a new car or new curtains or a new fridge, and when she got them they weren't good enough for her."

"I did my best to hide behind a show of courage."

Both Opal and Charmian were talking to Earl, while pretending to ignore each other, and he marvelled that Colin Kemp had deliberately chosen to move into such an unpleasant atmosphere. "Where did you find Sandra's key, Charmian?" asked Earl, hoping that his intervention would avert a full-scale battle.

"I told you; I found the key on the kitchen floor where *he* dropped it." Charmian snapped out the words so defiantly that Earl doubted her story even more than he already had done.

"The kitchen's tiled. He'd have heard a key hit the floor."

"How clever of you to think of that," said Opal, eager to ally herself with Earl against Charmian. "It must be the detective brain making you see through her lies."

"I *did* find Sandra's key on the kitchen floor," maintained Charmian, scowling.

"When?" asked Earl.

"Last week. Friday. I told you."

"Why did you keep it?"

"Because she's a thief as well as a liar," said Opal.

"I just kept it." Charmian looked sullen, and she certainly would never help Colin Kemp by returning any missing item of his, but even if Charmian had found the key where she claimed, the door it opened would remain unidentified.

"How did you know that it was a key to Sandra's house?"

"She didn't know," scoffed Opal. "She invented the entire rigmarole simply to make trouble."

"But I bet that key opened Sandra's front door," Charmian said to Earl, savouring her victory.

"What absolute nonsense," decreed Opal, turning to Earl for support, but he failed to respond, and she protested, "No! No, it's too absurd. I don't believe any of it. This is some trick of Charmian's."

"Everyone in Bethanyville says that *he* was Sandra's boyfriend, and so I knew who must have given him the key." There was no magnanimity in Charmian's triumph, and she smirked contemptuously at her mother's startled face.

"I know exactly what happened," declared Opal, refusing to be daunted. "Charmian saw Sandra Stoddard drop a key in the street weeks ago, and the wretched thief pocketed it."

The theory was a possibility, but however Charmian had acquired the key, the girl was now complacently aware that she had the power to hurt her mother and perhaps damage the relationship with Colin Kemp. Earl had no idea how he could get some truth out of the kid, assuming that Charmian was lying, and she seemed determined to stick to her account.

"I found the key on our kitchen floor," Charmian stated, calm now that Opal was agitated. "And I saw the murderer who killed my Dad go into our garage and steal the car."

"Liar!" cried Opal. "You didn't see anyone. You couldn't have. The car never left our garage that night."

"It's all true." Charmian gazed steadily at Earl, as though attempting to hypnotize him into accepting her story in spite of his scepticism. "Albie believes me."

"But you thought the man you saw going into the garage that night was your Dad," said Earl.

"Yes," Charmian admitted reluctantly. "But now I know who it really was."

"She didn't see anybody," declared Opal. "She made the whole thing up."

It had been Earl's opinion as well until a key opened Sandra Stoddard's front door, and that one event altered everything. "Describe what you saw, Charmian."

"She didn't see a thing. Don't take any notice of her," protested Opal. "She'll only come out with another string of lies if you encourage her."

"The moon was shining, but a shadow from the garage just made him a figure in the dark." Charmian frowned, eyes narrowing as she struggled to see the picture in her mind more clearly. "He went into our garage, and then the car came out slowly. But he hadn't turned its engine or headlights on."

"A pack of lies," maintained Opal. "She's telling them because she wants to be the centre of attention."

"Was it a tall figure, Charmian?" asked Earl.

"There was no figure," insisted Opal.

Charmian frowned again, staring intently at nothing. "He was person-shaped. I didn't look properly because I thought it was Dad."

"Even when the car engine wasn't switched on?"

"The car never left our garage that night," said Opal. "It's a waste of time listening to her."

Opal could very well have been right, but Charmian was plainly striving to recall something, anything, distinctive about the figure she claimed to have seen, and her frustration seemed genuine.

"Did you think it odd that your Dad hadn't switched on the car engine or headlights?" asked Earl.

"It was just what happened, and I never thought about it until later on."

"When she invented the whole thing," Opal stated. "The silly girl's telling you one lie after another."

"No, I'm not," retorted Charmian.

"Yes, she is, and the wretch won't stop trying to fool everybody while you go on listening to her twaddle."

"I saw Dad's murderer take our car. I'm a witness. It's a fact."

Fact or not, Charmian had produced a key to Sandra Stoddard's front door, and was adamant that the key had surfaced in the house where Colin Kemp was now living. The photographs of Sandra placed inside a book that possibly belonged to him could have come from the same house: a house where an aggrieved young girl also lived, and that girl was determined to establish Colin as a murderer. "Charmian, did you send some photos and a book to the police station?"

Charmian was taken aback by Earl's question, but she recovered quickly enough to look surprised. "Photos? I don't know what you're talking about."

****

"A key to Sandra's house?" echoed Colin, untroubled. "No, I've never had a key to Sandra's house."

It was teatime, and most Barton workers went to Bethanyville Hostel's canteen for their break, but Colin was no longer a Nissen hut resident, and he ate sandwiches in the shade by the factory's main entrance, sitting on a conveniently low wall with his back to the concrete building. Earl had spotted him from the road, and decided that it was a good opportunity to catch a suspect off-guard and alone.

"You dropped a key in the Teal kitchen last week, and that key opened Sandra Stoddard's front door."

"As I didn't have a key to her house, I couldn't drop one anywhere," Colin pointed out.

"Charmian Teal says she found the key in their kitchen."

"Well, I didn't drop it." Colin continued to eat his sandwich, undisturbed by the presence of a policeman.

"Then where did the key come from?"

Colin shrugged, finished his sandwich, picked up the yellow-plastic bottle beside him and drank some water. The afternoon heat felt as heavy as if the air had solidified around them, silencing birdsong and turning the horizon to glass. Colin seemed to think there was no need to defend himself further, but Earl was too uncomfortably hot to be patient.

"How could Charmian have got hold of Sandra's door key?" he demanded.

Colin shrugged again, implying that the answer was Earl's problem, not his. "Sometimes I can't believe I'm thousands of miles away from home, but this isn't one of those times. It's like being plunged right into the middle of a film."

"How could a key to Sandra's front door end up in the Teal house?"

"In a film, the hero would keep quiet for some gallant reason, but I'm no hero. Opal and Derek made each other miserable."

"It's none of my business," said Earl, annoyed that Colin should attempt to justify deserting a wife and child.

"This might well be your business. I've heard rumours around the factory that Sandra and Derek were more than friends at one time."

Earl was forced to admire Colin's quick-witted sidetrack. With both Sandra and Derek dead, there might be no one who could now say for sure whether or not they had once been lovers, but the possibility gave a reason for Sandra's key to be found inside the Teal house. "You're claiming that Sandra and Derek had an affair?"

"I claim nothing whatsoever. I'm merely reporting that I've heard they were extra-friendly."

"Will his widow confirm this?"

"I don't think Opal can know about the gossip, or she'd probably have mentioned it by now. But she won't be hurt if anything emerges. It's all in the past."

"Who told you about Sandra and Derek?"

"I don't remember. It was ages ago. When I was still living on the Hostel. I didn't know Opal in those days." Colin looked surprised to realize how short a time had actually passed, and he added, "You imagine that a new life in a new country will turn you into a different person, and when it doesn't, other things have to change or you can't cope with the let-down of being the same old you."

Another attempted justification for running away from responsibilities made Earl frown, before he remembered that stern disapproval of lax morals should long since have been rejected together with all the religious bigotry and brainwashing of his early years. "So your theory is that Charmian found her father's key to Sandra's house?"

"I have an advantage over you here, because I know that I've never had a key to Sandra's house," said Colin, apparently unconcerned whether Earl believed him or not.

"Do you have a copy of *The Whitechapel Murderer*?"

"The Jack the Ripper book?" queried Colin. "Yes, I've got a copy of it somewhere. Why do you ask? Does reading a book about a murderer automatically make you a police suspect in Australia?"

"Do you know where your copy is?"

"Somewhere about. Unless I threw it away. Why?"

"How come you'd get rid of the book?"

"I was reading it when I heard about Sandra's death," replied Colin, wincing at the memory. "I put the book down and never looked at it again. Things are different after someone you actually know is murdered. Things are very different then."

They were, and Charmian had chosen carefully when selecting which of Colin's books to steal, leaving Earl wryly amused at the girl's thoroughness. "Do you have any photos of Sandra?"

"There's one of me standing next to her at the factory's Christmas party last year," replied Colin, his relaxed expression abruptly sombre. "The photo's still on the notice board because nobody's had the heart to take it down. Sandra organized the whole party and even hired a dance band, as well as getting presents for all the kids. She asked me what my daughter would want, and when I said Hester liked reading, Sandra got her a book called *Seven Little Australians* because Hester wouldn't have read it, and Sandra was right. She put a lot of thought into every one of those presents, but that was Sandra Stoddard."

"And yet you told me that you hardly knew her," commented Earl.

"You didn't have to know Sandra well to realize what a nice person she was." Colin sounded defensive, but most people did when answering police questions, and Earl tried not to see signs of guilt where none might be visible.

"Did Sandra ever give you any pictures of herself?"

"Why would she do that?"

"Did she?" asked Earl, noting an evasive reply.

"No. Sandra never gave me any pictures of herself."

"Then your fingerprints wouldn't be on any photograph of Sandra?"

"No. Why?"

"I'll get my notes typed up so that you can read and sign them," said Earl.

"OK." But Colin had stopped paying attention. He stared at the road, and when Earl turned to see what had distracted him, there was nothing to look at, only an empty highway with a few gum trees on the far side in front of Bethanyville's railway station. Whatever Colin Kemp saw existed only in his mind.

"You were fond of Sandra," Earl remarked, hoping for an unguarded reply.

"Everyone was fond of her," declared Colin, returning to the present. "You won't hear a bad word said about Sandra anywhere."

8

"I never met Sandra Stoddard, but she was what my mother would have called a slut," said Albie, and he waited for Detective Sergeant Lanyon to smile with him. "My Mum was English," Albie added, when Earl failed to react.

"How long have you known Charmian Teal?"

"I don't know her," replied Albie. "The first time I saw the kid was when she told me about Colin Kemp."

"Charmian mentioned that she knew a cousin of yours."

"She probably goes to Bethanyville School then."

Earl had hoped for more detailed information about the Teal family from Constable Fulton, particularly concerning Derek's relationship with Sandra, if one had existed, but Albie still only seemed to have gossip to offer, despite living in a Rosebery Avenue flat close to the places where two deaths had occurred: two deaths that might possibly be linked.

The sun's heat was bubbling tarmac at the edges of the police station's car park, and the afternoon air smelt dusty in a searingly hot wind that had travelled from the Northern Territory over desert. Earl was returning to his office when accosted by Albie, who had been too eager to hear the outcome of Charmian's interview to leave the station, and Earl wondered if Constable Fulton could be used to get some reliable testimony out of Charmian Teal.

"I want you to talk to the kid again. I reckon she's inventing most of the things she says, but Charmian produced a key to Sandra Stoddard's house, and there must be more to the story than finding a key by chance because Charmian knew precisely which door it would open. You were the one she picked to talk to, so let's humour her and see what happens."

Albie was convinced that good luck followed him around, but to work with Detective Sergeant Lanyon would give his ambitions a tremendous boost, and Albie imagined himself gleaning vital information from Charmian, information leading to the conviction of Colin Kemp for Sandra Stoddard's murder as well as the murder of Derek Teal, which would result in Constable Fulton's rapid promotion through police ranks until he achieved the glory of being addressed as Detective. No kid was going to hinder Albert Fulton's rise to the top, and he would get the facts from Charmian Teal if he had to beat them out of her. All girls lied, in Albie's opinion, lied consistently and fluently, but for once in Charmian's empty-headed life, she was going to tell the truth, and Constable Fulton would succeed where Detective Sergeant Lanyon had failed.

"Charmian admitted that she couldn't identify Colin Kemp as the man who took the Teal's car that night, assuming it was taken," added Earl. "But I reckon there's a possibility that she might have seen someone go into the garage."

"I'll find out exactly what she saw," declared Albie, confident in his ability to deal with females of any age.

****

Opal blossomed at the sight of a handsome young man when she opened the front door, not recognizing an out-of-uniform Albie as a policeman. In casual clothes, he became part of her world, a potential conquest, a certain admirer, and Opal could forget that she was no longer seventeen. An attractive man smiled at her, and Opal prepared to flirt, whatever his reason for ringing the doorbell. Then, to her astonished indignation, she heard Charmian's excited voice.

"Albie! Do you want to talk to me again?" Charmian pushed past Opal in the joy of seeing her beloved, and she demanded, "Were they pleased that you solved the case? Will you get promoted?"

"I'll be promoted if I can find some more evidence," replied Albie.

"I'm sorry that I didn't give you Sandra's key, but I'd totally forgotten I had it. What sort of evidence do you need?"

"Are you the policeman who was forced to hear Charmian's string of lies?" Opal attempted a carefree laugh, but she was decidedly taken aback to be upstaged by her plain and stocky daughter. It was a bitter foretaste of times to come when she would be sidelined by age, and young girls without a quarter of her looks would be preferred simply because they were young. Colin had left a wife for the beautiful Opal, but when she grew older, he might desert her for a youthful challenger, and the betrayal would be unendurable. Opal was her looks; her looks were Opal. She had no other identity, and wanted no other identity, because admiration was her food and drink, the air she breathed, the sunshine that warmed her. Deprived of male worship, Opal would shrivel away to nothing.

"Your daughter's been a great help to us," said Albie, hoping that they would assume he had already been promoted to the splendours of plain-clothed detective work.

"The girl tells lies," snapped Opal.

"Every single word I told Albie is true," declared Charmian, light-headed with happiness at having been praised by her hero. "What more do you want to know, Albie?"

"How come you had a key to the Stoddard house?"

"She's going to tell you another pack of lies," Opal predicted.

"If I'd been lying, that key wouldn't have opened Sandra's front door," Charmian pointed out with considerable smugness. "You can ask me any questions you like, Albie."

****

"So Charmian Teal produced a key to Sandra Stoddard's house." Walter Grissom was intrigued by such unexpected news but realized that he could easily find the solution, as became a mighty Detective Sergeant. "Colin Kemp must have dropped it, like the kid said."

"Kemp denies ever having had a key to Sandra's house," reported Earl.

"So would I, in his situation," declared Walt. "Wouldn't you?"

"Opal says Charmian must have found the key in the street, but that doesn't explain Charmian linking it to Sandra."

"Unless she saw Sandra drop it."

"Then how come Charmian hung onto a key she knew belonged to Sandra?"

"Who knows why kids do anything?" Walt shrugged, dismissing the unfathomable, and added, "Colin Kemp's the likeliest source of that key."

"Kemp claims Derek Teal was very friendly with Sandra."

"That's a clever move by Kemp," commented Walt, smiling his appreciation of Colin's shrewdness.

"I reckon Charmian sent us the photos of Sandra and the book. Kemp admits to owning a copy of *The Whitechapel Murderer*, but denies ever having had a photo of Sandra."

"He'll say the pictures were Derek's, and we'll have a job proving they weren't if Kemp wiped his fingerprints off those photos."

"In that case, Sandra's prints wouldn't have been on them," argued Earl, and Walt shrugged again.

"Prints or no prints, I reckon Colin Kemp's the local murderer, and you're looking for complications when there aren't any."

Walt could have been right, and Earl knew it, but still the doubt remained. "Did you check if Derek Teal's prints were on the photos?"

"Of course not," Walt replied, offended by what he perceived to be an accusation of negligence. "Surely you're not listening to Kemp's hogwash? There's never been any evidence that Derek was involved with Sandra."

"It might be worth checking. Charmian now admits she didn't recognize the figure she saw going into the Teal garage, and assumed it was her Dad, but I don't know how much is true, or if any of it is."

"She's a kid. There isn't much you can do to pile up the pressure," sneered Walt, aggravated by unsolicited advice on how he should do his job. "Condemn her to extra arithmetic? Cancel the school holidays? Ban all lollies until she cracks?"

"I've sent Constable Fulton to ask her more questions. She chose to talk to him, so he might get closer to the truth."

"The Bethanyville heartthrob?" Walt shook his head in disbelief at the idea of such a time-wasting interview. "She'll want to please him, so there'll be even more elaborate stories, and Fulton's green enough to swallow them."

****

Albie was still officially off-duty, but he went straight back to the police station after talking to Charmian. Punctiliousness would surely be noted, single him out from commonplace workmates, and prove how seriously Albert Fulton took the job. He was pleased to find Earl Lanyon in his office, and even more encouraged when Detective Sergeant Grissom saw Albie and followed him into the room.

"Ready to make your first arrest, Constable?" asked Walt.

Albie half-smiled in an attempt to hide annoyance at being made fun of, and he tried not to snap out his words. "Charmian Teal sent some photos of Sandra Stoddard here. They were in a book belonging to Colin Kemp, and the face had been scribbled over with biro ink in all the pictures. It made Charmian angry because she liked Sandra Stoddard."

"The kid knew Sandra?" queried Earl in surprise.

"She arranged for Charmian to get a diamond necklace at the factory's Christmas party last year, and it was what the kid wanted. I don't reckon it was a real diamond necklace though."

"I don't reckon so either," agreed Walt, raising his eyebrows at such an unnecessary comment, and further irritating Albie who had been hoping for praise.

If Colin Kemp hated Sandra Stoddard so much that he literally defaced photographs of her, why had he kept pictures that could be used against him? Earl had a higher opinion of Colin's intelligence than to do something as stupid as store proof of hatred in a book entitled *The Whitechapel Murderer* and then keep such evidence with him when he moved into the Teal house. The pictures had presumably been regarded as spoils of victory, but Colin would have recognized the danger they were to him when policemen began asking questions, and he was more likely to have destroyed the photos than leave them where they could be found. There was a possibility that the pictures might have belonged to Derek, who later turned against Sandra when she rejected him for another man, and also a possibility that Opal had discovered photos of Derek's girlfriend and tried to obliterate Sandra's smiles in a fury. Charmian then found the pictures, and Charmian had a habit of hiding things away until they could be useful to her. And the photographs certainly made excellent ammunition in her campaign to rout Colin, especially after she purloined his copy of *The Whitechapel Murderer* as an ideal finishing touch to the parcel.

"Where did Charmian claim to have come across the photos?" asked Earl.

"Hidden inside the book behind a kitchen cupboard," replied Albie.

"Colin Kemp appears to have a great fondness for kitchens," Walt observed. "Between his keys, photos and books, there can't be much space left for pots and pans, never mind food."

"I reckon the kid didn't want to admit in front of her mother that she'd been going through Kemp's things," declared Albie, to show how sceptical he would always be of any witness's tale. "Charmian probably found the evidence against Kemp in a suitcase or a wardrobe."

"Maybe, but how come this ruthless killer didn't lock the supposed evidence away somewhere a bit more secure, if he hadn't got sense enough to destroy it?" enquired Walt. "Would you leave such photos of the victim lying around in closets or cases during the murder investigation?"

"No," Albie said hastily, and Walt smiled.

"Good to learn that Constable Fulton's too level-headed to keep incriminating evidence against himself in a kitchen cupboard."

Albie knew that any response would lead to more ridicule, and he resented being mocked after going out of his way to help Detective Sergeant Lanyon. Walt Grissom was only passing on the derision he had been forced to endure as a young constable, but Albie was in no mood to forgive. "The kid saw Colin Kemp go into the Teal garage and steal their car on the night her Dad was killed."

"She claims to have seen *someone* go into the garage, but it might not have been Kemp," Earl pointed out. "Charmian admitted to me that she couldn't be sure."

"And there might not have been anybody in the garage at all," added Walt. "This kid doesn't sound like the most reliable of witnesses."

"She saw Kemp in the street with Sandra Stoddard," declared Albie, alarmed at the prospect of his painstakingly gathered testimony against Colin being dismissed as a vindictive kid's fantasy. "Charmian says that she often saw the two of them out together."

"Unfortunately, no one else appears to be blessed with the Charmian Teal powers of observation," Walt commented. "Did you think to ask where and when these sightings took place?"

"Yes, of course," replied Albie, longing for the day when he would be a Detective Inspector and Walt Grissom a retired nobody. "Charmian told me that she saw Kemp and Stoddard together in the street far too many times to remember one specific occasion. And she often saw Kemp go inside the Stoddard house using his own key to open the front door."

"None of Sandra's neighbours recall seeing her with a man answering Colin Kemp's description," said Earl.

"That doesn't mean Charmian's lying," argued Albie.

He was right, but the fact remained that Charmian yearned to see Colin Kemp arrested, and it made everything she alleged suspect. "Did she say anything about her father and Sandra?" asked Earl.

"Her father?" repeated Albie, taken aback. "Was he one of the Stoddard blokes? No, Charmian only mentioned her Dad when she told me how Kemp stole their car to kill him."

"The death of her father being one of the very few events in Rosebery Avenue that Charmian Teal doesn't claim to have witnessed," remarked Walt.

"She had a key to the Stoddard house as well as those photos," said Albie. "How come Charmian got hold of them if Kemp wasn't involved with Sandra Stoddard? The key and pictures must have belonged to him."

"Thanks, Constable. You can leave now, but we'll keep your deductions in mind."

The belittling words sent a blast of anger through Albie that made the urge to punch Walt Grissom in his supercilious face almost overwhelming, but nothing must get in the way of the future Detective Inspector Albert Fulton's progress, and Albie struggled to keep a blank expression as he walked out of the office. If Earl Lanyon wanted to know about Charmian's Dad, then Albert Fulton would get all the information necessary and show everybody that he was no thickhead like Walt Grissom. Albert Fulton had brains and knew how to use them. Albert Fulton was no washed-up has-been.

"That imbecile swallowed the kid's story in one gulp," said Walt, amused at the gullibility of a young and raw constable. "We've all got to learn, but Fulton's taking longer than most."

"At least we know now that those photos of Sandra did come out of the Teal place, just like the key, and it means Derek, Colin or Opal must have taken them into the house."

"Or Charmian."

"Or Charmian," Earl conceded.

****

Albie had previously not given much thought to Derek Teal. The victim of a road accident was hardly worth attention, but Earl Lanyon's query about Charmian's father changed everything. If proof were found that Colin Kemp had killed Derek, all of Charmian's accusations would be credible and might lead to Colin's arrest for killing Sandra Stoddard as well as Derek Teal, and Albie was eager to see someone charged with Sandra's murder. He needed more information, and knew that a visit to his aunt would undoubtedly result in gleaning a detailed harvest of whatever gossip circulated about any Bethanyville inhabitant, whether past or present. If Derek Teal had had a secret, Aunt Brenda would know the particulars.

The evening followed a day of clammy humidity and sun-glare: the sort of day that made Brenda Dean recall London's foggy gloom with sentimental yearning. She had no wish to go back to England and endure the icy blast of northerly winds that carried snow rather than desert temperatures but, even so, Brenda would never fully adapt to the Australian climate. She had emigrated reluctantly as a teenager with her newly-married sister, rather than be left alone in London, but managed to build a life for herself by falling in love with both her new country and Leonard Dean. The only blight was the enervating heat of those long summers in Victoria.

The shop was closing for the day when Albie arrived, but his appearances were usually timed to coincide with meals, and Brenda smiled. "Only salad, ice-cream and fruit. It's too hot to cook."

"I hadn't even thought about cadging a free feed," said Albie, and for once it was true. He had more important matters on his mind than salad. "I want to ask you about Derek Teal."

"He was a good bloke," declared Lenny, preparing to empty the till after Brenda locked the shop door.

123

"How come you want to know about Charmian's Dad?" Ginevra's daily chores included dusting the shelves before she wiped the counter, and any distraction was welcome. "You should be looking for the driver who killed him."

Albie ignored his cousin and turned to her parents, knowing that he could rely on them for details of any local scandal. "When Lanyon asked you about Derek Teal, what did you say?"

"That Derek was a good bloke," replied Lenny.

"And he really was," added Brenda. "I don't care what anyone says."

"And what do people say?" Albie demanded.

Brenda glanced hesitantly at Ginevra, who protested, "I'm not going to tell Charmian a thing. I've never said a word about her Dad and Sandra, not to anybody."

The news was as good as Albie had dared to hope, and he asked eagerly, "How come you didn't tell Earl Lanyon about this affair?"

"Why should I?" said Brenda, hurt to be thought so insensitive. "Both Sandra and Derek are dead. There's no need for his wife to find out. It'd only make things worse for her. Not that she can have been all that devoted to him, shacking up with another woman's husband before her own was cold in the ground."

"How come you know Sandra Stoddard had an affair with Derek Teal?" In a mere matter of seconds, Constable Albert Fulton would discover more about Rosebery Avenue's secret life than two Detective Sergeants had, and Albie was thrilled at the confirmation of his superior talents. "Did Sandra Stoddard talk to you?"

"Of course not. She was no gossip."

"Then how come you know about the affair?"

"Everyone knew," declared Ginevra.

"They weren't very discreet," acknowledged Lenny. "Could be Derek hoped that his wife would find out, or perhaps he just got careless."

"I saw them in the street together loads of times," said Ginevra. "Everyone did."

"Then how come nobody's told the police?" But Albie already knew the answer to his question. No true Australian would volunteer such information to anyone with Governmental authority. It contradicted the rules of fair play. "What about Colin Kemp?"

"What about him?" asked Lenny.

"You know what I mean," retorted Albie, impatient with the lack of solid evidence against Colin. "He bought Sandra Stoddard a spider in here on the very night she died. Were they having an affair?"

Lenny shrugged, and Brenda smiled. "If I looked like Sandra, men would buy me drinks too."

"She was a slut," said Albie. "That's what my Mum would have called her."

"Not if she'd known Sandra. Everybody liked her." But someone had hated Sandra Stoddard; someone had killed her. Brenda flinched at the memory, and marvelled that she could have forgotten Sandra's fate even for a few moments.

"I need evidence, not gossip and feelings," Albie pointed out. "Colin Kemp has to be stopped before he kills again."

"*He* didn't kill Sandra," said Lenny.

"How could you know that?" demanded Albie. "You don't know anything about it. You can't know."

"Colin liked Sandra," replied Lenny.

"In our English lesson the other day, Mrs Lang quoted from a poem about people always killing the thing they love," remarked Ginevra.

"Don't you believe it," said Lenny. "There's never any love involved in killing. It's hatred, and that's that."

"Then Albie must have hated Rosamund."

"Is Gin ever going to shut up about that?" Albie retorted in exasperation. "She's nagged on for years and years."

"And I'll go on nagging for years and years," Ginevra declared. "I reckon Colin Kemp could never be as mean as you are, never."

"It wasn't my fault," claimed Albie, annoyed at being criticized in any way. "In fact, it was your fault for leaving the thing just lying around."

"Rosamund wasn't a thing," said Ginevra, pleased with the opportunity to remind Albie that he sometimes failed to live up to the glossy image he had of himself as a peerless upholder of right and justice.

"You shouldn't drink, if you can't handle it," Brenda advised Albie.

"Of course I can handle drink. I'm no fall-down drunk. I tripped over a doll; that's all. Does Colin Kemp drink?"

"Not that I've ever heard," replied Brenda.

"A secret drinker," decided Albie. "They're the worst, but a man isn't responsible for his actions when he's drunk."

"Yes, he is." Lenny and Brenda spoke simultaneously, then they laughed and linked little fingers to avert a jinx.

"There's no such thing as bad luck," Albie declared. "You make your own luck, and that way it stays good."

"You've got a lot to learn," observed Lenny.

****

"I don't like Albie," Ginevra announced after her cousin had gone.

"And you make it very plain that you don't like him," commented Brenda, as she tried and failed to sound reproving. "Albie's on his own now, and we're the only family he's got, so you ought to be nicer to him."

Brenda was actually reminding herself why she should be more sympathetic to a conceited and self-absorbed nephew. Her sister Eunice had regarded Albie as the last word in mankind's evolution, and he seconded that opinion. His father had died young, leaving Albie the centre of Eunice's attention, the reason for her existence, the reason the earth kept spinning, and that was fine by Albie, who expected the world to continue the adoration after his mother had thoughtlessly let him down by ceasing to breathe. He was accustomed to getting his own way, and considered anything else an aberration of the natural order.

"Albie reckons he's such a brilliant detective, he'll be the one who gets Hester's Dad charged with murder," said Ginevra.

"Nobody's going to charge Colin Kemp with anything," declared Lenny. "And I don't care how many stories you tell me about him being a bank robber."

"It's what everyone says," protested Ginevra, but she laughed as she spoke. The tales that were so plausible in school sounded very different when Ginevra relayed them to her practical parents, even though she would usually attempt to defend the stories. "Mr Kemp can't be worth much or he wouldn't have walked out on Hester and her Mum."

"That doesn't mean he'd rob a bank," said Brenda. "Or that he'd have hurt Sandra. Albie's on the wrong track."

"Not for the first time," muttered Lenny.

"Albie's ambitious. It stops him thinking clearly." Brenda knew that both Lenny and Ginevra remained unpersuaded by her efforts to pass off Albie's arrogance as a mere quirk of character. Other people were created simply to assist Albert Fulton get whatever he wanted, and nothing would alter his viewpoint, but admitting that Albie cared only for himself would be too disloyal to Eunice. "Ambition's a good thing," Brenda added, trying to look convinced by her own words.

9

Ginevra had almost reached the wire gates of Bethanyville State School when she heard Charmian call to her from behind one of the gum trees that lined the road. "Are you wagging school again today?" demanded Ginevra, eager for a news update. "You'll miss all the end-of-year fun if you stay away much longer."

"I'm not going to school any more," replied Charmian, as she flourished a letter in greeting. "Give this to Mrs Lang. It's a note about us moving to Melbourne, signed by my mother."

"Your mother?" Ginevra laughed, although she took the envelope from Charmian without hesitation. "There'll be nothing but trouble if you're caught. It's against the law to wag school, and so is forging somebody else's signature."

"Albie will make sure that there isn't a row," declared Charmian, adding proudly, "I'm working with him on the case against Colin Kemp."

"My parents don't think that he killed your Dad or Sandra."

"Albie and I know better. I'm seeing him later," announced Charmian, trying to make it sound like a date, as became the adult status of someone whose schooldays were in the past whether or not the authorities would agree. "I often see Albie."

"Sooner you than me. I haven't forgiven him for stamping on Rosamund's head, and I never will."

"Who's Rosamund?"

"She was my doll."

"You still play with dolls?" enquired Charmian, her tone loftily sophisticated.

"I couldn't play with dolls now if I wanted to. I only ever had one, and then none at all after Albie tripped over Rosamund five Christmases ago when he'd drunk too much. Albie got so angry that he stamped on poor Rosamund's head, and kept stamping until she was smashed to pieces." Ginevra sighed deeply, affecting a tragic air that was not entirely fake. "My parents were going to buy me another doll, but I couldn't bear the thought of replacing Rosamund. I buried her remains in the backyard, and never recovered from my grief. Albie's a swine when he's drunk."

"You shouldn't have left a doll lying around for him to trip over," Charmian retorted. "Poor Albie might have hurt himself."

"Poor Rosamund was the one who got hurt. I said then that I'd never forgive him, and I never have and I never will."

"You don't understand men," declared Charmian, happy to educate a less-worldly female. "You can't expect Albie to bother about a doll. He's got far more important things on his mind, and when he arrests that murderer, Albie's name will be in all the papers. He'll be the most famous detective in the world."

"He isn't a detective," Ginevra pointed out. "He's only a constable."

"At the moment, but they'll have to promote him soon because he's a genius."

"Not that I've ever noticed."

"You're just jealous," scoffed Charmian.

"Of Albie!" Ginevra laughed again, then hastily waved a hand at Charmian, and started to run toward the high gates of the schoolyard as Sousa's *Washington Post* began to blast from a loudspeaker. Charmian watched Ginevra disappear into the crowd of children forming lines as they got ready to march into school with a straight-backed discipline worthy of soldiers, but there would be no such acquiescence from Charmian Teal ever again, because she had taken charge of her own life and was determined to stay in control. The morning sun felt gently warm, with none of the ferocity it would develop by noon, and hours of freedom stretched ahead during which Charmian could do exactly as she pleased: perhaps get a bus to the beach or a train into Melbourne, and really live instead of frittering away a futile existence in a stuffy schoolroom. But first she would check to see if Albie's car was parked outside his flat, just in case he planned a day out as well, and might perhaps appreciate the companionship of a young woman liberated from chalk dust and boredom. It would also be a good opportunity to make sure that no rival was attempting to infiltrate his life.

****

"Hester, Charmian's wagging school again today," muttered Ginevra, as she hurriedly joined the end of Grade 6's marching line and prepared to stamp her way into the assembly hall accompanied by Sousa.

"There'll be one heck of a row soon," Hester predicted.

"Only if her mother happens to run into Mrs Lang or Mrs Hexham. Charmian's forged another excuse note."

It was audacity that Hester would never be able to match, and she felt ashamed of her cautious restraint. Fear of consequences limited all possibilities, and Hester longed to be reckless enough to have adventures, but she was only herself and that seemed to condemn Hester Kemp to a lifetime of conformity. "Where does Charmian go the whole day?"

"I don't know. She said something about seeing my cousin Albie, but I reckon she made it up."

Hester knew better. Charmian had often trailed Albie to check which girl he might be dating or if he patronized Bethanyville's Friday Night Dance, yet Albie never appeared to notice that he was under surveillance. There were always kids around, and as Charmian was too ordinary to stand out in a crowd, she had remained invisible to Albie. Charmian yearned for a fairy-tale ending that refused to happen, and once upon a time Hester might have been sympathetic, but Charmian was muddled up in the mess surrounding Colin's transferred loyalty, and Hester was homesick for a life that had gone forever. She lived in sunshine, but one of London's bleaker backstreets had acquired its own golden glow and Hester Kemp was out of place among antipodean children who marched in step to loudspeaker music across a playground's dust-dry soil. Hester Kemp now belonged nowhere, and the sense of rootlessness made her feel so lonely that she tried to forget everything but the actual moment she was trapped in. "Do you think Mrs Lang's going to believe another excuse note?"

"Charmian's problem," replied Ginevra.

****

The very next morning, all of Charmian's problems apparently solved themselves. She was brooding on what further evidence could be produced to convince the police of Kemp's guilt, when the bedroom door opened. Angry that her privacy had been invaded, Charmian looked up to see Opal leaning against the frame, tearfully trembling. "I was wrong. You were right. I'm so sorry I didn't listen. What should I do?"

"Do about what?" Charmian demanded, always suspicious of Opal's little-girl voice.

"Colin threatened me, and I've never been so frightened in my life." Opal started to cry, and for once her sobs were genuine. "What can I do?"

"Throw him out," declared Charmian.

"But he said he'd kill me, just like he killed your father and that Stoddard woman."

"He admitted it?" Charmian had spent many hours mulling over ways to get the killer hanged for murdering Derek, but never once had she imagined that Colin Kemp would make her task easy by being fool enough to confess his guilt. "He actually admitted it?"

"Colin said that I had to get rid of you, and when I refused, he was livid."

"I didn't hear shouting."

"There wasn't any. His voice just got colder and colder, but his eyes —" Opal was unable to go on, terror in every gesture and movement.

"I'm going to get Albie," Charmian announced, elated that she had at last been proved right.

"No! Don't leave me alone," begged Opal. "You can't even go to school today. I've never been so afraid."

"But the killer isn't here now. I heard him go out to work."

"He might come back. Phone the police. It's an emergency, tell them, and I need protection from a murderer."

After so much having gone wrong in Charmian's life, the speed of a turnabout was bewildering, even though she had always known that retribution must surely catch up with Colin Kemp one day. Opal's part in the unmasking was an astonishing element of his downfall, but the police were going to listen to Opal, and the enemy would be removed without ever again getting a chance to ruin Charmian's existence. It was a day of jubilation, a day of victory that Albie ought to share, and she rushed past Opal into the hallway, eager to hasten Colin's defeat. Charmian had long since made a note of the police station's telephone number in case she found an excuse to summon Albie to her side, and as Charmian dialled, she was certain that every wish she had ever made would be granted because a murderer was going to face punishment for his crimes, and the first of Charmian's wishes came true when she heard Albie's voice on the other end of the phone line.

"You've got to arrest Colin Kemp straightaway, Albie. He's just this minute made some terrible threats and confessed to killing my Dad, and Sandra as well. It's a dire emergency. You've got to get here before he comes back to kill me. And my mother too. This is Charmian, by the way."

"Yes, I know," said Albie, but seeming more bewildered than sure of anything. "I recognized your voice."

"Really?" asked Charmian, thrilled to have made such an impact. "You knew it was me?"

"Yes." Albie paused, and then added, "Did you say that Kemp had confessed to killing Sandra Stoddard?"

"And my Dad too. He'll kill me as well unless you get here and stop him." Charmian knew that she sounded childishly excited, and hurriedly attempted to adopt a more adult tone. "I'm in dreadful danger, Albie, but that doesn't bother me in the least because I know you'll save my life before he gets a chance to murder me."

"Kemp told you that he killed Sandra Stoddard?" Albie demanded. "He actually said it to you?"

"No, he didn't tell me. He told my mother," replied Charmian, proudly producing the trump card of an unimpeachably grown-up witness to Colin Kemp's villainy. "Mum's petrified in case he comes back to the house and murders us, so she told me to phone you for help. He's supposed to have gone to work, but I bet he'll be here at any second to kill us, now that we know all about him."

"Is your Mum there?" asked Albie.

"Yes, of course. She's far too scared to go out. Do you want to talk to her?" As Charmian spoke, she beckoned imperiously at the bedroom doorway where Opal was still wilting and shaking. "You've got to tell Albie what happened."

Opal began to cross the hall, her legs so unsteady that she gave the impression of having abruptly grown much older, and Charmian could see that her mother really was afraid, with none of the usual Opal pretence. Quite plainly, Colin Kemp had terrified her.

"Hurry up!" Charmian ordered, signalling with the phone receiver. "Tell Albie what you told me. He's waiting."

"It's all so awful," faltered Opal, "so horrifying. I don't know what to do."

"Talk to Albie, of course," said Charmian, impatient with Opal's shilly-shallying. "Albie's going to protect us."

"Colin Kemp threatened me," Opal sobbed into the telephone. "He said that he'd kill me, just like he killed Derek and Sandra Stoddard."

"You see!" Charmian said in triumph, snatching back the receiver. "You've got to save us, Albie; please save us."

"I'll get help," Albie decided.

"We only need you," declared Charmian, surprised that Albie should even consider sharing the glory of arresting a killer and solving two murder cases in one go.

****

"I spoke to the mother," insisted Albie. But standing on the wrong side of a Detective Sergeant's desk, he was beginning to think that the telephone call might have originated in his imagination, and Albie was glad that Walt Grissom, official investigator of the Stoddard case, had not been around.

"Opal said Colin Kemp told her that he'd killed Sandra and Derek, and then he went to work?" Earl was used to dealing with stupid criminals, but had never before encountered one that much of a dope. "Kemp threatened her, confessed to two murders, and then went out, leaving Opal free to contact the police?"

"Perhaps he thought she'd been intimidated," said Albie, but the idea was unconvincing even to him, and he added, "Charmian had to make Opal talk to me. They're both terrified."

It all sounded like another of Charmian Teal's ploys to get Constable Fulton's attention, but Opal was an unlikely co-conspirator, and Charmian had somehow managed to produce a key to the Stoddard house. Earl stood up, his chair scraping on the floor.

"Do you want me to go there with you?" asked Albie, eager to witness the close of the investigation into Sandra's death. "Charmian talks to me."

"But Opal's doing the talking this time, it seems."

"My aunt and uncle say that Sandra Stoddard was having an affair with Derek Teal, as well as Kemp," Albie reported.

"Gossip or fact?" asked Earl.

"Everyone in Bethanyville knows all about it, so there'll be truth behind the story. Kemp must have heard he was being two-timed, and got so jealous that he killed the pair of them. You should talk to my Aunt Brenda again. She'll tell you that both Teal and Kemp were having affairs with Stoddard."

"If Colin Kemp has confessed to murdering two people, I won't need to trouble Aunt Brenda," said Earl. Constable Fulton's dedication to the job was doubtless laudable, and his dealings with Charmian had revealed a link between Sandra and the Teal house, but Albie's habit of rushing into Earl's office to relay speculation had become tiresome. "Thanks for your input, Constable, but I reckon I might be able to handle getting a statement from Opal Teal."

Albie struggled to hide his anger at the snub after he had found the evidence essential to close two murder cases, but Lanyon and Grissom were fools who could be bamboozled by anyone, including a twelve-year-old girl, and they deserved Albie's scorn. The future Detective Inspector Albert Fulton was offended, and he would neither forgive nor forget.

****

When Earl arrived in Rosebery Avenue and opened his car door, Charmian was in the front garden of the Teal house, tossing a jacket over the wattle hedge's yellow flowers onto a pile of clothes by an empty suitcase in the Kemp driveway, while a bemused Noreen called from her verandah, "Charmian, I don't want his things. Colin doesn't live here any more."

"He doesn't live in our house either," retorted Charmian as she hurled a book, aiming it to land neatly on top of the clothes.

"Does your mother know what's going on?" Noreen enquired, trying not to laugh aloud.

"Of course she does. Mum told me to get rid of his stuff," Charmian said cheerfully, before turning to Earl. "We don't need you. Albie Fulton's on his way to arrest the murderer."

Noreen looked at Earl, expecting him to resent his dismissal, but he merely nodded at her as he followed Charmian up the Teal verandah steps and into the house, where Opal was pacing up and down the hallway, too nervously agitated to be still.

"There are only a few more bits, and then all his rubbish is gone forever," cried Charmian, grabbing a blue shirt and using it as a makeshift sack for a pair of shoes and the half-dozen books still littering the floor.

"I know it's undignified, Sergeant," said Opal, well on her way to more tears, "but I simply can't bear the idea of anything that belongs to a murderer being inside my house."

"There's nothing left now," declared Charmian, rushing out of the front door with her bundle.

"She's so protective of me." Opal struggled against overwhelming emotion at the thought, but compelled herself to go on speaking. "Colin said that I had to get rid of Charmian, but how could any mother part with her own child? There's nothing stronger than the maternal instinct. It's my guiding force through life, and always will be."

"That's the end of him," announced Charmian, jumping up the verandah steps and brushing her hands one against the other to cleanse them of Kemp contamination. "Has Albie gone to Barton's to arrest the murderer?"

"It's all so dreadful," sighed Opal. "I'm too trusting. I should have realized that a woman on her own would be targeted by criminals."

"I told you he was no good," Charmian pointed out. "I even told you that he was a murderer."

"Oh, darling, if only I'd listened," wailed Opal.

"Well, you didn't."

"What exactly happened?" asked Earl, to stop Charmian and Opal getting embroiled in a long bout of reproaches and remorse. He walked into the living-room and sat down as a further sign that he was in charge, and had questions requiring answers.

"It was awful," declared Opal, sinking weakly into the chair opposite Earl. "I'm still in shock. I don't know where to begin."

"At the beginning, of course," said Charmian, keen to speed up any process that would lead to Colin's execution.

"He told me I had to get rid of my daughter." Opal's voice thickened with tears, and she looked at Charmian as though a long-lost treasure had at last been restored.

Earl could see that Opal was genuinely upset, but still she had to put on a show to impress a man, a reaction that probably dated back so many years, it was now ingrained. She might make an appealing witness in a court, but not necessarily a convincing one, and Earl would need some rock-solid evidence against the plausible Colin Kemp to make any allegations stick. "Where and when did he tell you to get rid of Charmian?"

"We'd just had breakfast in the kitchen," replied Opal. "As Colin stood up to go to work, he told me that my little Charmian had to be thrown out onto the street before he got back."

"He knew I'd given Sandra's key to the police," Charmian informed Earl, as Opal's voice again faltered. "And he knew I wouldn't rest until I'd found even more evidence against him."

"Were you in the kitchen as well?" asked Earl.

"No, I was in my room," said Charmian, regretting the missed opportunity to play a starring rôle in Colin Kemp's trial. "I wouldn't eat at the same table as a murderer, so I didn't hear any of his threats."

"I thought Colin must be joking," continued Opal, unsuccessfully attempting to stop a shudder by clasping her hands tightly together.

"But it wasn't a joke. Colin told me that I had to get rid of Charmian and do whatever he said from now on, or he'd kill me the way he killed Derek."

"And Sandra too," added Charmian. "I'd have heard the threats, but he didn't yell them. He was cunning enough to make sure that he spoke quietly. His voice was cold and distant, but his eyes glittered with evil."

"That's right," said Opal. "That's exactly what I sensed in Colin: evil."

"And then?" prompted Earl.

"Then he went to work. Colin must have thought that he'd terrified me into submission, but a mother will always find the courage to protect her child."

Earl wondered which film Opal was taking her lines from, and yet the woman had gone through some sort of frightening experience. If Kemp's words were being reported to him by Charmian, Earl would have dismissed the account as fantasy, but clearly something had happened to turn Opal against Colin, and that something unnerved her.

"Will Albie have arrested the murderer yet?" demanded Charmian. "We need police protection until that killer's hanged, so you've got to send Albie here to guard us."

****

Noreen, still on her verandah, was surprised that the sight of Colin's homeless possessions strewn over the driveway made her happier than she had ever expected to be again. Colin imagined that all the choices were his, but some parts of life he would never be able to control. Opal probably knew nothing about Charmian's tantrum, and Noreen realized that she ought to feel ashamed of being so petty, but the thought of any upset in Opal's perfect house was a comfort, and Noreen only regretted the absence of a rainstorm to drench the mound of clothes and books.

Earl Lanyon walked down the Teal driveway to his car. He took some keys out of a pocket, glanced back at Noreen, hesitated for a moment, and then turned towards the Kemp gate.

"I'm not touching any of Colin's things," declared Noreen, smiling at the memory of Charmian's ruthlessness. "And I don't care if it's against the law to leave rubbish lying around a garden. Colin can pick up his own stuff by himself."

"I won't enforce any tidying-up laws that might exist." As Earl approached the verandah, he was relieved not to be facing an emotional Noreen distressed by the scattering of her estranged husband's belongings over a garden path, and Earl continued, "I want to ask you something."

"Yes?" prompted Noreen as he paused.

"Was Colin ever violent or threatening towards you?"

"No. Not once. What tale is Charmian spinning now?" Noreen laughed, and felt even better. "The girl claimed that Colin was a bank robber at one point, according to Hester. He's got a fearsome reputation in Bethanyville School, apparently, but Hester seemed quite content with the situation."

"What happens when Colin loses his temper? Does he shout?"

"No, but he hasn't really got much of a temper to lose. He gets impatient with stupidity: bosses at work not listening, things like that. Otherwise, Colin's fairly easy-going. Why? Is Charmian claiming that he rants like a madman and smashes up furniture with his bare hands?" Noreen suddenly realized that she was talking about Colin as an acquaintance, not a husband. He had moved out of the present and into the past: somebody she remembered but no longer knew. Colin had left her in more ways than one.

"So, in your opinion, it'd be out of character for him to make threats," Earl concluded.

"Definitely out of character. Don't listen to a word Charmian tells you about him." Noreen hesitated, noting Earl's guarded expression, and then added, "But you're not listening to Charmian; of course you wouldn't be. Who told you that Colin made threats? Surely not Opal Teal."

"It'd surprise you?"

"It'd flabbergast me." Once, Noreen would have refused to believe many of the things that Colin had done lately, but still she shook her head. "If Opal told you that Colin threatened her or was violent, she's lying."

"Why would she do that?"

"I've no idea. What did she say?"

"That Colin confessed to killing both Sandra Stoddard and Derek Teal, and then told Opal that he'd kill her too if she didn't get rid of Charmian." Opal's melodramatic statement seemed more bizarre in the peace of a summer morning that was tranquilly approaching midday with bird and cicada song the loudest sounds, and Noreen started to laugh again.

"Now I know where Charmian gets her imagination from. Opal must have found herself a richer man, and wants to ditch Colin. Perhaps he did have a fling with Sandra. I don't know. But I do know that he wouldn't have killed her or anyone else." Noreen was sure of what she said, without understanding how she could be so certain, but a susceptible Colin seducing attractive women, or being seduced by them, was a very different matter from a homicidal Colin, slaughtering his way to Opal. Surely no one changed that much, not even Colin.

****

The temperature inside the concrete building was inescapably dictated by its oven-air atmosphere, and outdid the northerly breeze following Earl into the biscuit factory, a sultriness that made him long for the cool freshness of winter, but the constant din of machinery must have been the worst part of working at Barton's. Earl waited in a hallway by the entrance while a petulant girl from the reception desk grudgingly ceased varnishing fingernails for a few minutes, swirled the wide skirt of her pink dress, and tottered off on stiletto heels in search of Colin.

If nobody could find Kemp, Earl knew that he would regret leaving the Teal house unguarded. Opal had no apparent reason to lie, but Colin did not seem a violent man, and to threaten before walking away was the tactic of a bully with intimidation rather than murder in mind. Earl had long since realized that it was impossible to know what any man or woman might be capable of doing, and there must have been some type of confrontation to upset Opal so much, but whatever had happened in the Teal house that morning, it was obvious special attention should now be paid to Colin Kemp, whether or not he had actually claimed to be a killer. Opal was unlikely to have misheard such a confession, or such a boast, but it seemed just as unlikely that a murderer would really have said the words. Cases refused to solve themselves so easily, in Earl's experience, and when Colin emerged from the midst of the other figures in white overalls on the factory floor, he certainly looked untroubled as he laughed and chatted with the young receptionist, who was no longer sulky but smiling at Colin in a way that girls never smiled at Earl.

"You want to see me?" said Colin, reluctantly transferring his attention.

"More questions," replied Earl, ushering Colin outdoors to avoid both an audience and the machinery noise. "Did you tell Opal that you killed Sandra Stoddard and Derek Teal?"

Colin stared at Earl in disbelief, and then demanded, "What are you talking about? If this is supposed to be a joke, it isn't a funny one."

"You deny telling Opal that you killed Sandra and Derek?"

"Of course I deny it. What's Charmian invented now? You only have to ask Opal, and she'll confirm that nothing of the sort has ever happened outside Charmian's imagination."

Colin Kemp was very plausible: firstly affronted by questions that insulted his integrity and then wearied by again becoming the target of Charmian's malice. Earl would have been surprised if Colin had agreed with the Opal version of events, but his denial was very well done.

"You don't get on with Charmian?"

"What's the girl been telling you?" Colin relaxed and began to smile, although jadedly rather than with amusement. "Have I branched out as a murderer, in addition to my career as a bank robber?"

The whole thing certainly did sound like one of Charmian's extravagant creations, but she was not even a witness to the scene related by Opal, and Earl persisted, "Before you came to work this morning, what did you and Opal argue about?"

"We've never argued," replied Colin. "Charmian does her very best to make trouble, but we don't take any notice of the kid."

"Did you tell Opal that she had to get rid of Charmian?"

"No, of course not."

"Opal says you did, and that you threatened her."

"You mean Charmian told you," said Colin, ruefully resigned. "I swear that kid spends each waking hour just thinking up schemes to frame me for every crime committed in Australia during the last year."

"It was Opal who told me about your threats."

"No," Colin stated, firmly and decisively. "Don't listen to Charmian. There wasn't any arguing and there weren't any threats. You should have realized by now that you can't believe a word the girl says."

"Charmian didn't hear your threats. Opal told me what you said to her." Earl watched Colin, but could detect no sign of anger at Opal's betrayal, merely bewilderment. The expression on Colin's face looked genuinely puzzled, as genuine as the shock and fear that Opal had so undoubtedly experienced.

"What did I say to her?" Colin was asking himself more than Earl, and evidently trying to recall a memory that had left no trace in his mind.

"You confessed to killing Sandra and Derek, and told Opal that you'd kill her too if she didn't get rid of Charmian." Even though Earl had expected stout denial, he could still admire Colin's baffled disbelief, so convincingly portrayed.

"You're making it up," declared Colin, suddenly sure of himself again. "Yes, you've made up a story to see if you can trick me into confessing something or other, but I won't oblige, and that's because I haven't done whatever you think I've done."

"Then how come Opal's had all your belongings thrown out of her house? How come she wants police protection from you?"

"It won't work," laughed Colin. "You'll have to find another suspect to intimidate. Opal and I were talking about a drive to Mordialloc for a meal after I finish work today. That's what happened this morning. No argument. No threats."

"Not according to Opal."

"It's probably against the law to tell a policeman he's lying, so I'll be very polite and say that you're mistaken. It was a good try though, but you're clutching at straws."

I'm not, but you might be, thought Earl.

****

The sight of a jumbled pile of clothing and books next to an empty suitcase in the middle of the Kemp driveway made Hester stare when she arrived home from school at lunchtime, and Noreen, still relaxing in the shade of the verandah, smiled at her daughter's bemused expression.

"What's a heap of clothes doing in the garden?" called Hester, intrigued by the mystery.

"Charmian threw them there."

"Why?" demanded Hester, running to the verandah.

"Because Opal's kicked your father out, and those are his things."

It was the best news that Hester had ever heard, and she could hardly believe that everything wrong was right again. The world had reverted to normality, and she could feel happy once more.

"Leave his stuff where it is," ordered Noreen, as Hester turned to retrieve Colin's possessions. "Your father can pick up his own belongings after he finishes work."

"But Dad's clothes can't just lie around the garden," cried Hester. "All sorts of snakes and spiders might get inside them. You don't want anything like that in the house."

"His clothes won't be coming into the house."

"But this is Dad's home."

"Not any more."

Hester looked astounded, and Noreen felt guiltily aware that pride would never permit her to forgive Colin, and pride had very little to do with love. In far-off days, she might have loved him as much as he had once claimed to love her, but it was a love that Colin could ignore when a younger and more attractive woman showed interest in him. The Kemps were no Romeo and Juliet; the Kemp story was about trivial feelings and trivial motives, not grand passion.

"But where will Dad live now?"

"I don't know, but he'll find somewhere. Hester, he won't want to come back here." It might have been true, but Noreen said the words to make herself seem less callous. If a daughter rejected her as well as a husband, there would be no reason to get up in the morning and struggle through another day. "Your Dad's started a new life, and we've got to respect his decision."

"But he can't have a new life today: not without somewhere to live," argued Hester. "This house belongs to him too, and Dad's got as much right to be here as we have."

"He'll prefer to go to a hotel for the night. He won't want to be next door to Opal."

Nor did Hester, but she appeared to have no choices, trapped on the fringes of other people's lives. Colin and Noreen refused to listen to their daughter, although she was supposed to obey them, and the Americans or Russians could destroy her with atom bombs at any moment. The whole world had become a sham, and it was time she accepted that nobody cared about Hester Kemp or her wishes. She was an also-ran.

****

"Your things," said Earl, pointing.

Colin gazed incredulously at the driveway of the house that he had so recently shared with Noreen, and then said firmly, "Charmian did this; Opal wouldn't."

"You don't like Charmian much," remarked Earl. They were in his car, and he waited to see how angry Colin would get. Even skilled actors had difficulty disguising loss of temper.

"Charmian? She's a spoilt brat, but this is carrying one of her outbursts to an absurd level." Colin spoke absently, and then added with sudden determination, "Charmian's not going to wreck my relationship with Opal."

"Opal told me that she doesn't want to see you again," said Earl. "She's too upset by whatever went on this morning."

"That's ridiculous. Charmian made the entire scene up."

"Bur it was Opal who told me about your threats."

"Impossible," stated Colin. "Charmian's behind these lies; I know she is. Talk to Opal. She'll tell you."

"She has."

"I don't believe you. Nothing happened this morning. I was there. I know."

Opal Teal or Colin Kemp? Which one was the liar? Opal had no reason to lie, but Colin certainly did if threats had been made, and his dislike of Charmian was very plain. Yet a wife ought to know her husband's character after years of marriage, and Noreen had defended Colin, despite being alienated from him.

"I can drive you to a hotel," Earl offered, knowing that Walt Grissom would have arrested Colin instead of acting as chauffeur. "Whatever was said this morning, Opal doesn't want you in her house. She's afraid of you."

"This is all wrong," protested Colin. "It's crazy."

"Opal's house, so Opal's choice who lives in it. Get your things and we'll leave."

"None of this makes sense."

Colin appeared genuinely confused, just as Opal had seemed genuinely frightened. Rosebery Avenue was producing more than its fair share of mysteries, although Colin Kemp could probably answer every question the police had, and Earl attempted shock tactics. "Did Sandra Stoddard change her mind about you, the way Opal has?"

"Sandra? What's Sandra got to do with all this?" Colin frowned at Opal's house as if it would tell him something, but there was no enlightenment from blank windows and walls.

"Did Sandra turn against you, just like Opal?"

"Sandra would never turn against anybody. She was straightforward, almost straightforward to a fault, and treated people honestly. Sandra wouldn't tell lies about someone and then hide away." Colin shrugged, giving up the effort to understand what was happening to him, and he added, "I don't care what you say. I know the whole mess goes back to Charmian somehow."

"Sounds like you knew Sandra well."

"Everyone who met Sandra knew her well. I thought I knew Opal too, but I can't figure out any of this."

"I'll help you collect your things," said Earl, opening the car door and climbing out into the glare of sunlight.

Colin hesitated, but then he left the car and followed Earl to the mound of clothes and books on the driveway in a garden that had so recently been Colin's. The front door of the house opened, and Hester jumped down the verandah steps, frantic to grab at any opportunity that might end the cataclysmic events that were wrecking her life.

"Dad, Mum says you won't want to come home, but you do, don't you?"

"Not if I have to face your mother," said Colin, trying to turn his answer into a joke. "This is just a misunderstanding with Opal. Don't worry about it."

Hester's main worry was that Opal and Charmian would get over whatever tantrum they were jointly throwing, and allow Colin back into the Teal house. It would be easier to see him go away than that, and she helped Colin to pack his suitcase and put it into Detective Sergeant Lanyon's car, which gave Hester the uncomfortable feeling that her father had been arrested, particularly as he was making an effort to look untroubled. The hot November sun and perfect afternoon seemed to mock the aliens, just as much as Charmian would, and Charmian was doubtless gloating behind the windows of the next-door house while she rejoiced in Colin's humiliation.

"Dad, this is your home. You can't just walk off and leave us here."

Colin already had, but he ignored the fact. "We'll go somewhere really special next weekend: any place you like. It'll be your choice."

Hester was beyond an age when she could be bribed, or even distracted, by a promise that offered nothing she wanted, and Colin ought to have realized it. "We should never have come to Australia, Dad. Let's go home."

"Being in London wouldn't make any difference now." Colin was right, and Hester knew it. The damage had been done, and was irreparable.

A policeman's car drove away, taking Hester's past with it, and her whole life seemed to be coming to an end. She thought that matters could not possibly get any worse, but she was mistaken because the sight of Charmian rushing out onto the Teal verandah and the sound of her triumphant laughter was unendurable.

"He'll go to prison forever and then be hanged. You'll never see your horrible father again."

"Of course I will," retorted Hester, trying to appear amused. "You're talking codswallop as usual. Dad's gone back to work now, but he'll be home with us this evening."

"He'll be in jail this evening, and Albie's coming to stay here to protect me from your murdering father."

"Why would Albie need to, if Dad was in prison? Albie thinks you're just a silly schoolkid, and he's right."

"You don't know anything about Albie. You haven't even met him," jeered Charmian. "Albie and I worked on the case together. I found the evidence that proves your stupid father killed my Dad, and Sandra too."

"Rubbish!" snapped Hester. "There's no evidence."

"Yes, there is. And Albie said that, without me, he couldn't have solved the case. He's going to take me to the very next Bethanyville dance as a reward."

"He wouldn't be seen anywhere with a kid. If Albie goes to the dance, he'll be there with another woman like Sandra. You know that as well as I do."

"Albie's taking *me* to the dance," Charmian bellowed. "We've got a date."

"A date to spy on him that he doesn't know about," scoffed Hester.

Hearing raised voices, Noreen appeared at the front door, called Hester's name and beckoned her daughter inside. It felt like defeat, but Hester was glad to turn her back on Charmian. They could shout at each other for hours, but nothing would alter the fact that Colin had been discarded by Opal and then driven away from Hester by a policeman. It was Charmian's victory.

"The neighbours have seen and heard quite enough for today without us adding to their entertainment," said Noreen, closing the front door behind Hester. "Things will actually be easier now that your father's not living in Rosebery Avenue."

However, Opal and Charmian still were: enemies in a way that Colin could never be to Hester, no matter how many times he let her down, and he had let his daughter down badly by caring so little for her. She blamed Australia, but the country had not made Colin's choices for him.

****

Earl drove down Rosebery Avenue, passed the spot where Derek Teal had died, and then the car turned a corner to where shops, biscuit factory and railway station formed Bethanyville's commercial centre. "Find a hotel or back to work?"

"Back to work," said Colin.

"What did happen this morning?" asked Earl, slowing the car as they approached Barton's factory.

"I've already told you."

"Tell me again."

"We talked about driving to Mordialloc for a meal after I finished work. That was more or less it, and Opal wanted to go. She feels trapped in the house because of the situation with Noreen, and can't wait to sell the place. Opal's very sensitive."

"What about Charmian?"

"What about her?"

"Was she there?"

"At first. Charmian said that she wasn't going anywhere with us, and Opal pointed out that she hadn't been invited."

"What did Charmian do then?"

"Refused to eat breakfast, flounced off to her room and slammed the door."

"What did you say to Opal about that?"

"Nothing. It's normal behaviour for Charmian. Opal and I talked a bit about driving, and then I went to work." Colin frowned, as though searching his memory for any detail that would explain a mystery to him. "I don't know how Charmian persuaded Opal to lie, but that's what must have happened."

"Driving? How come driving was the topic of conversation right after a scene with Charmian?"

"It wasn't a scene; it was just Charmian being Charmian as usual. We ignored her, and went on talking about our trip to Mordialloc."

However, the 'we' had become Opal and Charmian since that morning, with Colin now the outsider, and Earl had difficulty believing in such a bland account of the tête-à-tête that so distressed Opal. "There must have been an argument."

"It wasn't an argument. Opal didn't want to drive the car to Mordialloc, and I said OK I would, even though I knew I'd be tired after work because I'm still not used to this Australian heat. But Opal was adamant that she wouldn't drive."

"Opal can't drive."

"I thought that as well, until I found Opal's driving licence this morning. She lost her nerve after a collision back home."

"You've made a mistake," said Earl, tempted to declare outright that Colin Kemp was a liar who deserved to be hanged for his crimes. "It must have been Derek's driving licence you found."

"No, it was Opal's. I hadn't known before that she'd got a middle name, but Opal hates being a Cora and so tries to keep quiet about it.

Hardly a reason for her to start claiming I made threats though, and then throw me out of the house. Even if she's met someone else —" Colin left the rest of the words unsaid, and shrugged at the impossibility of understanding what had happened to him. "This all goes back to Charmian; I know it does."

****

"Why didn't you arrest him?" demanded Walt. "You'll have to keep the Teal house under surveillance now, and any overtime will be queried for sure. Kemp's certain to try and silence Opal, and he's already killed twice."

"He wouldn't be fool enough to murder Opal," said Earl.

"And he wouldn't be a killer if he had any sense."

"Assuming that he *is* a killer."

"Best to work with a theory," said Walt, relying as usual on inspiration rather than deep thought about the available evidence. "Kemp wanted Opal, so he had a reason to kill both Sandra and Derek. Now Kemp's decided that the kid's got to go as well. You should have arrested him."

"It's Opal's word against his that he confessed to murder."

A mere detail, as far as Walt was concerned. Two cases were closed in his mind, proving that he had been right all along and could boast of yet another success for the famed Grissom instinct, a gift that made the judicial process appear rather superfluous to Walt.

"Opal lied to me about being able to drive," said Earl.

"She probably meant that she preferred not to drive."

"It's a possibility." But it was also a possibility that Opal had deliberately lied because she wanted to be classed as a non-driver and, if Opal knew how to drive, Charmian's guess about the circumstances surrounding her father's death could be expanded to include an additional suspect. Opal and Derek argued, he left the house, she

151

followed in a fury, and slammed the door that had woken Charmian. "No," muttered Earl.

"No?" queried Walt.

"Nothing." If Sandra and Derek had had an affair, there might have been arguments between Opal and Derek about his lover, but with Sandra dead, it would be a somewhat belated clash on the night that Derek died. "No," repeated Earl.

"No to Opal killing her husband?" Walt was taken aback to discover that the dull Earl Lanyon could rival his own leaps of imagination, and he hurried to rout a trespasser on Grissom territory. "Kemp made up the story of a driving licence in an attempt to save his skin."

"He'd know that I can check the British records."

"And in the meantime, Colin Kemp vanishes. Anyway, what if Opal once had a driving licence? She probably told you she didn't drive, not that she couldn't. The next thing, you'll suspect her of murdering Sandra Stoddard. Kemp's done a good job with his smokescreen."

Walt was right. Colin had done an excellent job of putting doubts into Earl's mind.

****

"If Colin Kemp tries to get back inside the Teal house, arrest him," Earl instructed Albie. "I'll arrange for someone to take over when your shift ends, but I want you there first to talk to Charmian unofficially: just a casual chat when her mother's not around. The kid might have persuaded Opal to get rid of Kemp."

"How?"

"That's for you to find out. And ask Charmian if the figure she claims to have seen by the garage that night could have been a woman."

"You reckon Opal killed her own husband?" Albie looked intrigued, and then added eagerly, "If Opal knew about Derek's affair, she could have killed Sandra Stoddard as well."

"And perhaps Charmian killed Sandra. I need evidence, not guesswork." Earl had little hope of Constable Fulton producing information that would convict either Colin or Opal, but if Charmian ever talked openly, she was more likely to select her beloved Albie as the confidant than anyone else, and so Fulton it would have to be.

Albie, however, regarded the opportunity as a definite career boost. He had been chosen by a Detective Sergeant to further an investigation, and further it he would. Charmian was a kid, no match for Albie's intelligence, and she wanted to please him, just like all females of any age. His clever questions were going to prise out everything Charmian knew, and make it obvious that either her mother or Colin had killed Sandra. "I'll get Charmian to spill the beans. If Derek had a key to the Stoddard place, Opal could have used it to get into the house when she murdered Sandra, and Opal might also be the person who dropped the key in the Teal kitchen, not Kemp."

Albie was showing every sign of developing into another Walt Grissom, over-reliant on guesses, which was a method of working that thoroughly annoyed Earl, even if it did occasionally produce results, and he retorted, "Don't answer your own questions. Listen to what Charmian tells you."

"Of course," said Albie, surprised that Earl should think him in need of such basic instruction.

****

"Albie!" cried Charmian, jumping down from verandah to driveway, and running towards him. "You've got to protect me. And protect my mother too. Our lives have been threatened by a murderer."

"I know. You told me on the phone." Albie stood by the gate, and noted that Charmian was jubilant rather than afraid, enjoying the drama but eager to pose as a damsel in distress.

"I'm in terrible danger, Albie, mortal danger. The murderer's eyes glinted with evil when he made his brutal threat, and he'll be even more determined to kill us now that my mother's finally realized the truth about him."

"You didn't hear any of his brutal threats though?"

"He waited until he got my mother alone so that he could terrify her." Delighted with the chance to show Albie how courageous she was, Charmian laughed scornfully at the craven tactics of a homicidal coward.

"So your Mum told you about Kemp's threat. You didn't actually see those glinting eyes of evil?"

"No, but my mother did." Charmian frowned, hurt that Albie seemed to be mocking her because it clashed with the character Charmian had awarded him. The Albert Fulton of imagination was a paragon, invariably sympathetic and caring; therefore, any blemish in his perfection almost turned the real Albie into an impostor. "If that murderer escapes from prison, he'll be straight back here to try and kill me."

"He isn't in prison."

"He's escaped already!" Charmian's yell sent garden birds skywards as a film jumped out of a cinema screen and into her life. She was the heroine, naturally, and Albie the hero: two stars brought together by fate for their guaranteed happy ending. "The very second you see that murderer, Albie, you've got to shoot him dead."

"We still need more evidence against Kemp." Albie liked the idea of himself as a man of action, and regretted the fact that Colin was probably too sensible to risk silencing Opal permanently. There would be no armed confrontation, and Albie felt cheated out of a superb opportunity to enhance his career. "Kemp denies threatening your Mum."

"Of course he'll deny it," said Charmian, glaring in the direction of the Kemp house. "But my mother's terrified of him now, and before this morning she wouldn't hear a word against the murderer. Isn't that proof enough?"

"It's a start," conceded Albie. "Are you certain it was Kemp you saw taking the car that night?"

"Positive," Charmian replied.

"Even though you didn't see the figure clearly?"

"Who else would it have been? Of course it was him."

"You told Detective Sergeant Lanyon that you thought it was your Dad," Albie pointed out.

"Well, it wasn't. It was that murderer."

"Could the figure you saw have been a woman?"

"*Mrs* Kemp?" queried Charmian, looking puzzled. "Why would Mrs Kemp kill my Dad?"

"Not necessarily her: any woman."

"It was that murderer," Charmian maintained stubbornly.

"But you didn't recognize him."

"I would have, if I'd looked properly and seen his face."

"But you didn't."

"No," Charmian admitted, saddened that a chance to help Albie was lost forever. "How could I have known what a killer planned to do?"

"So you might have seen a woman, not a man?" Albie felt exasperated by Charmian's refusal to give him the information Earl Lanyon wanted, and the impatience creeping into his voice made Charmian pause before answering.

"Do you think Mrs Kemp was in on the plot?" demanded Charmian, trying to work out what Albie hoped to hear. "I suppose it might have been her. But why would she steal the car for him?"

"We've got to look at every single possibility," explained Albie.

"Do we?" Charmian smiled, elated that Albie now considered the pair of them a team. "Then it's possible I saw a woman take the car. Yes, it's definitely possible. You're so clever to figure out what Mrs Kemp did to try and fool us. I never once thought of her."

Nor had Albie, and he congratulated himself on tricking Charmian into an admission that she could have seen a woman by the Teal garage. If Opal had killed her husband because of his affair with Sandra, Earl Lanyon and Walt Grissom might both be inclined to regard Opal as an extra suspect in the Stoddard case, which meant that Albie's future would be safely secured. He had found evidence linking the two deaths, and such astuteness should soon lead to Constable Albert Fulton taking the Detective Branch by storm. All he now required was a supplementary detail or two that would connect Opal even more firmly to Sandra's death.

"Did you remove any fingerprints off those photos of Sandra Stoddard?" asked Albie.

"Of course not," Charmian replied, proud to demonstrate that she was no bungling amateur, unaware of the importance of correct procedure. "Removing fingerprints would destroy crucial evidence against the murderer."

"Will your own prints be on the photos or the book?"

"No, because I knew how careful I had to be," laughed Charmian, exuberantly overconfident.

"Did you really find the photos among your Dad's things?"

"Yes: well, sort of." Charmian spoke hesitantly, taken aback by the question, and Albie smiled reassuringly.

"Colin Kemp must have planted the pictures."

"That's exactly what he did," declared Charmian. "And he hated Sandra so much, he'd scribbled all over her face in every single photo, and yet she was really nice, wasn't she? It proves that he killed her."

"Too right it does, and he's so cunning that I'll need even more evidence before we can arrest and charge him. Where did he plant the pictures?"

"In our garbage bin with a book that had belonged to my Dad, but I wasn't fooled. I knew Sandra's murderer wanted to get my Dad blamed for her death, so I tipped out the rubbish just like a detective would, just like you would, Albie, to make sure I got all the photos. I didn't know who Sandra's killer was at first, but the instant he targeted my Mum, I realized what his game was, and that he'd murdered my Dad as well." Charmian looked at Albie expecting more praise, and he obliged.

"You'll be the reason a murderer gets hanged."

Charmian smiled back at Albie, and he was pleased to gain such an easy victory. "So you found the photos after your Dad was killed but before Kemp moved in?"

"Yes, and that's another proof of his cunning. He must have been around here seconds after he'd murdered Dad to dump the pictures. If Mum had seen them, the killer reckoned she'd think that Dad had murdered Sandra, but I wasn't conned though, not for a moment."

Charmian was vindictively triumphant, too caught up in her own fixed idea to consider any other explanation of the photos' appearance amongst Teal garbage, and she might have been correct. Kemp could have planted the pictures to convince Opal that Derek had two-timed her, and so cause a grieving widow to become a vengeful one, ready and eager to welcome a new man into her life. It made no difference to Albie, who was quite willing for Colin, rather than Opal, to be charged with Sandra Stoddard's murder, whichever of them had obliterated her face in the photographs.

"You've got to tell Detective Sergeant Lanyon everything you've just told me," Albie urged Charmian. "You've gathered important evidence against Kemp."

"I'll talk to anyone you want me to, Albie, anyone at all. That killer will definitely be arrested now, won't he? And hanged as well?"

"Definitely. Not a chance of him getting away with it. I'll speak to Earl Lanyon, and then he'll come here to see you."

"Why?" asked Charmian, disdaining an outsider's intrusion. "You solved the case, Albie, not him. Will you get promotion because of it?"

"For sure, especially if you can tell me anything else."

"I wish there was more, but I've told you all I know. It'll be enough though, won't it? You'll still get promoted?"

"Of course." Albie knew that Charmian was congratulating herself on his promotion, and expecting him to be grateful. She had no idea that Charmian Teal's rôle in his life was now approaching its end, and not before time in Albie's opinion. Girls who were neither voluptuous nor pretty hardly seemed to be female, and there was only one more question needing an answer before he dismissed Charmian. "Did you really find that key to the Stoddard house on your kitchen floor?"

Charmian dithered, and then asked, "Does it matter where I found Sandra's key?"

"It might turn out to be the most crucial piece of evidence against Kemp that there is," said Albie, eager to prove how much better he was at getting truth out of a potential witness than the stilted Earl Lanyon would ever be.

"But I told that Detective I'd found Sandra's key in the kitchen." Charmian considered it an act of stupidity to admit to a lie in school, even though a teacher could only cane her on the hand or impose extra homework, and she knew that the consequences of lying to a policeman would be astronomically worse. "Can you keep a secret, Albie?"

"Anything you tell me will stay our secret, if that's what you want. I won't tell anyone." declared Albie. "Where did you find the key?"

"It was in the garbage bin along with the photos," revealed Charmian, ecstatic to be sharing a secret with Albie. "I had to make up a story to try and get that stupid Lanyon to arrest the killer before I got murdered as well. I was acting in self-defence, forced to act in self-defence, so it doesn't really count as lying, does it? But you won't tell anyone, will you, Albie?"

"I promise."

Albie smiled at her again, and for the first time in weeks, Charmian's life appeared to be full of hope.

****

"The photos and key might have been planted in the Teal house by Colin Kemp before he moved in, or they could have belonged to Derek," Albie pointed out, apparently imagining that Earl required the full nuances and ramifications of Charmian's latest story to be explained to him in detail. "If Opal found the key among her husband's things, it means that she had access to the Stoddard house."

"*Could* have had access to Sandra's house," amended Earl. "It'd depend on if and when Opal found the key, and that's assuming Charmian has told the truth at last. And the girl had access to Sandra's house herself as she's the one who produced the key."

Euphoric now that he had proved his ability to contribute so significantly to an investigation, Albie laughed at the idea of a kid as murderer. "Charmian's certain that Colin Kemp planted the key and photos, and she could be right. Finding them in a book of Derek's would make Opal think that her husband had two-timed her, and it'd be much easier for Kemp to work his way into the Teal house."

All variations of the scenario were possible, even one that featured a stranger attacking Sandra after discovering an unlocked door or open window by chance, but Colin had become more of a suspect now that Opal was insisting he had confessed to killing both Sandra and Derek, although Opal Teal had her own track record of telling at least one lie. Questioning Opal about the key and photographs should determine how much of a liar she was, and might add evidence against Colin or throw doubt on Charmian's most recent stories.

"I told the kid that she had to tell you the truth," added Albie, proud to have more influence than a Detective Sergeant over a witness. "She won't take you for a ride now."

Earl hoped that the same could be said of Charmian's mother.

****

"You told me that you'd never learnt to drive."

Opal had welcomed Earl as her saviour, and the childishly wide eyes still gazed at him in adoration as she replied, "No, I never said that I *couldn't* drive; I said that I *can't* drive now. It's so silly of me, I know, but I completely lost my nerve after a collision back home. I don't even like being a passenger in a car these days. It's positively shameful to be a coward, but I'm terrified of driving, and I hope you won't despise me because I'm such a timid soul."

"But you do know how to drive a car."

"I did once, but I've tried to forget all I knew about driving and cars. I still suffer from nightmares about the accident even though it happened ages ago, and I don't think I'll ever fully recover from such a horrible experience. It's quite true what they say about your whole life flashing through your mind because that's exactly what happened to me." The wide eyes became even wider as Opal beseeched Earl's compassion for her fragility, so guileless and so feminine.

"When did you find the key and photographs of Sandra Stoddard?" asked Earl, annoyed to be distracted by Opal's wistfulness. Good-looking people would always have an easier life, simply because they pleased by appearance without having to make any effort, and Earl resented the way Opal could manipulate him into feeling protective towards her, even though he knew that she had lied about being able to drive.

"What photographs?" Opal looked puzzled, an imitation of a little girl baffled by the adult world, but an act that might possibly contain some genuine emotion as she had hidden behind an infantile mask for so long that it was now a part of her. "I don't know what you're talking about."

"The photos of Sandra Stoddard that you threw into your garbage bin, along with a key to her house."

"Albie promised! Albie promised me that he wouldn't tell you," cried Charmian, abruptly flinging open the living-room door. "You stole Albie's notebook; you stole it, you thief!"

"Charmian, you mustn't shout at people," said Opal, so gently reproving that it was more like advice than a rebuke. "It's such bad manners, and I'm quite sure Detective Sergeant Lanyon never stole anything in his life."

"He stole Albie's notebook; he definitely stole it," Charmian retorted, furious at the crime. "How else could he know about the garbage bin? Albie wouldn't tell. He promised me that it'd stay our secret. Why, he practically crossed his heart."

"Charmian and I are both so upset today," said Opal, turning to Earl. "It'll be much better if you postpone your questions until later on. I can't think straight after all I went through with Colin this morning. And my daughter's just as distressed by the whole thing. She's so protective of me."

"I'm going to tell Albie what you've done," fumed Charmian, glaring at Earl. "You're jealous because he solved the case when you couldn't. That's why you stole his notebook. You'll get sacked and he'll be promoted."

"Perhaps any further questions could wait until tomorrow?" suggested Opal, smiling wearily. "I really don't feel well enough to cope with anything more today. Have you arrested Colin yet, Sergeant?"

"He let him go," snarled Charmian. "Albie told me."

"But, Sergeant, you've got to protect me," pleaded Opal, and she could not have cowered back with more fear had Colin just walked into the room. "You've got to protect me from that man, that killer. Please, Sergeant, I beg you."

"He won't protect us," scoffed Charmian. "Don't bother asking. It's a waste of time talking to him, but Albie won't allow anything to happen to us."

Like mother, like daughter, thought Earl. Charmian was also trusting a man certain to disappoint her, but Colin Kemp could have let Opal down merely by discovering that she had lied about knowing how to drive a car. In the drama of a relationship's unanticipatedly sudden end, Opal might have hoped that Colin would forget the minor detail of finding her driving licence, particularly as an accusation against him of threatening violence would add to any suspicion Earl might already have that Colin had killed Derek, and possibly Sandra as well. However, even in an attempt to incriminate Derek, Colin would be unlikely to plant defaced photographs and a key to Sandra's house so close to where he lived, especially as Colin had had ample opportunity to dispose of such signposts to guilt anywhere in Victoria. But if Charmian could be believed, Opal might have thrown out those symbols of hatred right after Derek's death, when perhaps she felt that all the old scores had at last been settled, leaving her free to start a new life with a new man.

"Charmian, you told Constable Fulton that you found those photos of Sandra and her key in your garbage bin."

"What Albie and I say to each other is nothing to do with you," declared Charmian, haughtily outraged.

"Colin!" gasped Opal. "It was Colin! He threw that key into the bin, along with photos of the woman he killed. Charmian, I'm so sorry that I permitted such danger to enter our home."

"I warned you enough times."

"Yes, darling, you did; indeed you did. You saw through him right from the start with total clarity, and I'm so glad you gave the proof of Colin's guilt to the police. Our nightmare's over, once and for all."

"Absolutely," stated Charmian. "And Albie's gone to arrest that killer before we're murdered as well. Albie's so clever, he solved the case entirely by himself."

Charmian glared defiantly at Earl, determined to stick to the latest version of her story, and he realized that nothing would induce the girl to backtrack. Opal knew how to handle Charmian more intelligently than Earl had expected, and he tried a different approach. "I've heard that Derek was fond of Sandra Stoddard."

"He barely knew the woman," declared Opal.

"Yes, he did," said Charmian. "Sandra asked Dad what I'd like for my Christmas present at the factory party last year. He told her I wanted a diamond necklace, and that's exactly what Sandra got for me."

"It's a cheap plastic toy." Opal smiled at Charmian's gullibility, glancing at Earl as though they were in league.

"My necklace wasn't cheap, and it's not plastic either," protested Charmian. "The diamonds sparkle in sunlight, and they're on a gold chain. Sandra chose it specially for me because Dad asked her to."

"Biscuit factories don't hand out diamond necklaces."

"You're wrong. Mum, because I got one."

"She'll be telling us next that she still believes in Santa Claus," said Opal, again trying to persuade Earl to share her amusement at Charmian's credulity.

"Both Dad and Sandra said that it was a diamond necklace, and they wouldn't ever have tried to fool me," retorted Charmian. "Sandra was lovely. You ask Albie."

"Oh, all right. The Barton Biscuit Company is an exceptionally generous one." Opal smiled again, a good-natured mother prepared to concede any wild claim her young daughter might make.

The whole of Opal's life seemed to be a performance that an audience was expected to admire and applaud, but many people put on a show in front of others, and Earl knew that there might be nothing behind Opal's façade apart from an empty existence she was eager to fill. All the same, her account of Colin Kemp's menacing behaviour somehow failed to ring true, unless Colin had developed more expertise as a deceiver than Opal ever would. One of them was lying, and Opal had already lied about being able to drive a car: a small lie, but a telling one given the circumstances of her husband's death.

****

"Are you sure Opal said that she couldn't drive?"

Walt prided himself on his intuition, but Earl was equally proud of his accuracy when taking notes, and he retorted, "Opal told me that she'd never learnt to drive. She made a big thing of it. Did you question her about Sandra's death?"

"You know I didn't. Why should I have?" demanded Walt, immediately defensive. His instinct had failed to select Opal Teal as a suspect, which naturally meant she must be innocent. "There's no evidence at all that one person killed both Sandra and Derek, even if a wife did chance to get rid of an unwanted husband."

"Two murders in Rosebery Avenue during the same month? Besides, there was a connection between Sandra and Derek. They're said to have had an affair."

"Since when did you begin listening to gossip? That's Constable Fulton's speciality. Anyway, Sandra and Opal appear never to have met, and Derek's death was most likely a hit and run. Why would I have questioned Opal about Sandra?" Walt felt that the conversation had turned upside down, and the somersault irritated him. It was most unusual for Earl to claim the dramatic high ground, and double murder should have been Grissom territory, with Earl restricted to the more mundane cases. "My money was on Sandra's ex-husband at first. Not that their divorce seems to have been acrimonious, as divorces go. They were just kids who married too young, quickly learnt their lesson and said goodbye forever. He went to live in New Zealand after the split-up, remarried over there, started a family, and apparently refuses to venture outside his house unless he's got at least six alibis."

"Have you come across any evidence linking Derek to Sandra?" asked Earl.

"Nobody's mentioned him to me. Sandra was a popular girl with quite a few admirers, but don't forget that she also had a fulltime job to fit into her supposedly frenzied private life."

"Was Colin Kemp's name among the few?"

"Apart from the incident of the infamous spider, he and Sandra are only thought to have flirted a bit at work. But if you're beginning to think that the two deaths might be connected, you should hand the Teal case over to me." Walt attempted to sound as though he had made a joke, but the idea of Earl somehow managing to solve both murders rankled because Walt considered himself gifted beyond the ordinary, and the very ordinary Earl Lanyon should never try to approach the status that Walt Grissom believed was his by right. "Give me all your notes, and I'll take a look at them for you."

Earl resented the patronizing tone when Walt was the policeman least likely to keep accurate records or to re-read them even while investigating his own cases, but finding answers to questions would always be the most important part of their job, and Earl persisted. "Derek was at work the night Sandra died, according to factory records. Did you check up on him?"

"There was no reason to. I don't know much about factories, I'm glad to say, but it seems that any Barton worker would have been missed if he'd abandoned the biscuits to kill Sandra. They were at conveyor belts most of that night, ate sandwiches together inside the factory during their break, and so half of Bethanyville's population can alibi each other."

"Opal was on her own."

"Perhaps not, given Colin Kemp's activities."

"He was still living in a Nissen hut on Bethanyville Hostel then, and hadn't met Opal. According to them, anyway. Sandra went to a dance that evening and left by herself before it ended, didn't she?"

"I can't imagine why any female in her right mind would desert the celebrated Bethanyville Friday Night Dance in mid-merriment, but that's what Sandra did, and she was probably followed home by the killer. Or he was already in Rosebery Avenue, waiting for her."

On the night she died, the key to Sandra's house could have been used by Derek, Opal, Colin or Charmian. Derek might have been told that the affair was over, but refused to accept Sandra's decision, and had somehow managed to sneak out of the factory despite his multiple alibis. Opal could have found photographs of her rival along with a key, and stormed up to Sandra's house. Colin had possibly got bored with a tediously clinging girlfriend, and wanted to liberate himself to concentrate on Opal. Charmian? No obvious motive, but a custodian of the key.

"The same people are linked to both victims," said Earl. "It can't be a coincidence."

"And yet coincidences happen," Walt pointed out.

****

If you got to know the victim, you got to know the killer, or so Earl had once been told. Learning about Derek had led to suspicion of Opal, and perhaps knowing Sandra would implicate Opal as well, building more of a case against her. Sandra, an uncomplicated good-time girl, had been the opposite of Opal, but both women could have attracted the same man. Derek would be reacting against his wife when he started an affair with Sandra, assuming that they had been lovers, and he might even have hoped for permanent escape from a marriage gone stale, but to Sandra it was just a passing fling. Had Derek lashed out at her when he realized the truth? If Opal murdered Sandra to eliminate a rival, why did Derek need to die as well? And if Opal's fury had been directed against her husband, would she attack Sandra and then wait a couple of weeks before killing Derek? If he had murdered Sandra, why did Opal kill him? Colin might be a double-murderer, but so far there was only one spider and some speculation connecting him to Sandra, rather than solid evidence, in spite of Charmian's energetic efforts. However, perhaps the answers could be found in Sandra's life instead of her death.

Albie was pleased to be summoned to Detective Sergeant Lanyon's office, yet another sign that the investigation could only proceed with the aid of Constable Albert Fulton's input, and such appreciation of his valuable services was as welcome as it had been expected. Albie felt that his worth was now established, and recognition along with speedy promotion inevitable.

"Sandra Stoddard," said Earl, ignoring his opportunity to praise Albie's intelligence and resourcefulness. "When did you first meet her?"

"I didn't," protested Albie. "I never met her. You asked me that before, and I told you then."

"But you knew who she was."

"My aunt might have mentioned her once or twice, but I wasn't really listening."

"You must have seen Sandra around Bethanyville."

"I guess so. I don't remember her."

"But you live in the same street that she did," argued Earl. "Sandra was practically a neighbour."

"But I didn't notice her. There are always so many girls buzzing about."

Rosebery Avenue girls were presumably more spectacular than film stars if they relegated flamboyantly attractive Sandra to the background, reflected Earl. "I got the impression that you'd known her: something Charmian Teal said."

As he spoke, Earl recalled that the impression had come to him via the girl's order to consult Albie about the investigation, and not only did Charmian regard Constable Fulton as omniscient, she had inherited her mother's fondness for inaccurate testimony as well as blatant lies.

"Charmian Teal!" laughed Albie. "Charmian Teal thinks that I've already solved two murder cases single-handedly. No, I never met Sandra Stoddard. I wish I had by the sound of her, but I can ask my mates if they know more about the numerous boyfriends. Most of the men who live south of Melbourne, by all accounts: one bloke after another, according to local rumour, with Derek Teal and Colin Kemp the two latest in a very long line. But I heard that you'd decided a jealous Opal Teal had killed Sandra Stoddard."

Deciding who was guilty and proving guilt were two very different things, thought Earl. Constable Fulton had a lot to learn.

****

Noreen and Hester were cleaning windows in the shade of their verandah, when Earl drove up. He intended to interview Opal again, but concluded that it might help intimidate her if she spotted him talking to Noreen first, particularly if he pointed at the Teal house during the conversation before turning back to Noreen. Tricks worked well for Walt Grissom, and when Earl's usual meticulous work had failed to produce a result, it was time to branch out.

"Do you want to buy a house?" called Noreen, looking around from a half-cleaned window at the sound of Earl's approaching footsteps. "I'm going to sell up, and I just hope there'll be enough money to get a place closer to the sea. Not that I suppose it feels much cooler by the coast on days like this."

"You're right. It's going to another part of a furnace," said Earl, pausing in the middle of the drive and trusting Opal would see him. "A move that far away would mean a new school for you, Hester," he added.

"I'll be changing schools soon, wherever we are." Hester tried to sound indifferent at the prospect, although the thought of yet more disruption in her life was daunting, despite the relief that getting away from Bethanyville would bring.

"Aiming for High School? Good on you." Earl's social chit-chat was now exhausted, and he gladly permitted his job to take over. "You both knew Sandra Stoddard. What was she like?"

"Nice," replied Noreen, determined to ignore the possibility that they might be discussing one of Colin's former lovers. "But the nicest people always seem to die young."

In that case Opal and Charmian would live forever, Hester reflected. Sandra had been cheated out of years, and all because the Opals went on and on, in spite of destroying everybody else's happiness. Life was not only unfair, it was cruel.

"Did Sandra ever visit the Teal house?" asked Earl, pointing at next door.

"I haven't a clue," said Noreen, surprised that Earl assumed she would need guidance to locate the exact building blighted by Opal's presence. Then the obviousness of Earl's plan struck Noreen, and she laughed. "You're trying to get next door worried. That's the tactic school bullies used in my day, and probably still do. They'd point at you, and then smirk at each other."

"I'm not smirking," said Earl.

"But you aim to make a certain woman think that we're talking about her."

"We are talking about Opal Teal."

"And you want her to know it. Would you like me and Hester to stand in the garden as well, so that all three of us can turn and stare at the house before we start talking again?" Once Noreen would have pretended not to notice what Earl had done, but since Colin's defection, she no longer tried to please people, and the freedom was exhilarating. "Come on, Hester, let's help put the wind up next door."

Even the smallest amount of revenge would feel delightful, and Hester jumped down the verandah steps onto the driveway. "Can I point at their house as well?"

"Of course," said Noreen. "Forget everything I've ever told you about it being bad manners to point, and point to your heart's content. I just hope that somebody's at one of the windows to see us."

Noreen and Hester were so clearly having fun that Earl knew his strategy to alarm Opal would fail. It was the sort of trickery that worked for Walt Grissom, but not for someone with limited acting skills, and Earl abandoned the attempted bluff. "When did Derek Teal crash his car into the mailbox?"

"The day before we came to live here," replied Noreen. "Derek was replacing the box when we arrived. That was the first time I met him."

The day before the Kemps moved to Rosebery Avenue had either been the day that Derek learnt of Sandra's death, or the day after he had killed her, and Earl asked, "Did Derek explain how the accident happened?"

"He'd just heard about Sandra, and the sun dazzled him."

It was an odd coincidence, in two cases full of coincidences, that the sun should only be dazzling enough to cause Derek to collide with a mailbox on one particular day. Coincidences happened, as Walt said, but something had apparently changed for Derek. "Did he mention what time of day the accident happened?"

"No. Why?"

"How did Derek seem when he told you about it?"

Noreen's mind raced ahead of the questions, not a difficult task as she had long-since decided that Sandra and Derek must have been far more to each other than mere acquaintances. The idea of Opal spurned for a younger woman brought great comfort with it, and although Earl had presumably made the connection, Noreen added helpfully, "We talked mostly about poor Sandra. It was only two days after she'd been killed and Derek was very upset, as we all were. Well, not all."

"Who wasn't upset?" asked Earl.

"Who do you think?" Noreen smiled, happy to destroy whatever fantasy Opal was likely to have spun for Earl. "Derek's wife, of course. Didn't have a good word to say about poor Sandra, and actually said that she deserved to get killed."

Earl had expected Colin's vengeful wife to be at her most uncharitable when discussing any aspect of Opal's behaviour, but Noreen sensed the scepticism and she turned to Hester for corroboration. "You remember her saying that about Sandra, don't you?"

"Yes. Mrs Teal didn't like Sandra at all, and was glad that she'd died," said Hester, as eager as her mother to turn the tables on Opal. "Ginevra Dean told me that Mrs Teal killed Sandra, and Ginevra must know because she's got a cousin who's a policeman."

Albert Fulton was plainly not the most discreet of Constables, and Earl wondered if the gossip would reach Opal. Her reaction might be interesting.

10

For once, Opal and Charmian were allies, sitting side-by-side on the sofa, but Opal smiled at Earl while Charmian glared.

"I write down what people tell me, and you said that you'd never learnt to drive," Earl reminded Opal. "It's all in my notebook."

"That explains how you made the mistake," decided Opal. "You were so busy writing, you couldn't concentrate on my actual words. It's completely understandable when you must have so many important things on your mind."

"Albie's the one who's done all the work on this case, and he'd never make a silly mistake like that," declared Charmian, scorning Earl's underhand attempt to blame Opal for his own carelessness. "You should go on stealing Albie's notebooks. It's the only way that you'll ever know what the real clues are."

"Charmian's so high-spirited," said Opal, making a feeble effort to laugh. "I only wish that I could be as strong-minded. She refuses to allow anything to get her down."

"And whatever that stupid Hester Kemp told you just now in their garden was a lie," added Charmian. "She and her mother were laughing because they deliberately sent that murderer here to kill us. Has Albie arrested him yet?"

"I won't be able to relax for a moment until Colin's locked away," said Opal, shuddering. "Each time the memory floods back of the horrific things he said to me, I can't stop trembling in sheer terror."

"I'm not afraid," boasted Charmian, imagining words of praise from Albie for her courage.

"I want to see your driving licence," Earl said to Opal, before Charmian could revert to the topic of Constable Fulton.

"I've destroyed it. Just too many memories connected with cars for someone as sensitive as me, and I need to rid myself of the past now that I've decided to move. This house has too much sadness in it, and I can never be happy here again."

It would require very little sensitivity for a woman to turn against any house after her husband's death, but Opal looked as though she had said something laudable, and seemed surprised by Earl's impassive response to her news. "Your car will be taken away for examination."

"That awful man washed it, and he'll have made very sure that all proof of his guilt was removed." Opal winced at yet another recollection of Colin's existence, and she glanced at Charmian for support.

"Yes, it's far too late now. He'll have got rid of every single clue, and the murderer insisted on driving Mum to Chadstone last week so there was a reason for his fingerprints to be inside the car." Charmian snorted her contempt at the idea of such slyly covered tracks, and she frowned at Earl. "You should have taken the car away before he got a chance to tamper with it."

Earl knew that he had made a bad mistake by not seizing the car as soon as Derek's body had been found, but he suspected Opal, rather than Colin, of benefiting from his former negligence. In all likelihood, the car would be useless as evidence, and worrying Opal was Earl's main purpose in getting it removed. "There are some tests that can still be done."

"What tests?" demanded Charmian. "The murderer will have an answer for everything, and you should know by now what a liar he is."

"I'm so frightened the whole time," lamented Opal. "Surely you can't leave Colin free to return here whenever he pleases. I thought the police were meant to protect people."

"We don't need the entire police force to protect us," said Charmian, glowering at Earl. "We've got Albie."

****

"They're taking Derek's car away," Noreen reported, unable to stop watching the activity, although she already knew everything that an observation post at the front window could tell her. "Why bother with his car now?"

"Because the police have finally worked out who killed Mr Teal as well as Sandra Stoddard." Every book that Hester had read told a story of virtue rewarded and evil punished, but real life was usually less obliging, and she felt comforted by how neatly justice would at last catch up with the enemy.

Noreen was equally appreciative of fate's apparent retribution on her behalf, although she felt less certain than Hester that Opal's downfall could be taken for granted. Conviction on a double-murder charge was revenge beyond Noreen's most cherished hopes, and she knew that something would go haywire because it always did. "Opal Teal's too small and feeble. She couldn't have killed Sandra."

"She could with a hammer," argued Hester, unwilling to be cheated out of the entrancing vision of Opal led away in handcuffs by a police escort.

Proof that Opal had killed Derek would be enough to ensure her removal from Rosebery Avenue, and a second murder tagged onto the charge would be unnecessary, as far as Noreen was concerned, but very satisfying. "Have you been listening to Ginevra Dean again? If we were back in England, I'd say that girl was going to end up working for the *News of the World*," declared Noreen, in a futile attempt to distance herself from the vengeful woman she had become.

"Sandra *was* having an affair with Charmian's Dad, and Ginevra actually saw them walking together hand-in-hand loads of times, so it's true, not gossip," maintained Hester, pleased with the idea of an ignored and lividly jealous Opal.

"That doesn't mean the police are next door with an arrest warrant."

"But it doesn't mean that they won't be soon."

Noreen smiled at the optimism in Hester's voice, but it was a hope that she shared. Life would be transformed if Opal had to face some sort of reckoning, even though it would change nothing else. Whether Colin was the seduced or the seducer, he had chosen to discard his family, and that decision could not be undone or forgotten, but still the thought of Opal being punished was delightful.

"How long will it take the police to prove that she murdered two people?" asked Hester, impatient to reach such a glorious conclusion.

****

"No, you're wrong," Walt announced. "Opal Teal didn't kill Sandra Stoddard."

"You can't be sure of it," said Earl, despite knowing that Walt's instinct was supposed to rule supreme.

"A man killed Sandra. She was punched: battered to a pulp, as the newspapers are so fond of saying."

"An angry woman could have done that."

"Your experience of women boxers must be greater than mine," laughed Walt, confident in his analysis of the facts. "My money's now on Colin Kemp. You should have got the Teal car examined right at the start."

Earl had little need of a reminder "There were traces of blood, Derek's blood group, and a bit of his hair underneath the car, but no sign of the door locks having been tampered with."

"Then either Kemp stole the keys or found the car unlocked or he's a skilled car thief. Whichever, the case against him is stronger, though I reckon his lawyer will try to argue that Derek hit his head working underneath the car." Two investigations were at an end, according to Walt, and he was sure that any further details were bound to support his opinion.

"Why would Colin kill Sandra?" Earl leaned against Walt's office door, prepared for a long wait before he was convinced.

"Murderers don't require much of a reason to kill anyone. Sandra told him to go walkabout or threatened to tell his wife. She might even have said that she'd tell Opal."

"Opal and Colin didn't know each other when Sandra died," Earl commented.

"So they claim," said Walt, amused by such credulity in a Detective Sergeant. "Anyway, Kemp's violent. He threatened Opal and confessed to both murders."

"So she claims."

"Why would Opal turn against him? The facts now point in one direction, and that direction is Colin Kemp."

Walt could have been right, but still Earl frowned. Opal had lied at least once, and that threw everything else she said into doubt. However, Colin had presumably lied to Noreen when he was supposedly a mere visitor to Opal's house, and a lie remained a lie whoever heard the words spoken. Either Colin or Opal could have killed Derek and perhaps Sandra as well, if only because it seemed unlikely that two murderers would be active in Rosebery Avenue at the same time. "Have you got anything solid against Colin Kemp?"

"About as much as you've got against Opal, but I know that I'm right." Walt always did, even when he was wrong, and would be tempted to fake evidence in support of his belief and also to shake Colin's nerve: a ploy that might, with luck, result in a confession. Any trick was justifiable after Walt's instinct had identified and condemned a culprit. "I'm going to haul Kemp in for questioning. It's time that he had pressure put on him. I'll throw in Derek Teal's death to turn up the heat, and let Kemp see that we're on to him."

"I'll talk to Opal again," Earl decided.

"Talk!" Walt smiled at the idea of such a feeble approach.

****

"Sandra Stoddard," said Earl.

"What about her?" asked Opal.

"You didn't like Sandra."

"I never met the woman."

"She was nice," said Charmian. "I liked Sandra."

"You didn't know her," declared Opal.

"Yes, I did. And she was really nice."

"Take no notice of Charmian," Opal instructed Earl. "She can't tell you a thing about the Stoddard woman."

"I'm not saying one single word to *him*," said Charmian, despising Earl's ineptness. "But he only has to ask Albie about Sandra, and wouldn't even have to steal any more notebooks to find out that Albie thought Sandra was nice as well."

Charmian's obsession with the wondrous Albie was rapidly becoming her most tiresome characteristic, and Earl struggled to keep his voice free of impatience. "Constable Fulton doesn't know anything about Sandra."

"That's what you want people to think," snarled Charmian. "You're jealous because Albie's a better detective than you'll ever be, and I'm going to tell him who stole his notebook."

"Charmian's so lively." Opal made an effort to sit upright, before collapsing against the cushions of her armchair in a piteous yet graceful pose that suggested overwhelming exhaustion, and she pressed a hand against her forehead as though the weight of a headache required support. "I had the same high spirits once, but life's brought me very low, and I've no idea how I can go on. Are there many more questions? You should be protecting, not interrogating, me."

"If I'm interrogating anyone at the moment, it's your daughter," said Earl. "Charmian, when did you meet Sandra?"

"Dad introduced her to me last year at the factory Christmas party." It was remembering another life, as far away as the one left behind in England. Derek had been laughing with Sandra as Charmian raced across yellowing grass in the paddock beside the factory to show him the necklace a perspiring Santa Claus had just given her: a necklace with beads that caught the sunlight and sparkled when Charmian opened the pink box that had her name on it.

"Sandra arranged all the presents. She asked me what you'd like most, and I told her a diamond necklace," said Derek, his voice warm with appreciation as he smiled his gratitude at Sandra. "What do you say now, Charmian?"

"Thank you, Sandra. Thanks so much, Dad. This is the best day of my life."

Bunting fluttered in a hot breeze, excited children ran around the field with newly-acquired toys, and the moment was good enough to last forever. Sandra, in a pink dress with ballerina skirts, had laughed again, enjoying Charmian's happiness, while on the other side of the paddock, a neglected Opal in pale green pretended to ignore them.

"Yes, I met Sandra with Dad at the Christmas party," said Charmian, and the loss she felt ached with a pain that was physical. The best day of her life, and she had imagined there would be more and more best days, just as perfect as that one.

"I don't think I could go on without Charmian's exuberance," declared Opal. "I'm shattered by the terror I feel."

"Don't worry. Albie's gone to arrest that murderer," declared Charmian. "And if there are any clues left inside the car, he'll find them."

"Colin's much too wily to leave evidence behind him." Opal sank further back into her cushions, and glanced wistfully at Earl, imploring his pity. "It was too late for the car to be of any use, much too late."

"No, it wasn't." Earl expected Opal to flinch at the news, but she merely looked blank.

"I knew Albie wouldn't give up until he'd found all the clues there are," cried Charmian, trying to replace grief for Derek with hostility towards Earl. "It doesn't matter how many notebooks you steal, you'll never ever be as smart as Albie. You don't even know as much as I do."

"What was found on the car?" asked Opal.

"Evidence it was the vehicle that killed your husband."

"I told you ages ago who stole the car," Charmian pointed out, angrily fighting back tears in her determination not to reveal weakness in front of an adversary. "I even told you why he stole it."

"Yes, she did," agreed Opal, jerking herself bolt upright. "Why haven't you done something to protect us from Colin Kemp? He's a dangerous man, yet he was still walking around free even after he confessed to murdering two people. It's almost as if you don't believe an iota of what we say."

"That's because he hasn't bothered talking to Albie," jeered Charmian. "Albie could tell him everything he wants to know about Sandra, every single thing."

"How come you think that?" asked Earl.

"Because it's true," snapped Charmian.

****

"Have you learnt anything else about Sandra Stoddard?" asked Earl.

"Nothing new," replied Albie. "I'll be meeting up with some of my mates after work, and I'll ask them if they know more."

Charmian's advertising campaign on behalf of Constable Fulton had been successful enough to make Earl summon Albie to his office again, despite being certain that Fulton would have pushed himself forward as the investigation's main witness if he had discovered any previously unreported fact or rumour about Sandra Stoddard. "You're sure you never spotted her in the neighbourhood with friends?"

"Not that I remember. Like everyone else in Rosebery Avenue, I'd heard tales about her string of men, but that was all I knew. Apparently, she flaunted herself like a film star." Albie laughed, scorning a small-town woman who dared to live the sort of life that he imagined belonged solely to those who had the wealth and power to defy convention. A factory typist should have accepted the ordinariness that went with the job, and not had such a good opinion of herself. "Sandra Stoddard was always going to come to a bad end."

"Nothing's inevitable," said Earl.

"Has Colin Kemp done a vanishing act yet?" asked Albie, sounding more amused than concerned.

"Should he?"

"Didn't he confess to killing Sandra Stoddard?"

"Not to me."

"You don't believe Opal Teal?" Albie frowned with the effort of trying to work out a reason for Earl's lack of action, before adding, "How come she'd lie?"

"How come anyone lies?" Earl was annoyed that gossip among the Constables apparently criticized him for not having been more decisive, but if Opal were lying about Colin, she had presumably lied in the hope of diverting suspicion from herself, and Earl wanted to see what would happen should Colin remain a free man, something Opal had plainly not anticipated.

"A confession's a confession," Albie commented.

"Only if the words were actually said," retorted Earl.

11

"Colin Kemp's here! He's outside the house! You've got to help me. You've got to arrest him."

Opal was panicking, her voice piercingly shrill, and Earl moved the telephone receiver further away from his ear. "There's a constable watching your house. He'll stop any attempt to get to you, but close all the windows and lock the doors. I'll be there soon."

Earl had judged Colin as too sensible to approach Opal, and it was possible that she might have invented the story, unaware that her house was being watched, but whatever the truth behind Opal's phone call, it was an interesting development, and one that would add to Earl's knowledge of both Colin and Opal: an advantage for a policeman not blessed with Walt Grissom's magical insight.

As Earl drove up Rosebery Avenue towards the Teal house, he saw Constable Henley Spencer on the opposite side of the street, sitting in a car with its door open, the better to take advantage of cooler air from the shade of a roadside willow tree. Henley was not in uniform, and his rusting vehicle looked as though it had been welded together from several others but, even so, Colin might have taken fright when he noticed a car complete with a driver who apparently had no intention of going anywhere, and as Constable Spencer was not escorting an arrested man back to the police station, Colin Kemp had presumably fled.

"No," said Henley, looking disappointed not to be relating a tale of action-packed drama. He was young but plain, tall and thin with pale-brown hair, and he had hoped to enliven his mediocre career by taking a murderer into custody. "A man answering the description did walk up the road, and I thought he was headed for the Teal place, but he stopped at the Kemp house, and a kid, a girl, opened the front door and he went inside. He's still there, but I couldn't arrest him for that. I don't think he even glanced at the Teal house, but Albie Fulton warned me that Kemp's clever."

Either clever, or Colin had simply intended to visit his daughter, and was in Rosebery Avenue for no other reason. Earl crossed the road and walked up to the Kemp house, certain that Opal would be stationed at one of her windows. She might hope to see Colin taken away in handcuffs, but unless he had threatened his wife or child, watch and wait would remain Earl's preferred strategy.

"What rubbish is Opal Teal spouting now?" enquired Noreen, opening the front door for Earl. "Either Charmian's hypnotized her or the woman's mad."

"Did you ask your husband to visit you today?"

"He isn't visiting. Colin's taking Hester to Mentone for the afternoon."

"Was it arranged beforehand?"

"Of course. Hester might have been out with a schoolfriend otherwise. Why? What does it matter?"

It mattered because Colin Kemp had a reason to be in Rosebery Avenue that was unconnected with Opal. His presence so close to the Teal house might alarm her, but whether or not Colin had actually spoken the alleged threats, Earl could hardly arrest a man for going to collect his daughter.

"If you want to talk to Colin, you'd better do it now before he and Hester leave." Noreen opened the front door wider, and Earl walked into the hall. A policeman in the house to question Colin about confessing to murder and threatening to add to the body count would once have seemed impossible, but the unthinkable had so rapidly turned into the norm that it was just another part of their new lives in Australia. Colin's rejection by Opal still felt like Noreen's triumph, because the man who had thought that he could choose between two women now had no choice at all. Colin might meet someone else, but she would be unable to break up a marriage that was already broken beyond repair. Colin had done all the damage he could do.

"What now?" asked Colin, taken aback by the sight of Earl in the living-room doorway. "I'm going to keep on seeing my daughter, whatever Opal says."

"When she spotted you in the street near her house, Opal was frightened."

"Why should she be afraid?" demanded Colin. "Opal lied about me, and she knows it."

"Perhaps she hears voices in her head or something." Life rarely punished beautiful women, but Opal Teal deserved to be an exception, and Noreen was comforted by imagining Opal locked up in a madhouse or imprisoned in a cell for wasting police time. And if Colin really had made threats, even better.

"Opal's lying about me, but I've no idea why," said Colin.

If Opal had lied, it was presumably to remove Colin from her house. She might have hoped he would immediately get sent to jail and be in so much trouble that the comparatively minor detail of a driving licence would be forgotten in the upheaval. However, Earl was still in need of proof, not speculation, particularly if Opal had killed her husband and possibly Sandra as well, but every answer he was given seemed to come from somebody with a reason to lie. "You told me that the first time you met Opal Teal was on the day you moved into this house."

"That's right," said Colin. "I'd seen Derek around Barton's and I saw him with Opal at the factory Christmas party last year, but I didn't speak to them then or know that they'd be next door when we came to live in Rosebery Avenue."

"Derek was nice. I liked him," Noreen commented, regretting that the wrong Teal was dead, and noting that Colin had been aware of Opal's existence for nearly eleven months.

"Did Opal know her husband was having an affair with Sandra Stoddard?" asked Earl.

"Was he?" Noreen tried to sound surprised, while she revelled in the idea of a policeman forcing Opal to acknowledge that she had had a younger rival. "I knew Derek liked Sandra a lot. I remember saying something to him about poor Sandra perhaps having been killed by a ditched boyfriend, and he told me that she never left bad feeling behind her."

"Everybody liked Sandra," said Colin.

"The person who killed her didn't," Earl pointed out. "What else did Derek say about Sandra?"

"That she didn't go in for lies or pretence." It was delightful to criticize Opal by praising Sandra, and Noreen smiled. "Derek told me that Sandra was a lovely girl, kind, generous, straightforward and pleasant to everyone. He'd obviously been very fond of her."

"Did Opal ever mention Sandra?"

"Not to me," said Colin.

"She hated Sandra," declared Noreen, more than willing to share the information with Colin. "She told me that Sandra deserved to be killed and finally had to pay the price for the way she lived. Those were Opal's very words. It was such a horrible way to speak about somebody as nice as Sandra that every bit of what Opal said has stayed in my mind."

"How did Opal sound?" asked Earl. "Was she joking or —"

"Joking!" protested Colin.

"She was vindictive, bitter, grimly satisfied," said Noreen, pleased to have another opportunity to damage Opal's little-girl façade of saccharine sweetness. "She actually seemed to relish the thought of Sandra's death; yes, relish it. I think she must have known all about Sandra and Derek."

"Opal never once mentioned Sandra to me," said Colin.

"Well, she certainly did to me." With luck, the charges against Opal might actually include the two murders of Hester's fantasy, and Noreen hoped that Earl pictured the same scenario: Opal killing Sandra and then Derek, after deciding that Colin would be a good catch. Every deserted wife should know that there was a chance of the usurper being sentenced to swing at the end of a hangman's rope, and Noreen smiled again. "Were you with Opal on the night Sandra died, Colin?"

"We hadn't met Opal then; you know that," said Colin, uneasy at the prospect of a confrontation with Noreen while a Detective Sergeant was present.

"Derek told me that he was working when Sandra died, so it looks like Opal Teal doesn't have an alibi for that night," Noreen remarked for Earl's benefit.

"You're talking drivel," declared Colin, but his attempt to laugh was unconvincing. "Opal's no murderer."

"She claims you are though," Noreen reminded Colin. "Did you have an affair with Sandra?"

"Who do you think I am? The Barton biscuit factory Lothario?"

"I don't know who you are these days."

"This isn't the time or place to discuss Sandra," said Colin, glancing at Earl.

"I think it's the ideal moment and the ideal place with a policeman here. For all I know, you might have developed a habit of going around threatening to kill people the way you killed Sandra and Derek. Isn't that what you're supposed to have said?"

"I was with you on the night Sandra died."

"How would I know? I'm not the one with insomnia."

The conversation was more interesting than Earl had thought it would be, and he sat back to allow Noreen the freedom to hurl her questions at Colin, but unfortunately she was silenced by Hester's voice from the doorway.

"Dad wasn't with Sandra that night, Mum."

"You see, Noreen, Hester believes me," said Colin, grateful for any support. "She knows that you're talking rubbish."

Noreen was now liberated from English reserve by weeks of anger, but Hester had cringed to hear her parents making a scene in front of an outsider, and she was desperate to stop them. "You only have to talk to Ginevra's cousin Albie, Mum. He'll tell you that Dad wasn't at Sandra's house."

Earl sighed, impatient with the ill-timed interruption by another devoted member of Albie Fulton's fan club. It was unlikely that Colin would reveal any violent tendencies with a policeman in the house, but Earl had hoped to spot signs of repressed rage, and he was annoyed that a kid should intervene just when Noreen's questions might start to anger Colin.

"Well, thank goodness for Ginevra's cousin Albie," said Colin. "But who *is* this Albie, Hester, apart from being somebody's cousin and a heart-warming supporter of mine?"

"He's one of our Constables," replied Earl, "and if the two of you have never met, he won't be the most impressive of alibis."

"Mum, Albie can tell you Dad wasn't with Sandra that evening," Hester insisted. "You've only got to ask Albie, Mum."

"Good news, Colin. Two people in Australia believe you," remarked Noreen. "That only leaves twelve million or so still to be won over."

"Albie doesn't just believe you, Dad; he knows that you didn't take Sandra home from the dance," Hester assured Colin. "It's true, Mum. Ask Albie, and he'll tell you."

Noreen had realized that one day Hester's social world would start to expand, but a police constable seemed an unlikely addition to the kids at Bethanyville School. "How come you know Ginevra's cousin so well?"

"I don't; I've never met Albie," Hester replied. "But he can tell you for a fact that Dad wasn't at Sandra's house. You only have to ask Albie, Mum."

Constable Fulton had plainly bragged to a young cousin about the important rôle he was supposed to be playing in two murder cases, and Earl tried to end Hester's sidetrack in the hope of getting the conversation to head back in the right direction. "Constable Fulton doesn't know many facts at the best of times, and none about Sandra."

"Well, Albie knows Dad wasn't at Sandra's house that night."

Hester was as tiresome as Charmian with her insistence that Albert Fulton could single-handedly solve every crime in Victoria, and to Earl it seemed inevitable that Albie would develop into another overconfident Walt Grissom, regarding adulation as his right. "Constable Fulton isn't part of the team working on the investigation into Sandra's death. The cousin's exaggerated his importance."

"Ginevra didn't tell me," said Hester.

"I hadn't realized it was possible for Ginevra Dean to be silent, but if she has been for once and you've never met this Albie, what are you talking about?" asked Noreen, wishing that the normally reserved Hester had not chosen to make a fool of herself in front of a policeman.

"Albie took Sandra home after the dance, so he knows that Dad wasn't there. Ask Albie," Hester pleaded, anxious to persuade Noreen. "And Sandra couldn't have died around midnight like it said in the paper, because Albie was in the house with her then. She would have been safe."

"You can't possibly know any of that," declared Noreen. "You're not the one wandering around Bethanyville at night, claiming to have insomnia."

"Hester, did somebody tell you they'd seen Constable Fulton with Sandra that evening?" Earl knew he was probably dealing with third-hand or even tenth-hand gossip, but the wildest of rumours had occasionally indicated a pathway worth following, and there was a possibility that Sandra might have been seen on the night she died with a man who resembled Albie Fulton.

Glancing at her father for guidance, Hester dithered, uncertain how much she could say before the strict rules against sneaking were infringed, but Colin guessed the dilemma and hastened to reassure his daughter. "It isn't snitching to tell a policeman something, because he has to find out what you know to do his job."

"Somebody might get into trouble," said Hester, loath to go against schoolyard indoctrination.

As long as that somebody was anyone but himself, Colin had no objection whatsoever to Hester becoming a telltale, and he put more pressure on his daughter to speak out, no matter whose secret she was betraying. "Hester, it's a citizen's duty to give the police all the information you have. In actual fact, it's the law."

Perhaps both duty and law were adamant that she must turn into a sneak, but Hester still felt uneasy, convinced that she would be in the wrong, even though proving Colin's innocence to Noreen might bring about the happy ending promised by so many Hollywood films. After a few seconds, however, family loyalty defeated schoolyard propaganda, and Hester capitulated. "It was Charmian who told me that she'd seen Albie go into Sandra's house after the dance."

"Charmian wouldn't be out and about at that hour," objected Noreen. "She made up one of her usual rigmaroles."

"I don't think she did," said Hester, well aware of Charmian's long history of spying on Albie.

"Was Charmian out with her parents when she thought that she saw Sandra and Constable Fulton together?" asked Earl.

"No. Charmian was by herself." Hester realized that no one believed her, and it was the perfect upshot. Noreen and Colin had been stopped from arguing in front of an outsider, the sole reason for Hester's intervention, and Charmian would never know about the betrayal. It was worth being thought a liar.

Bethanyville dances were sedate occasions ending around eleven o'clock, but Earl agreed with Noreen that a girl Charmian's age was unlikely to be roaming the area alone at such a time of night. There was another possibility, however. "Did Charmian wake up, look out of a window, and see Sandra in the street with a man?"

"Even if she did, Charmian couldn't have seen Sandra's house from here," said Colin. "Hester, how did Charmian know that a man went indoors with Sandra?"

If becoming a police informer meant that Colin and Noreen might somehow be reconciled, acquiring a reputation as a sneak would be a lesser concern, and Hester resigned herself to a future of shame and scorn. "Charmian followed Sandra and Albie there."

"From the dance? You shouldn't believe a word Charmian Teal says," declared Noreen. "They'd never let a girl her age into the dancehall."

"She didn't go to the dance," said Hester, accepting her bleak fate. "Charmian told me she felt much too hot and sticky to sleep, so she —"

"It was cold that night," Colin objected.

"You recall the night in detail?" enquired Earl.

"Not particularly, despite your many questions, but it must have been cold because winter was the only comfortable time inside those hostel Nissen huts, so I'd remember if the temperature had been hot last August."

"Well, that's what Charmian said," Hester maintained, but conscious that a chance sighting of Sandra and Albie might have seemed more dignified to Charmian than admitting to a schoolmate that she had deliberately left the house to continue her routine surveillance of the adored Albie. "She told me that she got out of bed, went to sit on the verandah, saw Albie walk by with Sandra, and followed them."

"Why?" asked Colin.

"She wanted to see where they were going." It sounded a feeble reason, even to Hester, but explaining Charmian's obsession with Albie would be far too difficult. "She didn't have anything else to do, I suppose. So she followed them to Sandra's house."

"Charmian's lying," declared Colin. "Or she was talking about a different night."

"I don't think Charmian would muddle up the night that Sandra died with any other, would she, Dad?"

"Who knows? It's lie after lie with Charmian Teal." Colin said in exasperation. "The girl's one ambition in life is to make as much trouble as she can."

"I'll talk to her," decided Earl, noting Colin's eagerness to discredit the Charmian story. Colin Kemp was worried.

Hester imagined that no adult would be able to understand Charmian's fixation, but Earl had encountered the girl often enough to realize that trailing after Albie, or a man she had mistaken for Albie, was exactly what Charmian would do. Sandra had left the dance early, telling friends that she needed some air, but might in fact have gone for a discreet rendezvous with a married man: the man Charmian saw. A man resembling Albie Fulton, a fair-haired man, tall and broad-shouldered: a man like Colin who, on the night that Sandra had died, was still living on Bethanyville Hostel and still unknown to Charmian.

"She actually saw this man go into the house with Sandra?" asked Colin.

"That's what Charmian told me," replied Hester.

"She was absolutely certain it was on the night Sandra died?"

"Charmian was positive, Dad. So you see, Mum, Albie can tell you Dad wasn't with Sandra that night."

Charmian the fantasist would always be convinced by her own inventions, thought Earl; but there was just a chance that, for once, truth might lurk behind Charmian's tale of seeing a man accompany

Sandra into the Stoddard house, and Colin Kemp was looking decidedly perplexed to learn that a witness could have been present.

****

"Why haven't you arrested that murderer yet? Why is he still free?" Charmian demanded, hurling the front door open before Earl had even climbed the steps onto the Teal verandah. "You've got to throw that killer in prison before he murders me. Why are you leaving us in such danger?"

"There are a few questions —"

"We've answered all your questions," retorted Charmian. "Go and arrest that killer immediately. There's nothing left for you to ask us about."

Charmian was wrong, and Earl walked past her into the house, trusting that he would be able to sift through the kid's usual mix of exaggeration and downright lies to get evidence that might lead to Colin Kemp being charged with the murder of Sandra Stoddard.

"I feel so vulnerable while Colin's still roaming around wherever he pleases," complained Opal, moving away from the window as Earl went into the living-room. "I thought I'd see you take him away, but he's still next door."

"For the moment," said Earl. "I need to talk to Charmian."

"We've already told you everything we know. I'm beginning to suspect you of ulterior motives for visiting me so often." Opal attempted a flirtatious smile, but she was too apprehensive for her customary archness, and abandoned the pretence. "When will you arrest Colin Kemp? I won't feel a bit safe until you do."

"Don't worry, Mum; we'll be OK," declared Charmian. "I'll ask Albie to come here and protect us. He won't let anything bad happen."

"How long have you known Albie Fulton?" asked Earl.

"Ages." Charmian looked defiant, apparently daring someone to contradict her. "Ages and ages."

"You told me to ask Albie about Sandra Stoddard."

"Yes, because he knows more than you ever will. He even knows who killed Sandra," bragged Charmian, proud of having the astuteness to recognize Constable Albert Fulton's innumerable talents. "He'll arrest that murderer and get every word of his confession out of him all over again, while you're still going around asking silly questions."

"How come you're so sure that Constable Fulton's got any information about Sandra?"

"You haven't even bothered to ask Albie." Charmian laughed, scorning the lackadaisical approach to a police investigation. "You'll never detect a thing."

"What should I ask him?" Earl tried to keep annoyance out of his voice, but Charmian's attitude was disconcerting. A kid should be awed by his status, instead of openly mocking him, and Earl was irritated by the girl's air of smug superiority. "What information do you think Constable Fulton has? How come you imagine he's got any at all?"

"You don't even know that he was one of Sandra's friends," scoffed Charmian. "You don't know anything."

"You aren't being very polite, Charmian," said Opal, although her rebuke sounded more like admiration.

"I don't feel very polite." Charmian glared belligerently at Earl, the fool without the good sense to appreciate Albie's worth.

"How do you know that Constable Fulton was a friend of Sandra's?" asked Earl. "Did you ever see them together?"

"Yes, I did," stated Charmian, having the last word on the subject in her opinion.

"When?"

"What does it matter? You should go straight back next door and arrest that murderer, not waste time here."

"Charmian does things at once," explained Opal. "She's very efficient and practical, not a silly dreamer like me. Charmian never wastes time."

"No, I don't, and a policeman shouldn't either."

"Then tell me when you saw Constable Fulton with Sandra," bargained Earl. "It'll speed things up."

"How?" Charmian demanded. "By you stealing Albie's notebook again? I reckon that's the only way you'd manage to speed things up."

"It's the fear," declared Opal. "It's fear of Colin making Charmian so on edge. I know you'll understand, Sergeant. My daughter and I are living in sheer terror. You've got to help us by arresting that awful man before our nerves go completely."

Arresting Colin Kemp was precisely what Earl wished to do, despite Charmian's determination to thwart him, and he made another attempt to drag details out of her. "Are you quite certain it was Constable Albert Fulton you saw with Sandra Stoddard?"

"Do you think I don't know Albie when I see him?" jeered Charmian. "Of course it was Albie."

"How often did you see him with Sandra?"

"Just once, but they were good friends. I could tell."

"How?"

"He went inside Sandra's house with her," replied Charmian, adding pointedly, "Albie wouldn't barge into anyone's home without being invited. Albie's got manners."

"You wouldn't have been able to see him clearly at night," said Earl.

"What makes you think it was night?" retorted Charmian, suspicious of anything Earl said or did.

"Because Sandra would be at work during the daytime," Earl said quickly, hoping to camouflage his blunder. "Anyway, you couldn't make a positive identification at night."

"It was Albie," insisted Charmian. "I heard his voice, and I heard his laugh. He was laughing a lot. Albie told Sandra that she was getting a police escort right up to her front door, in case the Kelly Gang happened to be hiding behind one of the gum trees in the street. They couldn't be, of course, because the whole Gang's been dead for years, but Albie was joking. He's got a terrific sense of humour."

"You're sure it was Constable Fulton's voice?"

"Absolutely sure," snapped Charmian, indignant that anyone should suspect her of confusing Albert Fulton with a lesser being.

"Did you see him go into Sandra's house?"

"How would I know that he'd gone inside, if I hadn't actually seen him go inside?" asked Charmian, pleased to ridicule Earl's question.

"That Stoddard woman! So typical of her disgraceful behaviour," fumed Opal, suddenly and blazingly angry. "It was one man after another with Sandra Stoddard."

The description could also apply to Opal Teal's own life, but Earl was too taken aback by Charmian's latest tale to register the interruption. "You can't see Sandra's house from here," he argued.

"I was in the street." Charmian looked triumphant to have such a good reply, and Earl tried again to get her to admit that she had mistaken Colin for Albie.

"What time was this?"

"Probably around eleven. Bethanyville dances finish then, and Sandra went to the dance on the night she was killed. The newspaper said so. Poor Sandra. It's just not fair she's dead and her murderer's still alive."

"Constable Fulton didn't go to the dance that night. I've seen the names of everybody who was there," said Earl, hoping the fact would persuade Charmian to concede that she was wrong. "It must have been someone else you saw. Another man. Perhaps a man who looks a bit like Constable Fulton."

"Albie might not have been at the dance, but he was with Sandra afterwards," Charmian maintained stubbornly. "I saw them."

"You were out in the street at night? Alone? How come?"

"I went to sit on the verandah because it was much too hot to breathe inside the house," Charmian said smoothly, her excuse readily in place.

"It was a cold night," commented Earl.

"Well, I didn't think so. I'm from England. Australia always seems too hot when you're English."

Charmian felt proud of her answer, unwilling to admit she was an outsider in Albie's world, forced to keep tabs by stealth on his private life, and that Friday evening, she had crept out of the house to continue her surveillance and check whether or not he left the dancehall with a rival devotee. Lingering in shadows cast by the ex-barn now used for Bethanyville festivities, Charmian had swayed to the music to keep warm, watching blurred figures twirl past bright windows, while she imagined herself in a party frock dancing with Albie. Sandra appeared in the light that spilled from the hall's open doorway, a Sandra who looked like the star of a film prepared to play an artistically-lit scene, as she paused to turn and wave goodbye to someone still inside before starting the short journey home that would take her past the railway station to Rosebery Avenue. Then Charmian had heard Albie's voice.

"I heard Albie's voice, and saw him go by with Sandra."

"Did you shout hello to them?" asked Earl.

"No."

"What did you do?"

"I went for a walk," claimed Charmian.

Albie hurried across the road to Sandra, and Charmian had been pleased that he was shunning the dance, perhaps a sign that Albie remained girlfriendless. A woman as old as Sandra, so old that she was a friend of Charmian's Dad, could be of no interest to Albie, but he was a gentleman who escorted lone females to safety, and gallant Albie had plainly taken pity on Sandra's middle-aged solitude.

"It was just as stuffy on the verandah as in my room," said Charmian. "I thought there might be a breeze in the road."

"You were out by yourself at night?" Opal sighed at such folly in an area with a killer on the loose.

"I knew I'd be safe as long as I stayed close to Albie," said Charmian, quick wits neatly supplying a sensible reason for trailing after the couple. "When Albie went into Sandra's house, I came straight back home."

"Charmian, you couldn't have seen Constable Fulton that night," Earl stated. "He never met Sandra. Describe the man you saw."

"Albie's identical twin," said Charmian, offended by Earl's assumption that there might be any circumstance in which she would be unable to recognize her idol. "Albie's identical twin with Albie's identical voice. His name's identical as well, because when he wanted a beer, Sandra told him, 'I reckon you've had enough for tonight, Albie.' But then she said that he could go inside the house for ten minutes and have some tea."

"You heard Sandra call him Albie?" demanded Earl.

"I've just told you that I did."

"What sort of accent did the man speak with?" Earl was desperate for a link, any link, to Colin Kemp, but Charmian failed to perceive the opportunity on offer to her.

"Albie's got an Australian accent, of course. Even you should have noticed that."

"How close were you to this man?"

"A few feet away: five at the most. I stood by the gum tree that's outside Sandra's gate, but they didn't see me." Charmian smirked as she recalled the expertise of her tracking abilities, but then the smile faded. "They went into the house, and that was the last time I saw

Sandra. I bet Albie wishes he'd stayed longer than those ten minutes and protected her from that murderer."

"Did you see anyone else in the street?"

Earl waited for Charmian's reference to Kemp the Killer to jog her memory into realizing the actual identity of the man she must have seen that night, but Charmian replied, "I didn't see anyone except Albie and Sandra. There was nobody else to see then. That murderer wouldn't have the guts to go anywhere near Sandra's house while Albie was inside."

"Utterly typical of the Stoddard woman," muttered Opal. "Any man she could get."

"Charmian, you can't be absolutely certain that you saw Constable Fulton, can you?" pleaded Earl.

Charmian sneered at him, considering victory to be hers, and ordered, "Ask Albie."

"I will. Tell me again everything you saw and heard that night, Charmian, and I'll make some notes. Then you and your Mum can read what I've written and OK it," said Earl, aware that he had to get the story in writing and confirmed before Charmian got a chance to figure out the possible consequences for Albert Fulton of her statement.

****

"I never met Sandra Stoddard." Albie was very definite and very decided, facing Earl without any sign of concern.

"Charmian claims that she saw you go inside the Stoddard house on the night Sandra died," Earl pointed out. "Charmian's positive it was you with Sandra."

"Mistaken identity," Albie maintained. "I went to the beach that night. With mates. The girl's a liar. It must have been Colin Kemp she saw, if she saw anyone."

"Charmian's usually keen to blame him for everything, but she didn't even think of it this time."

"The kid's crazy. That's been obvious right from the start." Albie laughed, recollecting Charmian Teal's partiality for exaggeration and subterfuge, confident that no one would be likely to credit a word she said, and as he opened the door on his way out of Earl's office, Albie turned back to add, "Anyway, Kemp confessed to killing Sandra Stoddard, so what does it matter whether I met the woman or not?"

It mattered because, if Charmian had correctly identified him, Constable Fulton was lying, something that would remain a fact, even in the event of Colin Kemp being hanged for two murders, and Albie should have enough sense to work that out for himself. However, Charmian had a history of deception, and would mulishly insist on her version of anything she had perhaps witnessed until she heard that Allbie denied ever meeting Sandra, at which time Charmian's account might abruptly change. Luckily, dealing with the girl was now Walt Grissom's headache, and Earl gathered his notes together, more than willing to offload them.

"If the kid's a liar, why are you bothering to take any notice of her?" asked Walt, before Earl was halfway through his précis.

"Because there's usually some truth at the back of Charmian's wildest claims," replied Earl. "Besides, we can't ignore any allegation that could implicate a policeman in a crime. It's got to be investigated."

"Unless Fulton's the Chief Commissioner's nephew. Why did the girl go running to you with this nonsense? Has Fulton the Heartthrob told her to go walkabout, and she's eager for revenge?"

"It was Colin Kemp's daughter who first said that Charmian had seen Fulton with Sandra that night."

"Kemp's daughter?" Walt smiled and leant back in his chair, suddenly relaxed. "She's trying to help her Dad. He probably told the kid what to say."

"Perhaps, yet Charmian confirmed the story, and she hates Kemp. Fulton denied ever having met Sandra, but going by what Charmian said, he was drunk so might not have a clear memory of the night." It was an explanation stretching credibility, in Earl's opinion, but Walt nodded.

"That's the excuse I'd use, although outright denial's a good move too. But it sounds like you swallowed the kid's story in one gulp."

"Charmian admitted that she couldn't identify the person she saw taking the Teal car, despite maintaining it was Kemp," Earl pointed out, smarting at Walt's derision. "But this time Charmian's adamant she recognized Fulton. Of course it doesn't mean that he killed Sandra."

"But it wouldn't look too good for him either, even if the girl does decide to change her account." Walt frowned, mentally figuring odds on whose word was likelier to be accepted, a policeman or a kid. There had been many newspaper articles concerning the high number of police bullets that ended up inside civilians, often blameless civilians, and although Constable Fulton had never been involved in any of the more regrettable incidents, all members of Victoria's Police Department were now regarded with suspicion. A possible murderer in their ranks would be considered par for the course, whereas a girl might appear too young for slyness, and public sympathy would be on Charmian's side, especially as the police had failed to arrest whoever killed her father. "I reckon Constable Fulton will have to find himself a good alibi," Walt concluded.

"He said he went to the beach that night with some of his mates."

"Let's hope they're good mates then, ready to swear that Fulton wasn't out of their sight until hours after Sandra's body had been found."

****

"Of course my mates will back me up," insisted Albie, irked by the summons to Walt Grissom's office, and affronted that anything more than his word was required to clear him of all suspicion. "The Teal kid's a known troublemaker. She tells one lie after another, and has been a nuisance right from the start of both investigations. I never met Sandra Stoddard, not once."

"Make sure those mates agree with your story," Walt advised.

"Of course they will," declared Albie.

****

The picture of Charmian Teal in Walt's mind bore a close resemblance to memories of his ex-wife, a woman who became more deviously manipulative each time Walt recalled her. Charmian was evidently getting in some practice that would one day turn her into the sort of bitter harpy who flounced off with another man merely because a husband flirted harmlessly with a pretty girl or two at parties. Charmian Teal was making a determined effort to destroy Constable Fulton's career, and give Victoria's policemen an even worse record as trigger-happy mavericks. Not that Sandra Stoddard had been shot, but journalists would ignore the fact, and again start demanding to know why the Victorian Constabulary found it necessary to shoot more people than all the other Australian State Police Departments put together. Charmian Teal was trouble, and Walt Grissom recognized his duty: discredit every word the kid said.

"We've never met." Opal smiled, apparently assuming that the occasion was a social one as she ushered Walt into her living-room. "I'd love to help you, I really would, but I think I've only spoken to Constable Fulton once, although so many policemen have been here lately that I get a bit muddled. But I'd remember you."

"I'd remember you as well," declared Walt, ready to forgive Charmian anything if she resembled her mother. Opal was less vivacious than Walt's usual taste in women, but she had a face and figure that definitely compensated for any character shortcomings. "Yes, I'd remember you all right."

It was Opal's favourite type of conversation. An admiring man, ready to flatter, eager to please, had transformed a police cross-examination into an opportunity that might solve a few problems for Opal. A detective sergeant was likely to be well-paid, and Opal's mind raced ahead, escaping the limitations of Bethanyville and arriving in expensive Toorak with the more pricey Melbourne shops nearby. Walt Grissom was handsome and plainly attracted to her, a man she could easily persuade to be indulgent, which meant that, married to him, Opal would be able to forget the past with its many disappointments, and also find protection from the danger Colin Kemp posed to a defenceless woman. There was hope again, and Opal saw a glorious new future parade itself before her.

****

"Why is Opal Teal lying about you?" Noreen tried to sound indifferent, but she longed for Colin to admit that he had been a fool. It would alter nothing, but might help Noreen begin to look forwards rather than backwards. "Assuming that the woman actually *is* lying, of course."

"You know me better than that," Colin protested.

"I don't know you at all."

Colin had brought Hester back after a pointless outing to the coast that neither of them had enjoyed. When the first emigration brochures arrived at the London house, the Kemps could have selected a future home from the whole of Australia, an extraordinary country filled with boundless choices and possibilities, yet that freedom to go anywhere had led them to Bethanyville and the end of family life: a life destroyed as completely as by any Fry Day of nuclear annihilation with their world left poisoned by its fallout.

"I think Opal must be mentally ill," decided Colin. "She's delusional; that's the only explanation there is. And the police obviously know it too, because I'd have been arrested by now if they believed her."

"I gather Derek had an affair with Sandra Stoddard." Noreen was sitting on the verandah, wafting flies away with a newspaper, and Hester had gone indoors, but Colin stood at the top of the steps, an awkward visitor who had not been invited to sit down. "Is it true? Did Derek have an affair?"

"There was some factory gossip, but I've no idea." Colin pictured uncomplicatedly happy Sandra, and he was unable to imagine any man not being attracted to her. If Sandra had embarked on a relationship with Derek, he was a man to be envied, and even his untimely death would be less of a tragedy because life could surely never again be as special or as exciting after Sandra.

"Did Opal kill Derek?" asked Noreen. "Is that why the police took the car away?"

"I don't know that either." Colin would once have laughed at the idea of fragile Opal as murderer, dismissing it as Noreen at her most vindictive, but there was no more laughter in him.

"I suppose she could have worked out how to drive a car by watching Derek," Noreen suggested.

"Opal can drive; she's got a licence."

"She told me that she'd never learnt to drive," said Noreen, indignant to recall how she had automatically sympathized with Opal's lament about being reduced to using public transport.

"Did she say it before or after Derek died?"

"After." A couple of days after, which meant a couple of weeks before Colin had moved in with Opal Teal. Revenge was undignified but irresistible, and Noreen felt compelled to pass on a little extra information. "That police detective investigating Sandra's death — I don't know his name, but he's the tall, fair-haired one: a very handsome man. Well, he's been next door with Opal for hours, and the bedroom curtains were closed not long after he arrived. They're still closed. What do you think it means?"

"That the police suspect Opal of murdering Derek, and the handsome detective doesn't want to risk anyone witnessing his brutal interrogation methods. Or Opal's found herself another man, and you're more than happy to tell me the news."

"Quite right," said Noreen.

****

Earl had unlocked his car for the journey home at the end of a long day that was about to turn into night, when he saw Walt drive across the parking area behind the police station. Leaving his car door open in the hope of cooling its interior temperature, Earl called, "Charmian Teal? What do you reckon?"

"*Charmian* Teal?" Walt got out of his car, and looked at Earl in blank surprise before recollecting who answered to the name. "Oh, her. Opal told the kid to go to school after I arrived. A waste of time bothering with the girl. Opal said her daughter's a compulsive liar, always has been, always will be. Anyway, Colin Kemp confessed to murdering both Sandra and Derek."

"Only according to Opal," Earl pointed out.

"Her word's OK by me."

"Good news for Constable Fulton," Earl commented. "Are you going to arrest Kemp?"

"Too right, and it's what should have been done as soon as Opal told you about his threats."

"Kemp denies being that stupid."

"He's not going to admit confessing to murder," scoffed Walt. "And Kemp's not going to admit that he terrorized Opal either."

"And then he went out to toil among Barton's Biscuits, leaving Opal free to tell us what she claims he said?" Earl knew that Walt was susceptible to the lure of an attractive woman, but Opal Teal seemed to have had a mesmerizing effect, which made him as much of a fool as a confessing Colin was supposed to be. "Opal's account doesn't add up."

"That's what Kemp relied on: nobody believing her. The crazier the story, the more it'll be doubted." Walt pitied Earl for having so little insight into the criminal mind, a Grissom area of expertise, and he added authoritatively, "Kemp will have killed in England before he even thought of emigrating to Australia, and now he's overconfident."

To Earl, it appeared more likely that Opal had lied before and got away with her deception, perhaps by using the same seductive strategy that had recruited Walt Grissom as an enthusiastic supporter. "You know Opal could have killed her husband," warned Earl.

"Then he probably deserved it," laughed Walt. "Opal's as straightforward as they come: no pretence about her at all. She follows her feelings, and that's very unlike the usual run of women, holding out until they've trapped a man."

"Opal lied to me."

"You misheard. Her accent's still very English." Walt would only believe what he wanted to believe because otherwise he had put his career at risk, and Walt was an ambitious man in spite of a carelessness that came from overoptimistic faith in his value to Victoria's police as well as to womankind. "Colin Kemp murdered both Sandra Stoddard and Derek Teal."

"Apart from the famed spider assignation, nothing connects Kemp to Sandra outside work, and no proof that he ever visited her house."

"I know Kemp was involved with Sandra; I just know it." Walt's certainty came from the fact that he would have made a determined effort to seduce Sandra, if fate had engineered a meeting between them, and it was obvious to Walt that Colin would be equally unable to resist pursuing such a spectacular woman. "Every instinct I've got tells me Kemp was involved with Sandra, and you said from the start that a couple of killers busily operating in Rosebery Avenue at the same time was unlikely, and you were right."

"I still reckon there's only one Rosebery Avenue killer," said Earl.

"And you suspect Opal." Walt laughed again, ready to share his good humour with the world. "Or is Constable Fulton now the homicidal maniac? Don't forget that Colin Kemp's the one with motive, means, and opportunity to kill both Sandra and Derek."

"He was at work when Derek got killed."

Walt flapped a hand to dismiss irrelevant details. In his mind, Colin Kemp had been tried, convicted and hanged, while Walt enjoyed a dalliance with Opal, the victim who had escaped Colin's evil machinations. "If Charmian did spot Sandra with a fair-haired man, the kid would have been half-asleep at that time of night, and she assumed the man was Fulton because she hadn't met Kemp then."

"He isn't the only other fair-haired man in Victoria. Anyway, Charmian says she heard Fulton's voice." Earl knew that Walt would refuse to doubt himself, no matter how unlikely his inspiration was to stand up in a courtroom and take a bow. Guesses could be signposts to proof, but allowing them to pass as evidence offended Earl's thoroughness. "Charmian could have seen you with Sandra. You don't look like Fulton, any more than Kemp does, but the same general description would cover all three of you."

"You mean, I was having an affair with Sandra, got rid of her when I saw Opal, removed Derek from the scene, but then was thwarted by Colin Kemp, so now I'm framing him for the two murders." Walt looked impressed by the Machiavellian deftness hypothetically his, and then said regretfully, "No, it doesn't explain why Kemp confessed to the killings. I couldn't get him to do that."

"There's only Opal's word that he did confess."

"I know what happened," Walt declared merrily. "Opal had seen me from afar in Rosebery Avenue, realized there could be no other man for her, and decided that the quickest way to meet me was to provide testimony in the Stoddard case. Claiming that Kemp confessed had the advantage of getting him out of Opal's life, and she couldn't have timed things better because I was already in the process of framing him for Sandra's death. Is that elaborate enough for you? It's no more fanciful than your theory about Albie Fulton."

"I've been checking, and a couple of Constable Fulton's fingerprints are among those taken from Sandra's place, but they shouldn't be there. According to the record, he hasn't been inside her house during the investigation, and he maintains that he never knew Sandra."

Walt tapped on the car bonnet, impatient with Earl's refusal to share his merriment. The Grissom sense of humour had no equal, and Earl should at least make an effort to smile when Walt was in jovial mood. "Fulton's a young idiot who must have blundered into Sandra's house when the team was there dusting for prints. He isn't the first Constable to make a fool of himself that way, and he won't be the last."

"But Charmian Teal's certain he was with Sandra —"

"Charmian Teal! In the unlikely event that she's right, and telling the truth for once, Kemp also spotted Fulton with Sandra that night, got jealous, and killed her after Fulton went home."

Charmian's account had Sandra anticipating Albie's departure within ten minutes, which meant Sandra might have expected the arrival of a second guest that night, and Earl wondered ruefully if the celebrated Grissom instinct had just racked up yet another success.

12

The sensational tale of Colin Kemp's arrest was spreading around Bethanyville within minutes of the event supposedly happening, but Brenda Dean dismissed all rumours as empty gossip until the story's origin was revealed by a gleeful nephew, when Albie dropped in for one of those regular visits that chanced to coincide with a mealtime.

"Walt Grissom's hauled him in for questioning. Kemp confessed to both murders, although he's denying it now, but Colin Kemp's guilty all right, no doubt about it," reported Albie. "Two cases will be closed by tomorrow."

"I can't believe Colin Kemp would murder Sandra. I'll never believe that, even if he's convicted," declared Brenda. "And Derek Teal's death was probably a hit and run."

"Sandra's wasn't," Lenny commented.

"She was certain to come to a bad end sooner or later, the way she lived," said Albie.

"I don't see why," claimed Ginevra, but she would have argued the opposite, had Albie defended Sandra. His arrogance always annoyed Ginevra, and she was unable to resist contradicting him, despite her eagerness to glean details concerning the capture and downfall of Hester Kemp's infamous father. "There's no law against being as popular as Sandra was and having lots of boyfriends."

"There's no law against stupidity either," Albie pointed out. "And Sandra Stoddard was stupid: deliberately parading herself around Bethanyville to lead men on. One of those men was bound to kill the woman before long. Some things are inevitable."

"If you thought so little of Sandra, why did you pretend to be friends with her?" demanded Ginevra.

"I never met the woman," Albie retorted.

"You were with Sandra on the night she was killed. You walked her home from the dance. Charmian told me."

"I never go to those boring dances now. The Teal kid saw Colin Kemp." Albie sighed, irritated by Ginevra's antagonism. "It was Kemp with Sandra Stoddard that night. Grissom arrested him because of the kid's statement."

"You don't look much like Hester's Dad to me," declared Ginevra. "And Charmian wouldn't make a mistake like that. She saw *you* with Sandra."

"If Albie never met Sandra, Charmian must have been mistaken," said Brenda, as part of a long-running yet doomed diplomatic effort to avert warfare between her daughter and nephew.

"Charmian saw Albie," insisted Ginevra. "He's just scared it'll hurt his precious career if he admits to being out with Sandra that night."

"As I can't have gone out with a woman I never met, I'm not scared of a thing." Albie smiled derisively at Ginevra, the brat who refused to see him as he expected to be seen, as Albert Fulton deserved to be seen, and he turned to his aunt for support. "The Teal kid saw a man fitting Colin Kemp's description go into Sandra Stoddard's house with her on the night she died. It's part of the evidence against Kemp."

"Charmian saw *you*," Ginevra maintained obstinately. "She wouldn't even be fooled by your identical twin, if you had one."

"Albie will know more about the investigation than you do," said Brenda, hoping to close the subject yet unable to stop herself from adding, "But I still don't think Colin Kemp had anything to do with Sandra's death, whoever Charmian saw."

"What do you mean, *whoever* Charmian saw? The kid saw Colin Kemp. It's the reason, one of the many reasons, that Walt Grissom dragged Kemp in for questioning. Earl Lanyon should have made an arrest the moment he heard about the confession, but Lanyon's useless. While he was dithering around, Kemp could easily have killed again."

"But he didn't," remarked Lenny. "Not that I reckon Colin Kemp murdered Sandra or anyone else. He doesn't seem the violent type."

"That's how he blagged his way into Sandra Stoddard's house," declared Albie, frowning at the devious guile masked by Colin's apparent ordinariness. "Kemp did exactly the same thing when he conned Opal Teal."

"No, not exactly the same," objected Lenny. "Opal's still alive."

"Yes, but we know that Kemp planned to kill her. We got there before he had a chance to do anything." Albie spoke with the assurance of an insider with access to privileged information, his tone implying that Albert Fulton knew far more than he was ready to share. "Opal Teal had a lucky escape."

"No, she didn't," Ginevra stated. "Hester's Dad might be a bank robber, but he'd never harm a woman or a child."

"A bank robber!" Brenda smiled at the notion of a desperado who laboured through factory shift after factory shift to keep Australia supplied with Barton's Biscuits, and then she laughed aloud, recalling a similar wild tale from her own childhood. "When I was a kid back home, we had a new teacher at school, and within minutes of her arrival, a story flew all over the playground that she was a spy who'd send messages to Berlin about everything we did. God knows what we thought the Germans would learn by spying on our school, but we were convinced that she left coded reports in a tin canister at the side of the Odeon cinema for another spy to pick up."

"OK, perhaps the story of Hester's Dad being a bank robber was too good to be true," Ginevra conceded, the reality of home life behind a shop with down-to-earth parents banishing fantasies that were so persuasive in school.

Lenny and Brenda laughed with Ginevra, but Albie continued to frown. "For all we know, Colin Kemp might have a criminal background that includes bank robbery. It wouldn't surprise me in the least."

"It'd astound me," declared Lenny. "You don't know the man, Albie. He's a good bloke."

"Too right he's good: good at fooling people the way he's fooled you." Albie had a sudden suspicion that Lenny and Brenda were amused by his assertions about Colin, and Albie hated not being taken seriously. "Kemp threatened to kill Opal just like he murdered Sandra Stoddard. That's what Kemp said. He murdered her. And Derek Teal. It's fact, proven fact."

"I reckon Charmian invented those threats." For the satisfaction of thwarting Albie, Ginevra was willing to abandon more of Colin Kemp's scandalous activities, even though a backtrack made life less exciting, but combat always entailed sacrifice. "Charmian's cooked up all sorts of lies about Hester's Dad."

"And the kid lied about seeing me with Sandra Stoddard," Albie retorted. "Charmian Teal's a con artist determined to get everyone's attention."

"Her father died," said Lenny, his normally relaxed voice taking on a colder tone. "The girl needs to find out exactly what happened to Derek."

"She'd have found out a lot quicker if we hadn't been hampered by her lies." Albie snorted in contempt at Charmian's unwarranted meddling, and he added, "The kid's nothing more than a self-serving liar."

Lenny tolerated Albie for Brenda's sake, but there were times when that tolerance could wear thin. "You'll never make much of a career in the police if you don't try to understand people."

"What's there to understand in the Teal kid?" jeered Albie, disdaining so absurd an idea. "She's a liar; there's nothing else to be said about her."

Lenny had been an only son, sandwiched between four sisters, and he freely admitted to having profited from his mother's favouritism throughout childhood, but Albie was rapidly becoming a spoilt nephew too far, and Brenda hastened to intervene.

"You'll have to be patient and listen to all sorts of people if you stay in the police, Albie, and children are as important as any adult when they're witnesses."

"Yes, and Charmian knows who she spotted with Sandra," added Ginevra.

"She didn't see me," maintained Albie. "She saw Kemp."

"What a pity Charmian doesn't appear to know that," remarked Ginevra.

****

Derek's death would at last be avenged, and Charmian gleefully anticipated Colin Kemp's appointment with the hangman. She felt powerful, once more in control of her life, and ready to tackle a future that must eventually bring independence. Opal was playing the devoted mother with cloying sugariness, but Charmian had seen the performance many times before in days when Opal tried to get an ally against Derek, and the act was as unconvincing as ever. Charmian knew she had never been the daughter her mother wanted, but Opal would soon be left behind with the past.

Talk of Australia abolishing the death penalty was worrying, but it sounded as though any change in the law might be whole years away, and Charmian hoped that such an unenlightened measure would not stop Colin Kemp paying in full for his crimes. However, events finally seemed prepared to go her way, and Charmian dared to dream again.

In a matter of weeks she would be thirteen, on the verge of branching out into the world, getting a job and having her own money. She would be practically an adult, free to move to Melbourne, which was Albie's intended destination after his promotion, according to

Ginevra, and in the city a grown-up Charmian Teal and the grateful Albert Fulton would be friends, close friends, and go out on dates together. It was the only happy ending that Charmian could imagine, and of course there had to be a happy ending or she would never escape from the emptiness of sorrow. Albie was her only possible future.

****

Albie had gone, and the Dean household could settle down to an evening of peace without the bickering that inevitably occurred each time Ginevra encountered her cousin.   "You should be nicer to him," Brenda instructed Ginevra, despite the words having been said on many previous occasions with little effect. "You know that Albie hasn't got any family now except us."

"It's not a reason to like him when I don't," Ginevra pointed out. "I can't like him. Albie's horrible, and I'll never change my mind about that."

"You could try feeling sorry for him, Gin," suggested Lenny, but his own lack of sympathy for Brenda's conceited nephew had long been known to Ginevra.

"Only last week in Assembly, Mrs Hexham told us that we should have nothing to do with liars, and Albie lied about not walking Sandra home from the dance on the night she was killed. Charmian would never mix him up with someone else, never, so I reckon Albie murdered Sandra."

The stubborn hatred behind Ginevra's claim made Brenda smile as she asked, "Why would Albie want to kill Sandra?"

"Because he was drunk," snarled Ginevra. "Charmian told me at school the very next day about seeing them together, and she felt sorry for Albie, thinking he'd be upset when he heard Sandra was dead. Charmian won't believe a word against him, but I know what Albie's really like."

212

"Stamping on a doll isn't the same thing as murdering a woman," said Brenda.

"Might be to a kid," commented Lenny.

"A doll or a woman, it wouldn't make the slightest difference to Albie." Ginevra had no real belief in her accusation, but the words brought great satisfaction with them. "He'd kill anyone who got in his way or wouldn't do what he wanted. And he's nasty about Sandra, yet she was lovely. Sandra even said I looked pretty in my green dress."

"You do look pretty in it," said Lenny.

"No, I don't. That dress turns me into a lettuce leaf, but Sandra always said I looked nice and she didn't have to. I'll never forgive Albie for murdering her, never ever. And I reckon he killed Charmian's Dad as well."

"Albert Fulton: our very own Frederick Deeming," remarked Lenny.

13

According to Constable Albert Fulton, he had never met Sandra Stoddard. According to the records, Constable Albert Fulton had not been inside Sandra Stoddard's house at any time during the police investigation into her death. So how come Constable Albert Fulton's fingerprints had been found on a wall by the internal door between Sandra's kitchen and hallway, as well as on her backyard fence?

"There's been a mistake," Walt was still insisting. "Or else Fulton doesn't want to admit that he sneaked into the house when the team was there."

"But the newest and most dim-witted of young Constables would know that he ought to wear gloves, and even then not touch anything, if he has to go inside a house while it's being dusted for prints," Earl pointed out.

"Then Fulton's far more incompetent than average," decided Walt, resigned to the traditional stupidity of novices. "How come you're bothering about Sandra's death anyway? It's my investigation, not yours."

"You don't have anything solid against Colin Kemp," said Earl, avoiding Walt's question, "but there's a witness who spotted Fulton in Rosebery Avenue with Sandra on the night she died, and then saw him go into her house."

"A witness!" scoffed Walt. "Charmian Teal!"

"Fulton's prints were found inside the Stoddard house, but Kemp's weren't. How do you explain that?"

"Kemp's clever. He wiped the place clean after he killed Sandra," declared Walt, stubbornly loyal to his instinct. "And even Fulton would have enough commonsense to do that."

"Going by what Charmian said —"

"Huh!" Walt commented.

"Going by what Charmian said, Fulton was drunk that night, possibly too drunk to do a thorough cleanup job. He might have put a hand against the wall for a moment to steady himself, and was too befuddled to remember. He could have left by the backyard, got over the fence, and then walked alongside the railway line to his flat." The scenario made sense to Earl, but Walt never changed course easily.

"It's speculation," he protested.

"So are your suspicions of Colin Kemp. You should ask Fulton to explain how his prints came to be inside Sandra's house."

"The Chief Commissioner would go crazy if he heard that I was interviewing a police officer about a murder," grumbled Walt. "We get a bad enough press as it is."

"It'd be a good press for once. The editors will write sanctimonious claptrap about no one being above the law," Earl predicted. "You'll be their hero."

Walt laughed at the idea, but the thought of journalistic approval was alluring and his stance weakened. "I'll ask Fulton about the prints, but I'm not letting Kemp go. He's the only one who benefited from both deaths. Fulton would have no reason to kill Derek Teal, and you've maintained from the start that there's only one murderer in Rosebery Avenue."

"I've changed my mind," said Earl.

"So now you think that Fulton killed Sandra and Kemp killed Derek," Walt concluded. "They're very enterprising, these Rosebery Avenue residents."

****

Fingerprints might be Albie Fulton's downfall, and perhaps also Opal Teal's. The lies about her ability to drive only made sense if she had been the driver who killed Derek, and the story of Colin's confession and threats had followed his discovery of Opal's driving licence. There was no evidence that Colin had ever gone inside

Sandra's house, and his fingerprints were not on the photographs that Charmian had sent to the police station, but Derek's were, and a second match appeared when Earl checked the other fingerprints against the ones he had persuaded Opal to provide, supposedly for elimination purposes during the examination of Derek Teal's car. At some time, Opal had held the disfigured pictures of Sandra, those souvenirs of hatred.

****

"Surely I've answered every question there is in the world," complained Opal, but she was smiling, untroubled by Earl's arrival at her home, certain that she was in control. "There can't be a thing left for you to ask me unless you want to know my hopes, my dreams and my telephone number."

"Have you seen this picture before?" Earl put one of Sandra's photographs onto the glass-topped coffee table that stood between his chair and Opal's, but she leaned back without any trace of consternation.

"There's nothing to see," replied Opal, dismissing the picture with barely a glance. "It's just scribble."

Earl spread the rest of the photographs across the table, and asked, "You're certain that you don't recognize these pictures?"

"How could I? There's nothing to recognize. Has Colin been charged with Derek's murder yet? That's what you should be doing, not wasting time with scribble." Opal had gained self-assurance, convinced that she was now shielded by Walt, and could afford to add a touch of arrogance to her voice. "You ought to have charged Colin Kemp ages ago with threatening me, as well as with murdering poor Derek."

"You've never seen these photos before?"

"Why are you bothering about scribble when I'm in danger?" Opal demanded, piqued to encounter a man not prepared to do her bidding. "I refuse to speak to you any more. I'm only talking to Walt Grissom from now on."

"He isn't investigating your husband's death."

"Then you're the one who ought to have arrested Colin Kemp. He killed Derek. Colin told me that he'd killed Derek as well as that Stoddard woman. Why are you playing around with old photos of her, after my life's been threatened?"

"How come you know that these are photographs of Sandra Stoddard?" asked Earl.

"Of course it's her," snapped Opal. "Anyone could see that a mile off."

"Not when the face is covered with biro ink."

"You can still tell it's that Stoddard woman by the way she exhibited herself for the photographer, exactly the way she acted in front of every man." However, Opal knew that she had made a mistake, but the persistence of a spoilt child lingered inside her: a child who had once whinged and whined until she got what she wanted. Opal expected every word she said to be accepted immediately, and Earl was the person at fault for not acknowledging this. "If you won't protect me from a killer, then you can leave my house. And take your silly photos with you."

"You've never seen these pictures before?"

"Of course not. How many times do I have to tell you?"

"Then how come your fingerprints were found on them?"

"Because you're the sort of policeman who tries to frame innocent people like me. Did Colin Kemp bribe you? I suppose you hope that he'll soon be wandering around, a free man again, ready to murder me." Opal stood up to indicate that the interview was now at an end, and Earl gathered the photographs together.

"You can make a formal statement at the police station."

"I'm not going anywhere with you," declared Opal. "I'm staying right here and phoning Walt Grissom. He'll soon get rid of you."

****

The door to Earl's office crashed against the wall as Walt made a furious entrance. "You've no cause to arrest Opal, none at all. Are you insane?"

"She refused to talk to me, so I brought her in for questioning." Earl had anticipated a visit from Walt, and was quite prepared to tackle the susceptible Detective Sergeant. "She wants a lawyer, so I'm waiting for it to be arranged."

"Opal's gone through enough without being persecuted by you as well. Send her home at once." Walt was angry beyond anything that would be reasonable, and Earl's suspicions of a liaison between Opal and Walt were confirmed.

"She wouldn't answer my questions. Do you reckon I should treat her differently from any other suspect?" asked Earl.

"Suspect!" roared Walt.

"Yes, suspect. You said something about Colin Kemp having motive, means and opportunity to kill Derek Teal. Opal had all three as well."

"This is madness," protested Walt. "Opal's the gentlest woman in the world. She'd be incapable of killing anyone, even in self-defence, and she's been living in terror since Kemp made his threats."

"Assuming he made them."

"Are you calling Opal a liar?" Walt demanded.

"She lied about being able to drive," Earl pointed out. "And she claims never to have seen those photos of Sandra, yet Opal's fingerprints are all over them."

"Those pictures are part of my investigation. They're nothing to do with you, and I want them back now."

"Walt, think about it. I reckon Opal killed her husband, possibly because she found those photos of Sandra among his things. Derek's prints are on them too, remember."

Earl had thought that there would be no use telling Walt not to make a fool of himself and risk his career over a woman who probably imagined that an affair with a detective sergeant was going to protect her, but Walt's fury had already started to subside as he calculated the odds of his name being dragged into Earl Lanyon's investigation. It would only be Opal's word against his that anything had happened between them, and the word of a woman suspected of killing her husband, a woman who was not even Australian, seemed unlikely to harm the Grissom professional prospects as long as he distanced himself from Opal without delay. Walt believed that he was an ardent lover, a man of passion, but no woman could inspire the passion he felt for Walter Grissom and his chances of further promotion.

"Do what you want, if you won't listen to reason," Walt blustered, to disguise his rapid change of mind. "Opal's lawyer will make you see sense."

"Did Constable Fulton explain his fingerprints being found in Sandra's house?"

"Not very convincingly," snapped Walt, annoyed that Earl Lanyon appeared to have made a habit of being right.

"What's Fulton saying?"

"That jealous colleagues are determined to wreck his career by planting evidence against him. But I haven't got time to waste discussing Fulton with you. I'm in the middle of questioning Colin Kemp."

Walt left as abruptly as he had arrived, and with another slam of the door.

Opal was on her own.

14

Pelham Venn, ponderously middle-aged and sweltering in a business suit, had been told a multitude of unlikely tales over the years by his clients in police interview rooms, and Opal Teal's story was no exception, but her attractive appearance would be a definite asset in front of a jury because people expected killers to look as ugly as their crimes. Should Opal end up in court, she would seem vulnerable, a victim rather than the accused, particularly if as many men as possible could be crammed onto the jury.

"Did you have a happy marriage?" asked Pelham.

"Blissfully happy. Derek was a wonderful husband, so gentle and kind-hearted," replied Opal, sensing what the lawyer wanted her to say. "When Colin Kemp took over my life, I was too shattered with grief to resist his domineering character, even though it soon became apparent how cruel he is, but I was too frightened and too alone to escape from him. However, after he confessed to killing Derek and then threatened me and my child, I had to act and somehow found the strength to summon help. How was I to know that a policeman would turn against me, and believe every word the killer said? You've got to get me out of here. A murderer will be roaming free, if that dreadful Lanyon gets his way, and I'm terrified Colin Kemp's going to attack my daughter: kill my darling little Charmian."

Opal's performance was so good, it deserved a round of applause, but Pelham was a cautious man who never congratulated himself on success before it happened. "How do you explain your fingerprints being on those photos of Sandra Stoddard?"

Opal face crumpled like a child about to cry, and she sighed tremulously. "I found the pictures."

"Where?"

"Behind a cushion on the sofa. They must have fallen out of Colin Kemp's pocket. I took one look, then immediately threw the photos into my garbage bin, and tried to forget the whole thing." Opal shuddered, her sensibility affronted by so disturbing a memory.

"Was the key to Sandra Stoddard's house with the pictures?" asked Pelham.

"There was a key, and I threw that out as well. I wanted nothing to do with any of it."

"The key could have been a factory one connected to Kemp's job, or perhaps belonged to the house next door," said Pelham, admiring Opal's creativeness. "How come you got rid of it without first checking with him?"

"I didn't want Colin to know that I'd found the pictures. They sickened me."

Opal's replies were smoothly delivered, but Pelham's commonsense was adamant that no woman would have allowed Colin Kemp back into her house, or into her life, no matter how lonely she might be feeling, if the sight of Sandra's obliterated face had really been such an appalling shock. Opal Teal was lying again. "When did you find the pictures?"

"I can't remember," Opal claimed. "I was determined to put everything out of my mind, and that's precisely what I did."

"Why didn't you jettison Kemp after you saw the photos?" asked Pelham, to challenge Opal's resourcefulness, and she was instantly overcome by an excess of vulnerability which would be an effective strategy in front of a jury.

"I was so defenceless, so alone, so desperate for help to get me through the most awful time of my life. Colin Kemp targeted me, deliberately targeted me, and I was far too confused by all that had happened to heed the warning signs. My darling little Charmian told me enough times, and she's so astute, so intelligent, that I'll never forgive myself for not listening to her, never. I should have realized that Colin Kemp was a violent man when I saw the way he'd destroyed the poor woman's face in those horrible photographs." Opal pressed hand to forehead, aghast at her folly, and lamented, "I'm so naïve, but I suppose it's the inevitable result of a sheltered upbringing. Mr Venn, you're my one hope of surviving this nightmare. That dreadful Lanyon is framing me to cover his mistake in not arresting a murderer."

Saddened by the thought of police duplicity protecting a killer, Opal's head drooped over her arms, and she leaned helplessly against the table as though lacking strength to sit upright.

"Very good," remarked Pelham, admiring Opal's acting as well as her imaginative explanation of the inconvenient fingerprints. "Yes, I can expand something along those lines."

"You shouldn't have to work on my behalf at all. Why is life treating me so heartlessly?" wailed Opal, overwhelmed by her tribulations. "Why am I being made to suffer like this? What have I done to deserve it?"

Pelham reckoned that he could make a fairly accurate guess, but smiled reassuringly instead. "The only real evidence they've got against you are those fingerprints."

"Which I can explain," Opal pointed out.

"Indeed you can. Of course there's also Earl Lanyon's assertion that you lied to him about being able to drive, but —"

"If the man wasn't so intent on persecuting me, I'd be charitable and say that he misheard, but that crafty Lanyon is deliberately using the fact that I'm a timid soul who's never been able to drive a car since the awful day I was involved in a terrifying accident back home."

"Do the English police have a record of it?"

"No," admitted Opal, yet another explanation at the ready. "Please don't be cross with me, but I didn't report it. The driver sped off, leaving me so shaken and upset that I wasn't capable of doing anything. My whole life had just flashed before my eyes, and I was far too traumatized by the idea of my darling little baby almost having lost her mother even to think of looking at a number plate, never mind remembering it. There was nothing I could tell the police."

Opal added a touching shudder to her account, and Pelham thought again how effective she would be in a courtroom. "Did you get your car repaired in a garage?"

"It was a near miss, not an actual collision, but quite enough to put someone as nervous as me right off driving for good." Opal declared, fluently and swiftly. "I don't know why Detective Sergeant Lanyon told those awful lies about me, but perhaps he's jealous because Walt Grissom and I are such close friends. When can I talk to Walt?"

"Shall we get all the details sorted out first?" suggested Pelham, knowing that Walter Grissom's loyalty was solely to Walter Grissom, no matter how accommodating a friend Opal might have been. "Lanyon reckons you'll be intimidated by a police station, but stick to your story like glue and let me do most of the talking."

"Of course," said Opal, happy to agree to a plan that had been hers from the very moment she demanded a lawyer.

****

"A killer goes home," commented Earl as Pelham walked out of the interview room, plainly congratulating himself on a task successfully completed. "Doesn't the responsibility of getting her freed worry you?"

"Opal's no danger to anybody," replied Pelham. "I'm just doing my job, and doing it well. You jumped the gun. Blame yourself."

"She killed her husband," said Earl.

"Allegedly."

"You know that Opal's guilty."

"But you'll never prove it." Pelham smiled complacently, his victory not in freeing an innocent woman from custody, but in outsmarting an adversary.

"The fingerprints on those photographs of Sandra will be Opal's downfall," Earl predicted. Someone had once said that lost causes were the only causes worth fighting to the end, which sounded like a waste of energy to Earl, but Pelham's smugness was too irksome to be allowed to go unchallenged. "Derek had an affair, and Opal killed him because of it."

"Victoria's Police Department has got such a low reputation that any jury will regard Detective Sergeant Lanyon planting a spot of evidence as a credible defence, even if Opal didn't have a convincing explanation of everything you allege."

"You know that she's guilty," said Earl, exasperated by Pelham's slick hypocrisy. "You're practically her accomplice."

"And you're definitely a bad loser." Pelham laughed in triumph, but was unable to resist the temptation to show that he still had ammunition in reserve. "What's the story about Opal and Walt Grissom?"

"Ask Walt."

"Did he promise Opal that he'd disappear the phoney fingerprint evidence if she went to bed with him?"

"Walt isn't investigating Derek Teal's death."

"Are you persecuting Opal because she refused to sleep with you?"

Earl stamped down the corridor and into his office, pointedly closing the door. Pelham laughed again,

****

"They messed up evidence from the Stoddard woman's house, and now they're trying to cover themselves by implicating me," Albie complained.

Opal knew exactly how to portray herself as a helpless victim, but Constable Albert Fulton was angry and arrogant. If he went into a courtroom with that attitude, he would alienate both judge and jury when the best tactic was to make them believe that such a nice person would be incapable of any crime, no matter how damning the evidence, and Pelham realized that he might have a difficult job ahead of him, a task worthy of his ingenuity.

"What about the witness who claims to have seen you going into Sandra Stoddard's house with her on the night she was killed?" queried Pelham.

"Witness!" scoffed Albie. "A kid who does nothing but tell one lie after another. She didn't see me because I never met that Stoddard woman."

"Then how come Charmian Teal lied about seeing you?"

"How should I know? The kid saw Colin Kemp, if she saw anyone at all. Nobody's going to believe her."

With Charmian's track record, Albie was likely to be right, but Pelham never underestimated a witness, despite knowing that a child could easily be confused by a few complicated questions while giving testimony, even without the need for any bullying that might make a jury think the defence team was desperate. However, Albie's fingerprints placed him firmly inside Sandra's house at one time or another, and things would be much simpler if Albie acknowledged the danger he was in.

"There's a way out," said Pelham.

"Out of what?" Albie demanded, furious that a lawyer, who presumably expected to be paid by him, should doubt his story.

"All you have to say is that you went inside the Stoddard house sometime during the investigation."

"I wouldn't do anything as thick-headed as wander around the house leaving fingerprints all over the place," retorted Albie, his professional pride affronted. "On my first day with the police, I knew better than that. If I said I'd contaminated a crime scene, I'd never get promoted. It'd be the end of my career."

Pelham would prefer to be ousted from any job whatsoever than risk being hanged, but it was Albie's choice, and if he wanted to chance his life rather than invent a plausible excuse, he was quite free to do so. "The chain of evidence doesn't suggest a cover-up."

"No, of course not. That's why it's called a cover-up," said Albie, incensed by the stupidity of the man who was meant to be his advocate. "There are always mistakes when Grissom's involved. He relies on guesses, so his team's a careless one. You ask around."

"Have you heard any rumours about a relationship between Walt Grissom and Opal Teal?"

"Yes," decided Albie, pouncing without a second's delay on such unexpectedly useful information. "And that so-called witness is the woman's daughter. Grissom's bribed her in order to frame me and hide his own incompetence."

Pelham had occasionally succeeded with more unlikely defences, and juries were usually reluctant to send anyone to the hangman, so Detective Sergeant Grissom's frailty might turn out to be Constable Albert Fulton's salvation. "Earl Lanyon wouldn't talk to me when I asked him about Walt Grissom and Opal Teal," said Pelham. "Lanyon knows what's going on."

"We all do," declared Albie. "Grissom's as corrupt as they come. He'd do anything to give himself a better clear-up record, even framing innocent people like me, and Colin Kemp's going to get away with murder because of Grissom."

"What makes you so convinced that Kemp's guilty?" asked Pelham. "There doesn't seem to be much evidence against him."

"Only because it's easier for Grissom to frame me than do some real police work. He's probably bored with Opal Teal now, and so she's been framed as well." It was a wild leap of deduction, akin to the Walt Grissom method, but Albie felt inspired. "Colin Kemp murdered both Sandra Stoddard and Derek Teal, but Grissom's not clever enough to prove it, so he's resorted to his old trick of manufacturing evidence."

Albie had produced a triumph of imagination, and if Opal could be persuaded to talk freely, Pelham realized that pressure might be put on Walter Grissom to force him to drop the case against Albie. Earl Lanyon was likely to close ranks to protect a colleague at the threat of a Walt-Opal liaison reaching the newspapers, and the two Detectives might then concentrate their efforts on the unfortunate Colin Kemp who should have had the sense to recruit Pelham Vann as his defender. Kemp could be ill-wished with a clear conscience because Pelham's duty was to clients only, and he would enjoy giving off-the-record interviews about police corruption and ineptitude to all the journalists he could muster. Pelham might not have much luck refuting the evidence against Albie, but the reputation of the policeman investigating Sandra Stoddard's death could easily be tarnished, and Walt Grissom's poor judgment was going to be very useful in the cases of both Opal and Albie.

*****

"Have you seen this?" fumed Walt, brandishing a newspaper as he hurled himself into Earl's office. "There's no enquiry into my conduct. There's never been an enquiry into my conduct. And what's wrong with my conduct anyway?"

"You're not mentioned by name," said Earl.

"I don't need to be. It's obvious who they mean."

"They don't specify the case."

"How many murders are being investigated in Bethanyville?" Walt demanded.

Derek Teal might well have been murdered, but even a journalist would fail to imagine dour Earl Lanyon as the Don Juan of the Detective Branch, seducing vulnerable female witnesses. Not that Opal was a witness in the Stoddard case, and unless Charmian had now expanded her claims to include being seduced by a detective sergeant, the whole thing was a typically underhand manoeuvre by Pelham Venn, but Walt had his counteroffensive ready.

"I met Opal Teal once to interview her, and that was only for a few moments. The conniving woman's as much of a liar as her wretched daughter."

"It doesn't look good for Opal's chances, or Fulton's, if Venn's trying to discredit police officers rather than the evidence," commented Earl. "He must reckon that you're on the right track."

"I don't need Venn's approval," snapped Walt. It would be Detective Sergeant Walter Grissom's word against that of a Pom migrant, a woman who had welcomed another Pom into the marital bed only days after her husband was killed, a woman who had lied during the investigation into that husband's death. Despite Venn's wily skills, he might have difficulty portraying Opal as an ingenuous victim whose virtue had been assailed by a manipulative police predator. "I'll sue Venn for every penny he's got. And I'll sue the papers as well."

"More sensible to ignore the entire thing," advised Earl. "Venn planted the story hoping you'd react and provide reporters with copy for days."

"I'm being libelled," Walt protested, indignant at the idea of allowing anyone to get away with an attempt to damage his promotion prospects. "I've got to respond."

"It'd be an admission that you recognize yourself as the lecherous detective. Better to be amazed if it's ever suggested that the nonsense has got anything to do with you." Earl wondered why he bothered to speak when Walt so rarely listened to anybody but himself; however, self-preservation was occasionally joined by commonsense, and Walt paused for thought.

"Venn won't be expecting no reaction at all," Walt concluded after a few moments of prudent reflection. "If he reckons I'll back down over Fulton merely because a couple of scandal-sheets rant on about police misconduct, Pelham Venn can go to hell and think again. Anyway, a few articles won't be enough to justify an official enquiry."

The remnants of Presbyterianism were vanquished. Walt had accepted Lanyon advice to act as if he were innocent of the newspaper allegations, and Earl knew that he ought to disapprove of himself after helping someone get away with deceit. Opal might have deliberately seduced Walt on the assumption that he would then become her personal smokescreen, but Walt was still to blame for the ramifications because a detective sergeant should have known better whatever the attractions on offer, yet not the slightest twinge of conscience troubled Earl for supporting Walt. If the strategy to confound Pelham succeeded, Earl would feel that he had a share in Walt's triumph. Earl's own triumph was to free himself from the last vestiges of the rigid dogma forced on his childhood by parents convinced that their beliefs had come to them direct from a universe's creator.

"I reckoned Fulton was just a young idiot who blundered through a crime scene and then lied about it, but Venn's made me reconsider," said Walt, securing Albie's conviction for murder now a vendetta goal.

"Talk to Charmian before she gets a chance to realize what her testimony means," advised Earl. "The kid will probably change her story soon and argue that she saw Sandra with Colin Kemp, but there's still Charmian's original statement witnessed by Opal, and Venn won't be able to get around that one easily."

"There isn't the slightest bit of evidence placing Kemp anywhere near Sandra's house on the night she was killed," said Walt, determined to tolerate no more of Charmian's misinformation. "I'll get Fulton in the end, but Opal's going to walk away a free woman. Fingerprints on a few photos won't be enough. Venn will conjure up a story about her finding the pictures after Kemp left them lying around, and you could have misunderstood when Opal claimed that she didn't know how to drive."

"I didn't misunderstand anything," Earl stated.

"She'll walk, and Colin Kemp will always be a suspect because of it," predicted Walt.

15

"I don't believe it," cried Brenda. "Albie would never hurt anyone. I don't believe a single word of it."

"I do. The moment Charmian told me she'd seen Albie go into Sandra's house that night, I knew he killed her." Ginevra had known nothing of the sort, but was now convinced that her suspicion of Albie's guilt could be dated back to the very instant she heard the first rumours of Sandra's fate.

"Pelham Venn told me that Charmian's changed her mind about seeing Albie with Sandra, and now says the man was Colin Kemp." There could be only one topic of conversation during Dean family meals, as Brenda struggled to acquit her nephew of all charges, desperately hoping she would stumble on a way to expose the police cover-up that Albie insisted was making him Walter Grissom's scapegoat. "It means there's no proof Albie ever met Sandra, doesn't it?"

Lenny shrugged, unwilling to commit himself when fingerprint evidence apparently proved that Albie must have gone inside Sandra's house, despite his denials.

"Everybody's watching me in school and pointing me out, just because I'm a murderer's cousin," Ginevra complained, angry to find herself at the centre of a scandal instead of merrily spreading one about somebody else. "It isn't fair when I haven't done anything. I want to change schools. Charmian's left, and Hester will probably leave soon as she plans to go to High School. Why can't I switch too?"

"No reason at all," said Lenny. "You could get the train each day into Melbourne and go to a school where no one has ever heard of us or Bethanyville. It's a good idea. You shouldn't have to put up with any nonsense because of Albie."

"But it'd look like we think he's guilty, and that we're ashamed of him," protested Brenda.

Ginevra glanced at Lenny, wearied by her mother's refusal to see Albie as he really was, but Lenny prudently remained silent. The shop's takings were down that week, and he suspected they would plummet if Albie persisted in ignoring Pelham Venn's canny advice. Albert Fulton was likely to be found guilty of killing Sandra Stoddard, and the Dean family would have to live with the consequences of being related to a murderer: consequences that might include selling the shop and moving away from Bethanyville. Their future had become as uncertain as Albie's.

****

"Are you sure that you didn't go inside Sandra Stoddard's house while Grissom's team was there?" Pelham asked, offering a young fool yet another chance to grab at a lifeline.

"I've never been in the Stoddard house, not once," stated Albie, furious still to be on the wrong side of the table in a police interview room. "And I never met Sandra Stoddard."

"You're quite certain you don't want to say that you were told to give a message to one of the team, and didn't bother with gloves because you knew that you'd only be inside the Stoddard house for a minute or two?" Pelham implored.

"I'm certain," Albie confirmed, stubbornly and decisively.

If a man had a death wish, it was probably his right to gratify the aspiration, thought Pelham; but Constable Albert Fulton imagined that no judge or jury could possibly see him as a killer simply because it would never be the way he saw himself.

"Your mates say you weren't at the beach with them that night —"

"Mates!" Albie grumbled.

"And then there's the Teal kid's original statement, as well as the fingerprint evidence —"

"Evidence!" scoffed Albie. "Manufactured evidence. I didn't murder Sandra Stoddard. I didn't murder anyone."

Albie's main frustration was that the whole story could never be told. A full explanation would clear him of all suspicion and put the blame squarely on the person responsible for his predicament: Sandra Stoddard, the slut Albie believed went to bed with every man she encountered, yet who had had the effrontery to reject him. Sandra spun a tale about expecting a visitor, someone she knew from work, someone she was involved with: a humiliating brush-off, in Albie's opinion, and he could picture the tart laughing with all her friends, all her lovers, about his inadequate seduction technique. Sandra had smiled at him as she spoke: a smile that the drunken Albie decided was mockery, and it had been the alcohol that made him lash out at her to remove the derisive smirk, or so he told himself later, because Albie Fulton was a good bloke, but any man goaded by Sandra's ridicule would have reacted in precisely the same way. Albert Fulton was as normal as the next guy, no better, no worse, trapped in a situation that could happen to any bloke. In fact, Sandra caused her own death by rejecting Albie, because a mere punch, a punch that was really no more than a slap, would hardly kill someone, and she must have been telling the truth about entertaining another man that night: the man who had actually killed Sandra Stoddard. Albie Fulton was a victim, not a murderer, and he saw no reason why his ambitions should be ended because of a few drinks. During Albie's time with the police, he would be invaluable to society, upholding the law, righting wrongs, protecting the public from violent criminals, and making Australia a better country before nuclear war wiped out the planet's entire population. By comparison, the life and death of one Bethanyville hellhag faded to insignificance.

"Find the man who was in Sandra Stoddard's house that night," ordered Albie, angry with the lawyer who apparently expected him to sacrifice his brilliant career because of a fleeting hiccup that had no business transforming itself into a crisis. "Find the last man in the long list of her fools, and you'll have found the man who killed Sandra Stoddard."

Pelham felt that he had to look no further than across the table at Albert Fulton.

****

Opal Teal was a more rewarding client: a client who recognized the importance of heeding Pelham Venn's astute advice.

"Detective Sergeant Lanyon can't know the first thing about love. It's beyond me how he could imagine, even for one second, that I'd kill darling Derek, the most wonderful of husbands. You're my saviour, Mr Venn, my hero." Bewildered by the cruelties of life, Opal turned wistfully large eyes on Pelham, and declared, "Without you, I'd never have survived such a horrible ordeal."

Pelham liked appreciation and praise, but knew that Opal was a born survivor, and he could make a shrewd guess why Derek Teal had been killed.

No man rejected beautiful Opal; no man even looked at another woman when she was there. Yet the ungrateful Derek had hidden photographs of Sandra Stoddard, remembrances of Sandra Stoddard, in Opal's very own home, but not hidden them well enough. According to edited highlights of her memories, Opal would always have attracted men, been surrounded by men, handsome men, successful men, wealthy men, and why she had thrown herself away on a wastrel was a mystery that now baffled Opal. Derek had been a man she deigned to notice at a time when future husbands abounded, and he ought to have remained humbly besotted instead of wallowing in a sordid affair with a floozy, especially when Opal had been dragged down in the world by his meagre wages. After a confrontation, Derek walked off into the night and therefore Derek deserved to die, although no one apparently understood so basic a fact or seemed willing to accept her

233

unsupported word about Colin Kemp's confession, despite Opal's innocent eyes and delicate looks.

Pelham Venn knew that he was helping a killer go free, but his job demanded it, and he took pride in his work.

****

Charmian had harboured a subconscious belief that defeating Colin Kemp would immediately return her life to the way it had once been. Yet although the enemy was removed from the Teal house for good, nothing could ever be the same again, and fate appeared to mock Charmian. Her world was going to stay wrong, no matter what she did, because now Charmian knew that Derek was gone forever, whereas his death had previously seemed a temporary aberration. Worst of all, she had let Albie down, the Albie of her daydreams, the heroic Albie incapable of harming anyone. Charmian had supplied his foes with ammunition, and her replacement sighting of Colin Kemp as Sandra's escort that night convinced nobody, which made Charmian's future a pointless void. She had won without winning, and felt cheated.

"I've decided to move house," announced Opal. "Colin Kemp won't be able to find us in a city like Melbourne, and hiding from him is the only way we'll ever be safe. Mr Venn's such a darling and he says those trumped-up lies about me should be forgotten in a couple of days, despite that dreadful Lanyon man and all his scheming, so we can make a new start."

"But I've got to stay in Bethanyville," protested Charmian, appalled at the idea of deserting Albie in his time of peril. "That evil Lanyon's twisted everything I said. He hates Albie."

"Our safety comes first, and Melbourne's only a train ride away. You don't want to go on living next door to that spiteful Hester Kemp any longer, do you?"

"No," admitted Charmian. "And I'm never going back to Bethanyville School, never ever."

"You won't have to, if we move."

"OK then," Charmian conceded. She could still deliver her latest version of events at Albie's trial, and after he was triumphantly cleared without a blemish on his name, Albie would doubtless refuse to work at any police station that harboured the blundering Lanyon fool. Albie would be promoted to the job in Melbourne that was his supreme ambition, and Charmian's hopes could blossom anew.

"The sooner we're out of Bethanyville, the safer we'll be." Melbourne was a train ride away, as Opal had said, but her real plan extended across a wider area than twenty-five miles. She would sell the house, talk about moving to Melbourne, but go to Sydney instead and leave Australia by the first ship headed for Britain. Hidden among overpopulated England's millions, perhaps with a new surname, there would be less chance of a tenacious Earl Lanyon being able to carry out further persecution. A crime of passion was no crime at all, and Opal regarded herself as a passionate woman rather than a conniving one. She still had a youthful appearance, even with the drawback of a teenage daughter, the house-sale money would keep them going for awhile, and the world was full of men. Once free of Australia, Opal could turn her eyes from the past and look forward with confidence, ready to compel life to give the beautiful Opal Teal exactly what she wanted, particularly as she was determined not to repeat the mistake of throwing herself away on a man without money, the main cause behind all the trouble inflicted on a defenceless woman. Opal Teal had a future again.

****

Whenever Hester ill-wished somebody, magic would have nothing to do with her, and as usual an enemy continued to thrive. Opal was not going to be punished for the crime of destroying the Kemp family but perhaps Colin would return home after the obstacle of Teal neighbours had been removed, and it was a bewildering shock when Hester finally realized that her father had no intention whatsoever of resuming the life she regarded as his real one with the two people who ought to mean more to him than any fleeting attraction the outside world might offer.

Colin expected sympathy for his endurance, but Hester now seemed indifferent to her father's sufferings, and yet it had never occurred to Colin that she would or could be anyone but the daughter who admired him. Hester was polite, prepared to answer questions, but she apparently considered his rejection of Noreen as a rejection of herself as well, even though Hester had once been his ally rather than Noreen's. The girl was switching allegiance, and despite Colin's belief that his daughter would become more understanding as she grew older, he was beginning to suspect that Hester had written him off.

"I'll go talk to her." Colin had arrived to take Hester out for the day, but she was feigning illness and malingered in bed.

"The last time I checked, Hester was asleep, and she wouldn't be well enough to go somewhere noisy like Luna Park anyway." Noreen tried not to sound pleased, but the only achievement that she had felt in a long while came from Hester's sudden determination to avoid Colin.

Noreen looked older and the house, Colin's home until so recently, appeared unfamiliar with nothing of his remaining there. It was impossible to credit that he could once have relaxed in a place where he had become an outsider, and Colin was glad that Noreen would never pardon him for the Opal offence, which meant that any future blame for a father-daughter rift could be offloaded onto an embittered ex-wife.

"Hester can stay with me at weekends," said Colin, as proof that he refused to humiliate himself by begging Noreen for a second chance. Life with her would be a return to the past, a past far too monotonous after his adventures, and Colin craved yet more novelty, not retreat. "I've found a flat in Melbourne with a spare room."

"I've heard Opal Teal's going to Melbourne," commented Noreen, even though she was certain that Opal had no part in Colin's future. "Do the police believe what she said about you confessing to Derek's murder?"

Colin shrugged, unwilling to admit that he was excited by such a drastic detour from his formerly well-ordered existence. He had begun to feel almost like a film star instead of a mere audience member, and the change was exhilarating in spite of its dangers: a reminder of Colin's wartime experience. "I'm fairly sure they don't think I had anything to do with Derek's death. Nobody threatened to lock me up, anyway. It was just questions, and then a statement I had to sign. They've still got my passport, but that's probably automatic and luckily I wasn't planning to flee the country."

"The police might still decide to charge Opal with killing Derek. After all, she did lie about being able to drive."

"That doesn't prove she killed Derek."

"Do you think she did?"

"I guess so," admitted Colin. He suspected that Noreen was seeking an apology for his desertion, but he had no regrets to make him contrite because Colin had felt alone from childhood. Even while he and Noreen and Hester were supposed to be a family, Colin had known that they would decamp sooner or later. People always abandoned him, just as his parents had done, just as Hester was now doing, and Colin's subconscious insisted that he had merely left Noreen and Hester before they got a chance to leave him: an inevitable fate when being on his own was part of Colin's identity.

"What will happen to Charmian, if Opal's charged with murder?" asked Noreen.

"I don't know," replied Colin. "Charmian isn't my responsibility."

"No, of course she isn't." But Noreen despised Colin for saying the words aloud, even though she had no intention of concerning herself with Charmian Teal's welfare. "Derek once said something to me about his parents back home. Perhaps they'd look after Charmian."

"Perhaps." Colin dismissed the topic as irrelevant, and turned his attention to more important matters. "I phoned about a job at Hardy Spicer's, and they want to see me tomorrow for an interview. I was asked how soon I could start, so I'll probably get taken on. Do you still plan to move house?"

"Yes, of course," said Noreen, wondering why Colin needed to enquire. She wanted to be free of Rosebery Avenue as much as he did, despite the idea of a move daunting her with its complexities. Noreen had been forced to deal with many changes since childhood, yet instead of those experiences increasing self-confidence, she seemed to have reached the end of a limited supply of coping skills, but pride was adamant that Colin must never guess how beleaguered Noreen felt at times. "Someone made an offer for the house this morning that I might accept. I'm going to look at the Mordialloc area or maybe Black Rock: somewhere on the coast."

"It'd be more expensive than a place inland," warned Colin. "Don't get your hopes up too high."

Which hopes did Colin expect her to cherish after everything that Noreen once trusted in life had been removed? He was supposed to be clever, yet Colin had unthinkingly accepted Opal Teal's façade, and appeared to imagine that his relationship with Hester would be unaffected by the choices he had made. Whatever Noreen's hopes, they were now none of Colin's business, and she tried to sound carefree rather than scornful. "I'll find something nearer the coast anyway, and as Hester will have to change schools before long, wherever we are, she won't mind a completely new place. There seem to be plenty of jobs in every town out here; it's not like England and having to stay put because you won't find work anywhere else. I've heard Tasmania's cool in summer, so I might check the house prices over there."

Noreen wanted to prove that she had options and the possibility of a successful life without Colin, and knew that she had hoodwinked him when he frowned. "Tasmania? You can't take Hester that far away from me. Besides, you shouldn't get too ambitious."

"Why not?"

"Because you'll only be disappointed."

How disappointed could a wife get over a mere house while she handled the ramifications of her husband having waltzed off with another woman? Noreen wondered again why she once thought that she had married an intelligent man. "I'm not planning on luxury, and after living in a Nissen hut, I'm prepared to tackle anything."

And Colin was ready to abandon Noreen to that anything. He stood up, a free man with a free day ahead of him now that his daughter had shunned a trip to the tedious funfair attractions of Luna Park, but he was leaving behind a freed woman. When atom bombs started to fall out of the sky, Colin would be forcibly ejected from Noreen's mind, and the end of the world also meant the end of her troubles. Nuclear destruction, Noreen's worst nightmare for years, was beginning to present itself in the guise of an ally.

"Oh well, the future can look after itself," said Colin, happy to shelve such a low-priority matter as his one-time family's next home. "Things will work out."

"Of course they will, and the police should eventually accept that you told them the truth," added Noreen, although Colin's peace of mind was hardly a major or even a minor concern. "Now that they've caught Sandra's killer, they must know Opal lied when she claimed you confessed to murder. Anyway, why on earth would you kill Sandra? There was never anything between you and the poor girl. Or was there?"

"No, never," stated Colin. He headed towards the front door, eager to get away from Noreen, but then paused to marvel, "Can you believe all the things that have happened to us since we left London?"

"I'm starting to," replied Noreen.

****

Colin walked down Rosebery Avenue, sunlight and birdsong all around him, but there were too many memories connected with the road, and he would be glad when Noreen moved to a different area so that duty visits to Hester no longer reminded him of what he had lost: not the left-behind marriage or the left-behind relationship with his daughter, but Sandra. The lost Sandra who could have been everything to him, the hope, the promise, as well as the golden future. Sandra Stoddard had become a dream of a perfect life, representing total happiness that would never be spoilt by reality; she was the woman no other could match. Warm and generous Sandra had responded to Colin's admiration, and she was too straightforward to be coy. Seductive and beautiful Sandra wanted him, and a flirtation had grown into the possibility of an affair that might be without end.

"Only a couple of days to go, and I'll be moving from the Hostel to a house in Rosebery Avenue," said Colin, after he and Sandra had exchanged frantic kisses and taken their relationship more than a step forward behind the locked door of a factory office. "I'll be one of your neighbours."

"Then I reckon there's a good chance we'll be seeing each other outside work," laughed Sandra.

"Shall I call at your house and introduce myself as the new neighbour?"

"Anytime, Col: anytime at all."

"What about tonight?"

"I'm going to the Bethanyville dance, but I'll be home after eleven."

"Midnight then?"

"Sounds good to me. Do I still get that ice-cream you promised in return for all my hard work? The hard work slaving over a typewriter, I mean."

"You can have whatever you want from me, Sandra, anything you ask."

"I might ask quite a lot, Col, but I'll tell you what that is at midnight, and it won't be ice-cream. You know how cold these winter nights are."

"You'll never feel cold with me around, Sandra."

"That's another promise I'll hold you to."

The clear crisp air of an Australian winter's night, chilly enough for gloves and jacket, in a Rosebery Avenue of black silhouettes and silver moonlight with more stars than Colin had seen anywhere in the world. He passed the house that would soon be his, a house conveniently close to Sandra's, and walked up the path to her front door, noting that the shadow of a gum tree near the gate made him invisible to neighbours, which would be a great advantage when he had a wife living in the same street. Not that Noreen mattered any longer, because Colin had already left her in his mind. He would be unable to stay in a mediocre marriage after waiting the whole of his life for Sandra.

However, the Stoddard front door had remained closed that night, and even tapping on unlit windows with a garden pebble, cold through his gloves, failed to attract Sandra's attention. Colin knew that she was too good-natured to arrange a rendezvous, and then leave him on the doorstep without explanation, so he assumed that Sandra had fallen asleep while waiting and Colin left, sadly disappointed, decidedly frustrated, but full of hope for future assignations. She would laugh at her exhaustion, blame their office activity, promise to get a front-door key cut for him, and that would be a promise Colin was going to insist she kept.

One hour. Only one hour earlier, and he could have protected Sandra, saved her from Albert Fulton. Colin had known all evening that he would be unable to wait until midnight, and intended to abscond as soon as Noreen slept, but she had been restlessly anticipating their house move that night, adding afterthoughts to a myriad of lists, and forcing Colin to postpone his departure from the Nissen hut, something that he would never be able to forgive Noreen.

Colin had occasionally made a show of complaining about insomnia, but he savoured every moment of his time taken out of time. Sleepless nights belonged to Colin, offering freedom from his dull routine and escape from restrictions imposed by both work and family, which meant that Noreen had no place in those extra hours. They were Colin's, but Sandra could have been part of the magic. Sandra would have added to the magic.

Uncomplicated and happy Sandra was now Colin's ideal: the woman who would never leave him, the woman who would never let him down. Sandra had made Colin look beyond a predictable existence with Noreen, and rescued him from accepting mediocrity as his lot. Opal had simply thrust herself into the void opened by Sandra's abrupt death, because Colin already regarded Noreen as the past, and he had started the search for his future. That search would go on, even though Colin realized that Sandra could never be replaced. An hour earlier, just one hour, a mere sixty minutes, and he might have been able to save her. Instead, Sandra had saved him: saved Colin from tolerating a third-class life.

****

"I think I've got mumps," Hester announced at breakfast on the fatal Friday of Noreen's speech: the speech that would inexorably lead to a future filled with derision and disgrace. "I feel sick and my throat's really sore."

"You've had mumps," said Noreen, not bothering to glance up from her newspaper.

"There might be Australian mumps," pleaded Hester. "Like there are German measles, as well as ordinary ones."

"There aren't any Australian mumps, or Australian measles either. Drink some water and your throat will stop hurting." Every malady was minor with the lethal exception of radiation sickness, according to Noreen, and Hester felt close to despair.

"I might be infectious. Perhaps I should stay indoors today."

"Why don't you want to go to school this morning?" asked Noreen, putting her newspaper down on the table and studying Hester's face as though it would reveal more than words. "What's different about today? You never seemed to mind school before."

"It's all right."

"But not today. Why?"

Noreen looked tired, and Hester was guiltily conscious of being disloyal. Noreen ought to come first, before any stupid teasing or ridicule that a daughter might be forced to endure because her mother insisted on making a speech, but Hester was all too aware of being a second-rate person just like Colin, and knew that she would be unable to rise to the heights of self-sacrifice required to regard Noreen's attempts at saving Australia from radioactive doom as anything but an embarrassment.

"I always hated school," Noreen continued. "I hated school from the day I started to the day I left, but you can leave in a couple of years, if you want. Not that going out to work is much better."

Horrible school, horrible job, and then an agonizingly slow death by radiation poisoning. Noreen's world was both dreary and appalling, but it could not even begin to rival the bleakness of Hester's future on that benighted day. The sun would persist in shining, but her life had become one of stygian gloom, and she was depressed by the silence of the road, so very unlike any road in London, where even what was described as a backstreet would seem a bustling township in comparison to quiet Rosebery Avenue. England was so far away that memories were now akin to recalling a film Hester had seen long ago: a film that could be watched again in her mind, featuring Colin, Noreen and their daughter still living in the London house with no knowledge of the Teal family and the destruction they would bring.

"Hurry up," said Noreen. "I'll be going to work in a minute."

"You don't usually work on Fridays," Hester commented, too despondent to hope that Noreen had forgotten her afternoon appointment. "Are you doing an extra morning?"

"No, the whole day. I swapped with Valerie, mainly because I wanted an excuse to get out of making a speech. Do you remember that I said I'd talk at your school about surviving radiation? Well, I've chickened out, so you'll have to accept the fact that your mother's a coward." However, Noreen smiled, happy with her decision, and even happier to rejoin the vast majority who lived contentedly by ignoring death. "I suppose I should make the speech. Everyone says you've got to face your fears and conquer them, but I just can't be bothered, and that's that."

"I'd sooner take my chances with an atom bomb than stand up and speak in front of a crowd," laughed Hester, dizzily light-headed at her astounding deliverance from humiliation. She had started to assume that everything in life would go wrong for her because Hester Kemp was jinxed by destiny, but perhaps a tide had at last turned, and she might not always be weighed down by defeat.

It was a day of liberation for Noreen as well. Once she would have been compelled by a sense of duty to keep her word and give the speech, no matter how much she dreaded it or how uncomfortable she felt, but Noreen's life was now her own and she no longer needed to consider other people when making choices. "Elsie Moulton's going to speak instead of me, so your headmistress won't be in a mood about it."

"I don't care about Mrs Hexham." It was a statement that Hester could hardly believe she was able to say and mean what she said, but at that moment, she had no fear of anyone, including headteachers. Hester had imagined that she would never again be happy, but the news that Noreen had decided not to pass on her nuclear terrors to Bethanyville School seemed beyond a daughter's most optimistic hopes. Despite atomic warfare and radioactive fallout, even in spite of Colin's desertion, Hester Kemp had something to celebrate on a Fry Day and she could tentatively begin to tell herself that there might actually be more good luck ahead.